Obsession

Rebecca Deel

ISBN: 198197105X
ISBN-13: 978-1981971053

DEDICATION

To my amazing husband.

ACKNOWLEDGMENTS

Cover by Melody Simmons.

CHAPTER ONE

Lacey Coleman turned on lights in Coffee House, glancing through plate glass windows into the darkness beyond the cafe. Few lights glowed in the stores around Washington Square this early. On the main thoroughfare through Nolensville, a town on the outskirts of Nashville, Tennessee, traffic would already be moving at a good clip.

Grateful she no longer jockeyed for position in morning traffic, Lacey plunged into preparations for the first commuters who arrived in just over an hour.

She checked her watch again, concern knotting her stomach. Why didn't her mother call? Yvonne Coleman harped on the fact Lacey didn't call enough. She couldn't remember the last time her mother had been out of touch for this long. She'd called a week ago, but Yvonne should have been eager to pick up the phone and remind Lacey she should be a better daughter.

Ten minutes into her prep, Chase arrived. "Morning, Lace." He yawned as he shrugged off his coat.

"You look cold."

A snort. "If you didn't live above the shop, you'd know the temperature feels like it's ten below zero out there."

She glanced up from measuring coffee beans to pour into the grinder. "Are you serious?"

"Feels like it to me."

"As an Arizona native, you say that about any temperature below eighty degrees."

"Doesn't change the fact my fingers and toes are numb."

Lacey grinned. "Give me a few more minutes, and I'll have a pot of Ethiopian blend ready for you."

"Can't be soon enough for me."

A knock sounded on the door at the back of the shop. She checked the clock. "Right on time." Lacey checked the security camera and unlocked the door to admit their baked goods deliveryman. "Morning, George. How are you today?"

"Can't complain." He handed her paperwork to sign acknowledging delivery of products her boss, Rowan Maddox, ordered yesterday.

"Hi, George." Chase shook the man's hand. "Cold enough for you?" He followed the deliveryman out to the truck to help unload pastries for the shop.

Leaving them to trudge back and forth in the cold, Lacey finished prepping the coffeemaker, turned on the machine, and shifted to the next type of coffee.

Once the day's coffee selections were brewing, she stocked the displays with baked goods from Nolensville Bakery. As Chase and George talked about football, she eyed the apple strudel muffins. They looked and smelled terrific, and tasted even better.

She considered setting aside a muffin for herself. If there were any left by ten o'clock, she would eat one. Coffee House traffic slowed to a trickle between ten and eleven, then picked up steam as the lunch crowd dropped by for a midday energy boost.

By the time she and Chase completed their preparation, the sky had lightened to a smoke gray edging toward silver.

She poured a cup of Ethiopian blend for Chase and one of Arabica for herself.

"Thanks," her co-worker said on the heels of another wide yawn. "Did Yvonne call?"

Concern surged to the forefront of her mind. She shook her head. "I'm worried, Chase. She never gives me the silent treatment."

"You sure she's not trying a new tactic? Guilt trips haven't worked."

A lot Chase knew. Lacey had refused to give in this time, although the refusal hurt. "I can't believe she'd miss the chance to tell me how stupid I've been."

A hard look settled on her friend's face. "You aren't stupid, Lace. Breaking up with Frank is the smartest thing you could have done. He's an abusive jerk. You deserve better, and you mother should want the best for you. Take it from me, the best isn't Frank Gordon."

She blinked. Rowan, her husband, and a few of his employees from Fortress Security had said the same thing. She was almost one hundred percent in their camp. Perhaps five percent of her wondered if she would ever find someone to share her life. All the good ones were taken except for the dark-haired medic who frequented the shop and struck up conversations with her each time.

Lacey's cheeks burned. The handsome operative had frequent absences for his work, but when he was in town, he stopped every morning about this time.

She dragged her attention back to Chase. "You're right. I do deserve better than Frank, but he hasn't bothered me in months." Rowan's husband, Brent, and Adam Walker had escorted Frank out of the shop one day when he'd shown up, spoiling for a fight. Lacey didn't know what they said to him, but Frank had made himself scarce ever since.

"You'll tell me if he does, right?"

Her former boyfriend would make mincemeat out of the slender-built barista. Frank made liberal use of steroids and lifted weights religiously. The guy was built like a tank and hit like one, too. She knew from firsthand experience.

A knock on the door startled her. Lacey turned, ready to motion that they weren't open yet when she recognized Jake Davenport, the medic she'd been mooning about a few minutes earlier.

Knowing she risked others demanding early entry, she hurried to unlock the door. "Good morning, Jake." She hoped she didn't sound as nervous as she felt. Just being around this tall, built medic turned her into a bundle of nerves.

"I know I'm early." He smiled. "I've been up since three. I hope you will take pity on me and offer a tired soldier a cup of hot coffee."

As if she would turn away one of the Fortress operatives. "Of course." She opened the door wider. "Come in from the cold. We just stocked the displays. Browse while I fix your coffee."

"Don't you want to know my choice of brew for the day?"

She grinned. "You always order the Ethiopian blend when it's a coffee of the day."

When Lacey rounded the counter, she noticed Chase had made himself scarce. She looked toward the breakroom and saw the light was on. Maybe Chase forgot something.

"What looks good today?" Jake asked.

Besides him? "The apple strudel muffins always sell out early. It's a customer favorite."

"What about you?"

She grinned. "I'm a customer favorite, too."

The medic chuckled. "I already know that. Do you like the apple muffins?"

"I love them. I was debating whether I should set aside one for myself when you knocked."

"Sold." He climbed on one of the stools in front of the counter. "I'll take three of those with coffee."

"Wow. You must have worked up an appetite."

"Adam Walker is a slave driver." He gave her a wicked grin. "Feel free to share my opinion when you see him next."

She laughed, her nervousness fading away. "I'll do that. Will you take the order with you or eat in?"

"Depends. Have you finished your morning prep?"

Lacey tilted her head. "Yes. Why?"

"I'll eat in if you sit with me. I promise not to take long. I know the morning rush starts soon."

Why not? Rowan wouldn't mind since everything was ready to go. Another glance toward the breakroom. Still no Chase. Was he deliberately giving her some time alone with Jake?

"Are you working alone this morning?" Jake said as she poured his coffee and topped the cup with a plastic lid.

"Chase is in the back." Doing what, she didn't know. "He'll be out here before the rush starts." Lacey filled a plate with three strudel muffins, handed Jake the plate and his coffee before grabbing her cup. "Counter or a table?"

"Table, please." He chose a table in the corner with his back to the wall.

Why did all the men and women who worked with Rowan's husband at Fortress Security sit in the same place? She'd have to ask Brent the next time he came to the shop.

Jake took two muffins from the plate and set them on a napkin, then slid the remaining muffin to her. "I hate to eat alone."

She stared at him a moment. "Thank you."

He saluted her with his cup. "Any new Alexa stories to share?"

Thinking of Rowan and Brent's young daughter brought a smile. "Her latest mission is to convince her parents she needs a puppy."

Jake sipped his coffee. "Seems like a normal mission for a kid. I had dogs growing up."

She'd wanted a dog herself. Her mother had refused, claiming a pet was only another mouth to feed. A truth, but Lacey had been willing to work extra shifts to care for the dog. "I bet you didn't ask for a trained search-and-rescue dog. She met Heidi Gallagher's S & R Labrador retriever and immediately fell in love. Now, no other type of dog will do."

Her companion chuckled. "She's quite a character. Knowing Alexa, she'll wear Brent and Rowan down."

"Do you think Heidi would help her train the dog?"

"Probably. She's young, though. I think Brent will put her off for a few years. Why train the dog for S & R if the handler is too young to go on a rescue?"

Lacey finished the muffin before she replied. "No one should hold her back, especially not her parents."

Jake was quiet a moment, studying her. "Who held you back?"

Who didn't was the better question? And she needed to quit whining. She was an adult now. She made her own choices. Lacey opened her mouth to respond when her cell phone rang.

Her mother? She slid the instrument from her pocket and studied the screen, frowning. Not her mother, but the call was from the same area code. "I'm sorry. I have to take this," she murmured.

"Want some privacy?"

"Stay, please." She tapped her thumb to the screen and answered the call.

"This is Wayne Beckett, chief of police in Winston, Alabama."

Blood drained from her face, Beckett's voice hauntingly familiar. She still heard his voice in her nightmares. "Is Mom all right?"

"I'm sorry, Ms. Coleman. Your mother is missing."

CHAPTER TWO

Jake straightened as he listened to the one-sided conversation, concern growing by the second. Admittedly, the conversation wasn't much on Lacey's side. Less than a minute after the call began, she laid down her phone and covered her face with her hands.

"Lacey?" No answer.

He shoved back his chair and knelt beside her. "Lacey, talk to me." Knowing her history with an abusive ex-boyfriend, he chanced laying a hand on her shoulder and squeezed.

When she lowered her hands, her eyes were tear-drenched.

"What's wrong with your mother?" he murmured. If it was a medical issue, maybe he could help her interpret the medical jargon doctors loved to spout.

"She's missing."

He sat back on his heels. Not what he'd been expecting. "Who called?"

"The police chief in my hometown."

"Who reported her missing?"

"Her boss. She hasn't been at work for the past three days. Sonny went by her house to check on her and found no sign of her."

Jake brushed away a tear trickling down her cheek. "The cops have any leads?"

Anger burned in her gaze. "They aren't worried about her. They think she'll show up on her own."

The bell over the door rang as the first handful of customers streamed through the door. Jake rose and drew Lacey to her feet. "Need help with them?"

She shook her head as Chase returned and greeted their regulars.

"Mind if I borrow the breakroom to make a few phone calls?"

"Oh, sure." She waved at the hallway. "Take your time."

He grabbed his coffee and muffins. After making sure Lacey was settled enough to work, Jake walked down the hall, closed the breakroom door, and called Brent.

"Maddox."

"It's Jake. Is Rowan scheduled to come into the shop today?"

"She'll be in as soon as she takes Alexa to school. Problem?"

"Lacey's mother is missing, and apparently the cops don't care. From what I'm gathering, they aren't looking for her."

"I'll see what I can find out. Did Lacey call you?"

"I was in the coffee shop when the police chief called. I want in on this, Brent."

Silence, then, "You have a personal stake in this, D?"

He hesitated, not quite knowing how to answer the question. He'd had his eye on Lacey for months now although he gave her space as she recovered from the breakup with her ex. Rowan's assistant manager was a beautiful, intelligent, and capable woman who made a killer cup of coffee and served it with an engaging smile. Maybe now was the time to stake his claim. “Yeah, I do.”

“I see. Tell Adam you’re on Lacey’s protection detail.”

Jake’s gut tightened. “You think she’s a target?”

“Doubtful, but it’s better to be safe since she will want to go home for a few days.”

The same thought had crossed his mind. “I’m going with her. She shouldn’t be alone.”

“Agreed. Stay with Lacey until you hear from me. And Jake?”

He straightened. “Yes, sir?”

“If you hurt her, you’ll answer to me.” The call ended.

Jake flinched as he tapped in the number for his team leader, Adam Walker. He’d been on the receiving end of Brent’s tirades on more than one occasion over the last five years. They were never pleasant, but the boss always had his employees’ best interests at heart. This time, however, Jake had a feeling the dressing down might involve a punch or two from the Navy SEAL. Brent was protective of his wife’s employees, especially Lacey.

“Walker.”

“It’s Jake. I need some personal time, Adam.”

“Everything okay, D?”

“I’m fine. It’s Lacey.”

“If her ex has laid a hand on her again, the authorities will never find his body.”

Jake’s eyebrows soared, not sure his team leader was joking. “Lacey’s mother is missing. I’ve already received permission from Maddox to stay with Lacey.”

“She’s been threatened?”

“She’ll want to go home to see about her mother. I won’t let her go alone.”

“Need backup?”

Took him a minute to rid himself of the lump in his throat. “I don’t think so. Thanks, man.”

“We all like Lacey. If you need us, we’ll be there.”

A minute later, Jake slid the phone into his pocket. Since he was officially on duty as Lacey's bodyguard despite the remote likelihood of a problem here, Jake might as well make himself useful in the shop.

When he returned to the main room, the customers were six deep in two lines. He walked behind the counter and started bagging baked goods orders for Lacey and Chase. Ninety minutes later, the rush had slowed to a manageable level.

"Take a break, Lace," Chase said. "I've got this."

"Let me know if traffic picks up. Otherwise, I'll be back in fifteen minutes."

Jake kept pace with her as she walked to the breakroom and closed the door. "How are you holding up?"

She dropped into the nearest chair and doubled over.

He crouched at her side. "What's wrong?"

"My stomach is in a knot."

"Does the shop carry chamomile tea?"

She nodded.

"I'll be right back." He returned to the main room. "Lacey needs some chamomile tea."

Chase inclined his head toward the tea holders. "Chamomile is on the far left. Two bags. Hot water is in the dispenser beside the tea. If she needs it fast, drop in a couple ice cubes."

He could handle that. He'd been concerned the process of making tea for Lacey would be more complicated than that. "Will she want sweetener?"

"Nope. She says sweetener changes the taste."

He made a mental note not to add sweetener to her drinks. Grabbing a to-go cup, Jake plucked two bags of tea from the bin with tongs, dropped them in the cup, and filled the container with hot water. Figuring Lacey needed the tea sooner rather than later, he waited a couple minutes, then added two ice cubes and placed a plastic lid on the top.

When he returned to the breakroom, Jake found Lacey still bent over at the waist. He sat in the chair next to hers and laid his hand on her back. "I brought the tea. Try to swallow a few sips."

She straightened and took the cup he pressed into her shaking hands. "Thanks."

Although he removed his hand from her back, he remained close and silent while she sipped the tea. When she pushed the empty cup aside, he asked, "When do you plan to leave?"

Her head whipped his direction. "Why?"

"Answer my question."

"After work if Rowan can spare me."

"She'll work it out. If she needs an extra person or two, I'm sure Brenna Wolfe wouldn't mind helping out for a few days."

A slight smile curved her lips at the mention of the wife of a fellow operative. The woman also happened to be a bestselling author who was friends with Lacey. "Brenna would see it as a great research opportunity."

He chuckled. "If she lends a hand, I'd guess a future protagonist will work in a coffee shop. When is your shift over?"

"Two. Don't you have to be at work soon?"

"Trying to get rid of me already?"

"Of course not. I don't want you to be late."

"I'll be fine. We returned from deployment a few days ago, and I've already completed my PT for the day."

"You and the other operatives always have more going on than physical training."

True, but he didn't want to tell Lacey she was his latest assignment. That wasn't the most important reason he planned to stay. Besides, he did have tasks he could do while keeping an eye on her. "I have my laptop in the SUV. If you don't mind, I'll hang out in the coffee shop and work. I'd like to be close at hand."

Her brows furrowed. “Why?”

“In case you need me.”

Lacey stared at him a moment, then rose. “I need to get back.” She tossed her cup into the trash and walked out.

Jake blew out a slow breath, hoping he hadn’t screwed up his chance with the woman who had fascinated him for months.

CHAPTER THREE

Lacey filled order after order, smiling and laughing with her customers while her heart ached. Where was her mother? Beckett had insinuated Yvonne was off for a romantic holiday with a man she'd picked up.

Her mother's history shouldn't weigh into whether or not the police chief insisted his detective do the job for which he'd been trained. No one's disappearance should be ignored because she lived on the fringes of society. She mattered, despite Beckett's past poisonous relationship with Lacey's mother.

As she ground beans and brewed coffee, she kept a surreptitious eye on the drop-dead handsome medic who worked on his laptop. Hard to believe Jake had stayed in the coffee shop for hours in case she needed him. Lacey couldn't remember the last time a friend had put himself at her disposal for hours.

She should have insisted he go home or to Fortress headquarters. Jake had more important things to do. Something told Lacey she would be wasting her breath. She sighed. The least she could do was refill his coffee and give him a snack.

Lacey mentally tallied the number of coffee refills the medic had consumed, and reconsidered the choice of drink. Water, she decided, and a power sandwich, both good for a man who burned as many calories as she suspected he did each day.

She prepared his snack and grabbed a bottle of water on the way to his table. Jake glanced up as she approached. "Take a break." Lacey set the plate and bottle to the side of his computer.

He pushed the laptop aside. "Sit with me."

She grinned, her first genuine smile in hours. "I've heard that line before."

"Want half my sandwich?"

A grimace. "Pass. I don't think I could keep it down. Be a shame to waste a good sandwich."

"Stomach still bothering you?"

She shrugged, not admitting she wouldn't eat much until her mother was found.

Jake asked questions about the shop. Because he stayed with a neutral topic, the tension racking her body eased and the nervousness she'd experienced before with Jake was gone.

The bell over the door rang and cold air blew into the shop as Rowan rushed inside. "Sorry, guys. I was stuck in traffic. Five-car pileup on Nolensville Pike."

"No problem, Ro." Chase came out from behind the counter to take her coat and purse. "I'll take these to your office. I'm due for a break anyway."

"You're a lifesaver for staying, Chase."

"I'll remind you of that when it's time for my raise."

Since no customers were in the shop aside from Jake, Rowan dropped into a chair beside Lacey. "Brent told me about your mother. What can I do to help, Lace?"

She blinked at the sudden sting of tears. "I need a few days off. I have to go home." Just saying the words made her feel sick to her stomach. She hated Winston with a white-hot passion.

"Of course." Rowan squeezed Lacey's hand, her touch gentle. "Take as much time as you need."

"I can't afford to take more than a few days, Ro."

"Your job is secure, and your salary will be paid in full for as long as you're gone."

Stunned, she sat speechless for a moment. "I don't expect to be paid when I'm not working. I won't take advantage of you."

"You're not taking. I'm giving. You're my friend. Friends are there for each other. Besides, you've more than earned the time off. I've lost count of times you covered for me when you weren't scheduled to work."

Her gaze shifted to Jake. He gave her a slight nod as though he agreed with Rowan's statements. He viewed her as a friend, too? She couldn't deny a slight disappointment. Stupid. Why would he look at her as something more when he'd never indicated he felt anything different?

She turned back to Rowan. "I'll be gone long enough to nudge the police into looking for Mom."

"You don't think they'll look for her?"

"Not if they can help it."

"When do you plan to leave?"

"After my shift is over."

Her boss blinked. "That's three hours from now. I can handle the shop with Chase until Kristina gets here. Go pack your things, Lacey."

She shook her head. "It's better this way. I'd rather arrive in Winston after dark." She wasn't in the mood to deal with drama.

Beside her, Jake stiffened, his gaze locked on her.

Don't ask, she begged silently. *Please don't ask me to explain in front of Rowan.* "Packing won't take me long. I'll work out my shift, then leave."

"All right. If you change your mind and decide to leave sooner, let me know." Another squeeze of her hand and Rowan walked to the back of the shop.

Jake polished off his sandwich and water. "Why don't you want to go home?"

"I don't want to talk about it right now." She didn't want to tell a man she was fascinated with about her checkered past in that horrible town, about her family. He'd never hear the sordid details.

"I want you to feel comfortable enough to tell me the truth," he said, his voice soft. "Will you think about it? Please?"

"All right." She prayed it wouldn't be necessary.

When she returned to the counter, Jake pulled out his cell phone and had a quiet discussion with someone before he resumed work on his laptop. An hour later, Adam Walker walked into the shop with his wife, Veronica.

Lacey grinned. "Adam, Vonnie. Need a caffeine boost?"

"Who doesn't?" the dark-haired woman said with a smile.

She could use a pick-me-up herself. "What would you like?"

As she poured their choice of coffee, Jake approached the counter with the laptop under his arm. "More coffee, Jake?"

"Not right now. I'm heading out to run an errand, Lacey. I won't be long."

"If you don't make it back before I go, thanks for staying with me today."

"I won't be long," he repeated. He and Adam exchanged wordless glances, then Jake was gone.

What was that about? Before she could ask, Veronica and Adam sat on stools at the counter and started to tell her about their neighbor's twin boys. In minutes, she was laughing at the troublemakers' antics. One day, she hoped to have a family of her own to love and care for.

The lunch crowd began trickling in. Wouldn't be long before the place would be hopping again. As people streamed inside, Rowan and Chase arrived to help, and Adam and Veronica moved to the table Jake had vacated.

By the time the crowd thinned and she had a chance to check on Adam and Veronica, she noticed Jake had returned and sat with his friends. Pleased he'd made it back before she left, Lacey smiled at him and turned her attention to the next customer.

Finally, her shift ended. Like always, her legs and feet ached. "I think half of Nolensville wanted a cup of our coffee today," she said to Rowan.

"Must be the cool temperatures."

"I'm out of here," Chase said as Kristina arrived. "Got a class starting in less than an hour."

Envy bit hard. Lacey wished she was in school. Her savings account wasn't flush enough yet to allow her to register for classes. Maybe in the spring or summer.

She turned her attention to what needed doing. She couldn't remember how much gas was in her car, and hoped her fifteen-year-old, third-hand vehicle would make yet another trip to her hometown. With more than 200,000 miles on the odometer, that wasn't a guaranteed outcome anymore.

"Ready to pack, Lacey?"

Jake's baritone sent heat through her veins. She nodded.

"Come on. I'll walk you up."

"You're helping me pack?"

He shook his head. "I'll carry your luggage to the SUV."

Lacey stared. "What SUV?" She had an ugly green sedan.

"Mine."

"I don't understand."
"I'm going with you."

CHAPTER FOUR

"You can't." Panic swelled in a tidal wave through Lacey at the prospect of her worst nightmare coming true. No, thanks. She couldn't let Jake anywhere near Winston.

"Why not?"

Scrambling for any excuse, she blurted out, "You have a job."

"As do you."

"I don't need you." Pain shot through her heart hearing those words from her lips, the pain intensifying when hurt filled his gaze for a second before he masked his emotions. She laid her hand on his arm. "I'm sorry. That came out wrong. I don't need a companion for a trip home. I've driven myself many times. I can handle the drive."

"You may not need anyone, but you shouldn't go alone. You haven't been home for this reason," he murmured as he turned her toward the stairs leading to her apartment over the shop. "I want to go with you, Lacey. Let me."

"Why do you want to go to some back woods, dead end town?"

"We're friends and it's where you're going to be. You don't know what you'll face."

On the contrary, she knew all too well what was ahead and didn't want Jake to witness any of it. The people, the house, her past life. Remembering all of the drama and shame she'd felt growing up made her nauseated.

He followed Lacey up the stairs. "You shouldn't face this alone."

Lacey jammed her key in the door lock and twisted. Inside her haven, things were as she'd left them hours earlier. Orderly, neat, peaceful, unlike the chaos she still saw in her dreams. Just seeing the place that now bore the stamp of her personality eased some of the knotted muscles in her back.

"Let me know when you finish packing your bags."

She flicked a glance at Jake over her shoulder and nodded. Lacey hurried to her bedroom and hauled a scarred suitcase from the closet. Fifteen minutes later, her bag was packed.

Her gaze swept over the room to make sure she hadn't left anything important. Knowing Jake would be aggravated if she hauled the suitcase to the front room, she left it on the bed and went in search of the medic.

She found him in the living room, studying her pitiful array of pictures displayed on a table. One of her mother, none of her father, several of the neighbor's dog. A sad commentary on her life in Winston. "My suitcase is ready."

He turned, frowning. "One suitcase?"

She only had one, but that was beside the point. "I don't plan to be gone more than a few days," she reminded him. "I don't need much."

"My mother can't travel with any less than four suitcases, no matter how short the stay."

Four? All the clothes she owned would fit in half that many suitcases. "Wow."

Jake snorted. "If you had to haul them around, you wouldn't be impressed. Not only are there four, those suitcases are stuffed to the brim. If I didn't know better, I'd swear she packed rocks in them. They weigh a ton."

Incredible. Her gaze dropped to his shoulders, chest, and arms. With his build and obvious muscle tone, Lacey doubted he broke a sweat hauling his mother's clothes and shoes from one place to the other.

A moment later, he carried her battered hard-sided luggage into the living room. "Do you need to water the plants or pitch leftovers that will spoil before we return?"

Lacey got the sense that continuing to argue with the hot medic would be pointless. She knew when to give in gracefully and save her battles for something that mattered. "I have a few things that might be skating toward the science-experiment stage."

"I'll store your bag in the SUV, then take out the trash." He held up his hand, holding off her protest. "My father drilled manners into me as I grew up. I'm an expert at taking out the trash." His eyes darkened, seemed haunted almost.

He couldn't be talking about her kitchen trash, not with that reaction. Hmm. Maybe he'd be willing to share what caused such pain in his eyes if she wasn't so reticent about her past. Something to think about. Later.

While Jake carried her suitcase to his SUV, Lacey hurried to the kitchen and yanked open the refrigerator door. She scanned nearly bare shelves and tossed three takeout cartons into a garbage bag, then swept through the other rooms, dumping the contents from waste baskets. By the time Jake returned, the bag was full.

"Is that all?" he asked as he took the bag from her hand.

She nodded, glancing toward her kitchen. "Should I pack drinks and snacks for the road?" She might have enough snack food in the cabinets to keep them from starving. Maybe. Her paycheck wouldn't go in the bank for another four days which meant her food supply was low.

"Not necessary. I'll stop every two hours. We'll purchase whatever we need."

She forced a smile while mentally calculating how much cash she had in her purse. Not enough for food and a hotel room. She couldn't stay at her childhood home, and no one in town would offer her a place to stay. Hopefully, she had enough in her account to cover a room for a few days. If the money ran out, she would tell Jake she needed to return to work.

After she locked her door, Jake escorted her to his SUV and helped her into the front passenger seat. When they merged onto Interstate 65, Lacey twisted to face Jake. "Stopping that often will cause over an hour delay in reaching Winston. I usually stop once."

He regarded her, concern in his gaze. "Prevents DVT."

She blinked. "DVT?"

"Deep vein thrombosis. Blood clots, Lacey. You need to stretch your legs and get your blood moving every two hours."

Leave it to a medic to make her wonder how she'd made it home all those trips without having a serious medical issue. Lacey plopped her sunglasses on her nose. "Brent doesn't mind you taking off a few days?"

"My team is not due for another deployment for at least a month. Brent and Adam gave me permission to go with you."

"If your team is activated again, we'll come back."

He clasped her hand a moment before clutching the steering wheel again. "Don't worry. Tell me about Winston."

Instead of specifics, she told him about the funny side of small town life, everything from dealing with nosy neighbors to traffic jams caused by escaped cows.

When she kept breaking off in mid-sentence to yawn, he chuckled and said, "Looks like you didn't get much sleep last night."

"I'm a night owl. The mornings I draw the short straw for opening the store are tough."

"Why don't you take a nap? I'll wake you in two hours."

"I'd love to, but it seems rude to sleep while you drive when I'm the reason you're going in the first place."

"In the military, we learned to sleep whenever and wherever we could. Even a twenty-minute combat nap did wonders for us." He slid a pointed glance her direction. "Take advantage of the downtime to rest, Lacey. You may not have much chance when we reach Winston."

CHAPTER FIVE

As Jake drove, he cast an occasional glance at the woman sleeping beside him, thinking about what she'd said and what she hadn't. He didn't understand why, but Lacey was desperate to keep him away from her hometown.

At first, he'd been hurt at the rejection. Then he realized she wasn't rejecting him, but his knowledge of where she came from. Something to think about there. Jake had a feeling her childhood was a great deal different from his own.

His lips curled. Not too many people in his world right now were born with silver spoons in their mouths. In fact, instead of a silver spoon, his mouth would have been filled with an entire place setting. What would Lacey's reaction be when she discovered his background? More people than he wanted to count would slap him on the back, say how cool that was, and in the next breath hold out a hand for a loan or a cash gift.

Somehow, he didn't see Lacey doing that to him, and what a refreshing change that would be. No, his concern was she would turn away from him because of the wealth. Based on what he'd seen at her apartment, she didn't have much money and that made him wonder about her response to his flush bank accounts.

Jake drove on the striped asphalt ribbon in silence for the next two hours. Although he hated to wake his traveling companion, he also knew she needed to walk.

He exited the interstate and parked in front of a gas pump. Might as well fill up the tank. His SUV was reinforced with steel plates and bullet-resistant glass which made the vehicle great for safely transporting friends, family, and principals. Having the extra weight also burned fuel faster than normal.

He checked on Lacey. She slept on. He climbed from the vehicle and closed the door. When the tank was full, he parked the SUV in front of the convenience store and turned off the engine.

"Lacey."

She stirred and turned to stare at him through heavy-lidded eyes. "Where are we?"

"Two hours outside of Nashville. We need to walk a few minutes." Jake circled the vehicle to open her door. Twenty minutes later, he and Lacey resumed their journey.

"Thank you for the banana and water, Jake."

"I was hungry and thought you might be as well. When we stop next time, we'll find a place for dinner."

Her lips curved. "Do you always think about food?"

He shrugged. "We burn a lot of calories each day with our training regimen."

"You and your teammates are in terrific shape."

"With our jobs, we have to be in better shape than the people we go up against."

"How many hours a day does the training take?"

"Two or three hours a day for conditioning. If we're preparing for a mission, that time may be extended by another two or three hours."

"Good grief! No wonder Fortress operatives are in such great shape."

He grinned. "Noticed that, did you?"

Her cheeks flushed. "Hard not to."

"What do I need to know before we arrive in Winston?" he asked, his voice soft. Would she tell him? Man, he hoped so. Jake didn't want to be blindsided after they rolled into town.

Beside him, Lacey stilled. "I don't want to talk about it."

"Will you be able to keep your secrets when we're in your hometown?"

She sighed. "No."

"I need to know enough of the truth so I'm prepared for what I'll face."

"Winston law enforcement is very familiar with my family."

Huh. "Okay."

"That's it? You won't dig deeper?"

"If I need to know more, tell me the rest."

"I have a juvie record. I didn't do anything really bad, like kill someone."

Those words felt like a punch to the gut. Did Lacey see him as a killer? Jake didn't regret his military career and now his second career with Fortress Security. He saved people's lives. Unfortunately, saving innocents might mean taking the lives of those who weren't innocent to protect his principal. He never took a life lightly. He had yet to meet a woman who could handle his career or whose first question wasn't to know how many people he'd killed in the line of duty. Lacey hadn't asked for a scorecard. Would she be the one to handle the career? He supposed only time would give him the answer to that question.

Lacey dragged in a deep breath. "I need to shut up now. I keep saying the wrong thing to you."

"Do you see me as a killer?"

Her soft hand pressed against his arm where it rested on the console between their seats. "I see you as a protector, a defender of the vulnerable. I've heard Brent talk to Rowan often enough that I have a pretty good idea what you face each time you're sent on a mission." Her hand squeezed. "I'm sorry if I offended you by my choice of words."

"Don't apologize. I shouldn't be so sensitive."

"How many people have called you a killer?"

"Too many to name."

"They're wrong. They should be calling you a hero."

"I'm not a hero, Lacey. I'm doing a tough job in an ugly environment where there aren't any good choices." He turned the conversation back to the coffee shop. "Tell me stories about your customers."

She launched into funny stories about the interesting customers who frequented Coffee House. By the time she ran out of steam, Jake's mood had lifted and it was time to find a restaurant. He parked in front of a restaurant that served a variety of food. "Come on. Dinner is on Brent. He said if he had been the one driving you home, he would have insisted on paying."

"You're his stand in."

He slid her a pointed glance. "Yes, ma'am, but only for dinner."

"And for the rest?"

"I'm with you because I want to be."

When he and Lacey left the steakhouse ninety minutes later, he said, "Do you feel like driving for a while?"

Bright blue eyes turned his direction. "I'd love to. I promise to be careful."

Jake handed her the keys. "The SUV is heavier than your car. We'll have to fill up when we stop again."

"I'll watch the gas gauge."

"If anything makes you uneasy or you grow tired, wake me and I'll take over."

"You were up two hours before me this morning."

Three, but he didn't intend to tell her that. "Military training. I'm used to operating for days at a time with little to no sleep." He opened the driver's door for her and tucked her inside. Normally, he wouldn't be eager to cede the wheel to someone else's control. He'd deal anyway because having an active part in getting herself to Winston gave her control and he had a feeling Lacey needed that.

When they were back on the interstate with the sun setting in the distance, Jake reclined the seat and fell asleep in seconds. Sometime later, he woke when the SUV slowed to a stop. Lacey parked in front of a gas pump. "Any trouble?"

"The only trouble is I won't want to drive anything else after this. Your SUV drives like a dream."

"Yeah, it is pretty sweet." Jake climbed out and filled the tank. After walking around for a few minutes, he took over driving. "You want to nap for a while?"

"I better not. I'm afraid I won't sleep tonight."

"Do you like audio books?"

"Love them. I borrow them from the library all the time."

"I have a new Clive Cussler audio book. Want to try it?"

"Sure."

For the next four hours, they listened to a book featuring Dirk Pitt. Fifteen minutes before they rolled into Winston, Jake stopped the audio file and placed a call to Zane Murphy, Fortress communications guru.

"What do you need, Jake?"

"Did you confirm the reservation for me?"

"You and Lacey have connecting rooms at the Magnolia Hotel."

"Thanks, Z."

"Yep. Need anything else?"

He frowned, analyzing his friend's voice. "What's up?"

"The Shadow Unit's in a hot zone."

"Do they need backup?"

"Unknown."

Lacey laid her hand on Jake's arm again. "Hi, Zane."

"Hello, Lacey. How are you?"

"Worried about Mom."

"I'll be glad to help any way I can. All you have to do is ask."

"If this Shadow Unit needs Jake, call him in. I'll be fine on my own."

"We have several units available to send as backup."

"Jake is the best."

He kept his gaze fixed on the road. In his chest, however, his heart skipped a beat at her words.

"No argument there," Zane said. "If we need Jake and his team, we'll notify him, then send an operative to Winston to aid in the search for your mother. Brent and Rowan want you to have someone you can trust at your back."

"What did you find out about Yvonne's disappearance?" Jake asked. He needed to know and wanted to take the heat off Lacey.

"Not much. The cops' file is thin. Prevailing theory is she left under her own steam. They're assuming she'll return the same way."

"Any sign of foul play?"

"Not that I could find. No sign of forced entry at her house. No sign of her car, either."

"She doesn't have one," Lacey said. "Mom walks or takes the bus. Mostly walks."

"Your mother has a green SUV registered to her, Lacey."

"That's not possible. At the end of the month, she doesn't have two pennies to rub together. She works as a waitress in a dive, Zane. Mom can't afford a car payment, insurance, and gas for the tank. There has to be a mistake."

"Not according to the DMV records. Guess that's something you and Jake can look into while you're home."

"The SUV is like a hundred years old, right?"

"Try two years."

"Two..." Lacey's voice trailed off. "This can't be right."

Something in her voice had Jake glancing her direction again. She was mad, but there was something else under the mad. Hurt. More secrets from the woman who had caught his interest. Would she ever fully trust him?

She looked so alone. He shifted his arm and wrapped his hand around hers. "Keep digging, Z. Let me know what you find out."

"Copy that."

The silence inside the SUV stretched out long enough he chanced another sideways glance at her. The fact she hadn't moved her hand also struck him as interesting. "You okay?"

"I don't understand what's going on, Jake."

"We'll figure it out. We'll keep digging until we discover the truth."

"What if you have to leave to help the other team?"

"If you're still in Winston when the mission is finished, I'll come back to help you look for the answers."

"Why would you do that?"

"You matter to me. Do you know where the Magnolia Hotel is?"

"You can't miss it. The place looks like a throwback to southern plantations right on Main Street."

"Have you ever stayed there before?"

She shook her head.

"You must stay with your mother when you're in town."

Lacey remained silent.

Dread settled like a rock in his stomach. "Lacey?"

"I stay in a motel outside Winston."

"Your mother doesn't want you to stay with her?"

She turned her head toward him. "It's my choice to stay elsewhere."

CHAPTER SIX

"Turn right at the corner." Lacey peeked at Jake, grateful he'd dropped the subject of her odd sleeping arrangements when she visited her mother. He didn't understand. If he'd grown up in the same town and in the same house as she had, he wouldn't be sending her those puzzled looks.

She knew allowing Jake to drive her to Winston would be a terrible idea. Fortress Security was in the information business, and they were very good at their job. He wouldn't let this rest. As he dug into her mother's disappearance, the medic would feel compelled to uncover her secrets, too. Lacey hoped he still respected her when they returned home.

Jake parked in the hotel's parking lot, off to the side of the building. "Do you want to wait here while I check us in?"

Her first instinct was to say no, but chances were she knew several people who worked in this hotel. She'd rather put off the smirks and innuendos as long as possible. "Sure."

He squeezed her hand, climbed from the vehicle and walked into the hotel.

Lacey opened the passenger door and slid to the asphalt. She contemplated the beautiful landscape noticeable in the strategically placed lights. The hotel was three stories of white splendor, the Georgian architecture reminding her of houses in movies about the Civil War. She couldn't wait to see how the interior looked.

Headlights swept over the exterior of the hotel, drawing her attention. She stiffened. Really? They couldn't wait until tomorrow morning before starting the campaign to make her look like the worst criminal ever born?

Lacey wanted to hurry into the hotel after Jake, but that would only delay the inevitable. Besides, if she dealt with this now, maybe he'd leave her alone while Jake was with her. Not only that, she didn't dare turn her back on the Winston cop. He made her skin crawl.

Hoping the cop would move along before Jake returned, she folded her arms across her chest and waited.

"What are you doing here?" Will Beckett demanded to know, his voice a deep growl that sent a shiver of distaste through her.

"My mother is missing."

A snort. "Missing? Your mom is out of town with a friend." He sneered. "Probably a boyfriend or someone willing to pay her for sex."

Her stomach churned as old memories shoved to the forefront of her mind. "My mother isn't hooking." At least she hadn't been for a while. Was that how she'd been able to afford an SUV? Man, she hoped not.

"You're blind if you can't see what's right in front of you." He shifted closer until he forced her back against the side of Jake's SUV. "I don't see your clunker. How'd you get here?"

"It's none of your business how I came to town."

"I'm a town cop, baby. Everything and everyone in this town is my business."

"You have an inflated opinion of yourself. You're just a beat cop."

Will closed the last inch of distance between them, his face twisted with anger as he grabbed her upper arms and squeezed. "What did you say?" he snapped, rage filling his expression.

"Take your hands off my woman." Jake's hard voice had the cop spinning to face the unknown threat.

With his attention diverted, Lacey sidled out of his reach.

"What did you say to me?" Will swaggered forward.

"You heard me." Without taking his eyes from the cop, the medic held out his left hand to Lacey.

"I'm the law in this town. I have the right to stop and frisk anyone."

Jake wrapped his arm around Lacey's waist and pulled her against his side. "You need probable cause or a warrant. You don't have either."

"Who are you?"

"Jake Davenport."

"Got proof of that?" An ugly smile settled on his lips. "If I don't like what I see, you'll be spending time in the town lockup."

Lacey stared in disbelief. If he expected Jake to quail in fear at the threat, he was doomed to disappointment. Was Will really that stupid? Even a fool could see the man holding her against his side wasn't intimidated in the least.

"That would be a costly mistake on your part. My wallet is in the side pocket of my pants." He slowly reached down and pulled out his wallet, then removed his license for Will to examine.

"Wait here," he said curtly and stalked to his cruiser.

Jake turned and cupped Lacey's cheek with his rough palm. "Did he hurt you?"

"Not really."

His eyes narrowed. "Lacey."

"I'm fine, I promise. He scared me a little." A lot, but she didn't want to upset Jake more.

"Who is he?"

"Will Beckett. He's the police chief's son." He'd been the bane of her existence growing up along with his buddy, Noah Holt. The two of them had always watched her, a knowing look in their eyes. Hadn't taken her long to figure out Will's father had a big mouth. Didn't matter, she supposed. You couldn't keep secrets in Winston. Everyone knew everyone else's business.

"He'll be twitchy when he returns. When he runs my name, he'll find out I'm licensed to carry."

"He'll make trouble for you if he can. I'm sorry, Jake."

Jake's thumb brushed lightly over her cheek. "Everything will be fine. I'm covered."

She was about to ask him to explain that statement when Will returned, gun in his hand.

"Hands up, Davenport. Lock your fingers behind your head and get on your knees."

The medic handed a plastic card to Lacey, released her, then complied with Will's order. "Give the card to him," he said to Lacey, his voice soft.

She handed the card to the policeman and shifted closer to Jake. She didn't know what she could do if Will decided to rough up her friend, but she would do her best to help.

"Get away from him, Lacey. Your boyfriend is dangerous."

"He would never lay a hand on me in anger." Not like Frank. He was in her past, she reminded herself. She'd escaped his clutches.

"Then you're a stupid twit like your mother."

Jake didn't say a word, but he turned his head to stare at Will. Whatever the cop saw made him swallow hard and back up another step.

"You armed?" Will asked.

"Always."

"Take out your weapon, and put it on the ground, slowly. You make a move too fast, I'll fill you full of holes." Another sneer. "One or two bullets might accidentally hit your girlfriend."

Jake's eyes narrowed.

Not wanting things to escalate out of control, Lacey laid her hand on his shoulder.

He bent his head just enough to kiss the back of her hand and slowly unclasped his fingers. He tugged his pant leg up and pulled a gun from an ankle holster and laid it on the ground within easy reach.

"This is an Alabama carry permit. You live in Tennessee with Lacey. This ain't a legit permit, boy."

She started to correct his misinterpretation of their living arrangements, but thought better of it. If Will believed she and Jake were intimately involved, maybe the cop would keep his hands off her.

"The carry permit is legitimate. I work for a private security firm. We have agreements in place with every state."

"I'm confiscating your weapon."

"If you do, you can expect a call from Governor Chandler within the hour."

A snort. "I don't believe you."

"Try me."

Apparently thinking better of his plan, Will tossed the gun permit and driver's license on the ground in front of Jake. "Stay out of trouble, Davenport. I'll be watching you." He slid a glance toward Lacey. "I'll see you later, baby."

CHAPTER SEVEN

Jake rose and turned to Lacey. The sight of her pale face made an invisible band squeeze around his chest. He scooped up his license and permit, and opened his arms. "Come here."

She flew into his embrace. He held her tight against his chest, hating the belligerent cop had caused her to tremble. "It's okay, Lacey."

"It's not. I shouldn't have let you come."

"You couldn't have stopped me. I told you, I'm here with you because I want to be."

"Will Beckett will cause you trouble."

He tightened his grip across her back. "You are worth every hurdle I have to leap over."

She stared, her eyes widening.

Did Lacey understand what he was telling her? Sometime soon, he would have to spell it out. The beautiful woman in his arms didn't seem to do subtlety. "Come on. We're checked in, and I have our key cards."

He made himself let go of her and lifted the back hatch of the SUV. Jake reached inside and hauled out his mike bag and Go bag, then grabbed Lacey's suitcase before locking his vehicle. Wouldn't put it past the nosy cop to try poking around the interior if Jake was stupid enough to leave it unlocked. Never going to happen. Fortress operatives didn't take chances with their safety or those they cared about. His gaze shifted to Lacey. He cared about her. A lot.

"I can carry my bag."

"I've got it." He started toward the front door of the hotel. "We're on the third floor."

Lacey hurried to keep up with him. At the elevator, she punched the call button, glancing around as they waited for the car to arrive in the lobby. "This is really nice," she whispered.

He considered their surroundings, caught himself before he shrugged. The hotel was all right, but he'd stayed in much better when he lived with his parents. They had expensive taste when they traveled. With his years in the military and Fortress, Jake had learned to sleep any place that was dry. Most of his teammates had learned to sleep even in the rain, a skill he'd yet to learn for himself. He hated being wet, something he'd experienced more than once on missions.

They rode to the third floor in silence. When they reached her room, Jake set her suitcase against the wall and pulled the card from his pocket. A moment later, he placed her suitcase on one of the double beds in the room.

He unlocked the door connecting to his room. "After that incident in the parking lot, I think it would be wise to leave the doors unlocked between our rooms."

"He wouldn't dare come up here."

"Better to be safe." He wanted easy access to her room if a problem developed. "I'll drop my bags in my room, then we'll talk." And they would talk. Things weren't adding up here. The Lacey he'd come to know over the past few months didn't mesh with the one he was seeing in her hometown.

Lacey walked to the window to peer outside without replying.

Doubting she was interested in the scenery at this time of night, Jake figured she needed a minute to get herself together. He left her room and walked next door. His accommodations were the same as hers. Two double beds covered with blue comforters, several pillows heaped on the beds, curtains open to the view at the back of the hotel.

He laid his bags on one of the beds, and took a minute to splash cold water on his face, giving himself time to cool his temper. Will Beckett was going to be an irritant while he and Lacey were in Winston. But was he dangerous?

He pulled out his phone and called Zane. If there was something to he needed to know about the cop, he'd rather have the information up front.

"Miss me already, Jake?"

"As much as I miss a rash. Got a name for you to run. I'd do it myself, but I need a deep scan yesterday."

"Go."

"Will Beckett. He's a local cop. I need everything you can find on this clown."

"You've only been in Winston a few minutes, man. How could you run afoul of the cops this fast?"

"It's a gift. When I went into the hotel to check us in, Lacey remained outside. I returned to the parking lot and found her pinned against the SUV by this local cop. He put his hands on her, Z. She said he didn't hurt her, but I'm not convinced she was being honest."

"Did you lay him out?" Raw fury filled Zane's voice.

"I wish. I didn't want Lacey upset more than she already was. I told him to get his hands off my woman. If he hadn't complied, I would have taken him down and dealt with the consequences."

A soft whistle sounded over the phone's speaker. "What did Lacey have to say about you claiming she was yours?"

His gaze shifted to the still locked door leading from his room to hers. "Nothing yet."

"She will. Were you just giving her your protection or is there something going on between you two that I don't know about?"

Jake sighed. Should have known Z would pick up the implication. "She doesn't know I'm interested in her. I've been giving her some time to get used to me. After the trouble she had with her ex, I didn't want to move too fast."

"Wise. Frank's one of the sorriest excuses of manhood I've ever seen. He roughed her up a few times before Rowan got through to her, and Brent and Adam laid into him."

Jake's hand gripped the phone tighter. The thought of anyone hurting Lacey made his blood boil. No wonder Adam and Brent were so protective of her. "I didn't know Frank hurt her." Probably safer for the man. Wouldn't save him from Jake if he ever went after Lacey again.

"She doesn't talk about him anymore. Says he's in her past."

Right. Sometimes, though, the past had a way of biting you when you least expected. "While you're looking into Will Beckett's background, see what pops for his father as well. He's the chief of police in Winston." Another glance at the connecting doors. "I assume you're checking into Yvonne's background."

"I'll send the results of that to your email. From what I've learned so far, Lacey's mother has quite a checkered past. Looks like you've already raised some interest in town. Someone in the Winston PD is running your name through the system."

He frowned. "Will ran me a few minutes ago. This is a new search?"

"That's right. Seems you've caused quite a stir. I'll send the name of a top-notch Alabama lawyer who works with Fortress when our people run into legal trouble. A necessity where you're concerned."

Smart aleck. "Send the name. I hope I won't need it. Just make sure the lawyer has zero ties to Winston or the Becketts."

"Copy that. Anything else I can do for you?"

"Not right now."

"Keep me posted. We'll do whatever is necessary to help Lacey."

So would Jake, even if he had to take on the Winston police to protect her. After sliding his phone into his pocket, he unlocked the connecting door and knocked before walking inside Lacey's room. She hadn't moved from the window.

Although he didn't think there was much chance of Beckett or one of his buddies being in the courtyard, he didn't want to chance someone pinpointing Lacey's location if an observer happened to be in the area. He turned off the light.

Lacey turned. "Why did you turn off the light?"

"You were backlit by the light." He crossed the room and stood beside her, noting the balcony had an outdoor loveseat and a table.

Jake unlocked the door and stepped outside. He quartered the area, looking for possible threats to Lacey's safety. A minute later, he turned back, held out his hand to her. "Would you like to sit outside for a while?" Pleased when she took his hand, he led her to the loveseat. "Do you need something to drink?"

"I'd love some water."

"I'll be back in a minute." Jake found the vending machine down the hall, purchased two bottles of water, and let himself back into the room. He broke the seal on Lacey's bottle and handed her the cold drink.

They sat in silence for a while. When she'd finished half her water, Jake set his bottle on the table. When he sat back, he draped his arm across the back of the loveseat. He'd love to hold her in his arms, but wasn't sure she would welcome his touch right now. "Talk to me, Lacey."

"I don't want you to think poorly of me," she murmured, her gaze focused on the courtyard below.

"That's never going to happen."

"You don't know my background. It's not pretty, Jake."

"Everybody has a past. I wouldn't ask, but yours got in my face in the parking lot a few minutes ago." He risked resting his hand on her shoulder. "I'd rather hear it from you."

She turned to him, her expression resigned. "When you hear the details, you may decide I'm not worth the trouble I'm causing you."

He squeezed her shoulder. "Trust me."

Lacey shifted to face the courtyard again, as though she couldn't look him in the eyes while she told her story. "I grew up here in Winston. I don't have any idea who my father is, and the men in town know my mother all too well."

Oh, man. He still needed to hear her story, but he hated that she had gone through a tough childhood. Jake moved closer to her and draped his arm across her shoulders. She might not need his support, but he wanted to offer it anyway.

"My mother was in and out of jail for prostitution and public intoxication. As far as I know, she's been sober and hasn't turned tricks for six years."

"When did you leave Winston?"

"Six years ago, right after my mother got out of rehab." She sighed. "You probably think I'm heartless, but I couldn't handle another downward spiral until she was forced back into rehab or tossed in jail again for the drinking. Being known as the daughter of the town drunk and prostitute limited my job opportunities. The owners of the grocery store let me work for them during high school, but I couldn't make a career out of scanning groceries. Besides, most of my paychecks were going to pay for Mom's treatments or court costs if she didn't outright steal money from my purse or my account to buy liquor. I knew I would never get anywhere if I stayed in Winston so I got out. I left her to deal with her problems."

"She was taking you down with her, Lacey."

"Doesn't help me sleep at night. I feel guilty for leaving her, but I had to save myself."

His heart actually hurt listening to her story. "Where did you go when you left?"

"You aren't going to ask about my juvie record?"

"If it's relevant to what I'm facing, tell me."

"I was collared by the police for shop lifting more times than I can count."

He blinked. "What made you stop stealing?"

"The grocery store I was stealing from hired me as a stocker." She smiled now. "The owner was a gruff old guy, but he figured it would be better to hire me than to keep racking up court costs filing charges against me for stealing food. Turned out Mr. Grady had a soft heart underneath the gruff exterior."

Jake froze. "You were stealing food."

"What money Mom brought in she drank. I got tired of being hungry all the time."

He placed a kiss on the top of her head. "Where did you go when you left Winston?"

"I bought a bus ticket to Nashville. I worked at two grocery stores to have enough money for a studio apartment. I lived at a shelter until I scraped enough money together to rent the apartment."

Jake thought about what he knew of her activities. "Is that the shelter where you volunteer every week?"

She nodded. "I became good friends with most of the staff. I wanted to give something back for what they did for me."

Because they'd helped her when she needed it, Jake would be making a sizable donation in her name. "When did you meet Rowan?"

"A friend who was a coffee fanatic told me about Coffee House. The shop had been open a week, and Rowan was asking for recommendations for help. When Rowan heard about me, she called and asked me to come in for an interview." Soft laughter. "Some interview. Rowan was swamped with customers. She put me to work behind the counter. I've been working there ever since."

"Do you want to have a shop of your own one day?"

Lacey shook her head. "I love what I do. Although I know most of our customers by name and coffee preference, I want to do more with my life than pour coffee and hand out pastries."

"What's your ultimate goal?"

"Don't laugh."

"I won't. Tell me what your dream job is."

"I want to be a trauma surgeon."

Huh. He hadn't seen that one coming. "Do you have any college credits?"

Another head shake. "I've been saving most of my paychecks so I can register for classes."

And that explained why her apartment was filled with well-loved furniture and her closet was nearly empty. "Have you told Brent and Rowan what you want to do?"

"Not yet. I didn't see the point since I can't afford to start school yet."

"You should. Fortress needs another trauma surgeon. We only have one, and he's in Texas."

"I don't understand why Brent would be interested in my career goals. It takes a long time to become a doctor and I haven't even started."

He cupped her chin and turned her face toward him. “He will want to talk to you about working for Fortress. If you agree, there’s a good chance he’ll help you with your tuition.”

CHAPTER EIGHT

The next morning, Lacey sipped coffee from the local coffee shop and grimaced. She wished she could go behind the counter and show them how real coffee was made. If she brewed coffee this bad, Rowan would fire her for sure because they wouldn't have any customers.

"It's definitely not yours," Jake murmured. He sat next to her at the table in the shop, his back to the wall.

"Why do you do that?"

He paused, his coffee cup halfway to his mouth. "Why do I do what?"

"Why do you and your friends sit with your backs to the wall?"

"To see the occupants in a room along with the doors and windows. We never turn our backs to a room. That's a good way to end up dead because you can't defend against what you can't see."

Lacey frowned. "But Coffee House is safe. We've never had a problem."

"No place is safe. You work in retail. There's always a chance someone will come into the shop and demand the proceeds from the cash register."

Great. Nothing like smashing her security into a million tiny pieces.

"And don't forget the guy who broke into your apartment above the shop when your boss lived there."

"You can stop boosting my confidence in my safety at home and work," she said dryly. "Besides, Fortress installed a security system in both places."

"No security system is foolproof, not even ours. The best we can do is make the protection strong enough to discourage a thief from breaking in, and getting you the help you need."

The girl behind the counter called out, "Jake. Order up."

Lacey winced. Definitely not how Rowan's employees handled orders.

Jake returned to the table with a small tray. One plate held Lacey's blueberry bagel with cream cheese. The other plate contained his breakfast sandwich.

She spread cream cheese on one slice of the bagel. "Do we have a plan for today?"

"I thought we'd start at your mother's house to see if we can find any indication where she might have gone."

"If she left of her own free will."

Jake inclined his head as he bit into his sandwich.

She sighed. "Maybe I overreacted. What if the police are right and Mom is turning tricks again?"

"It's better to know for sure, Lacey. I though you said Yvonne hadn't returned to her old habits."

"As far as I know. I don't visit her that often. I talk to her on the phone every week. She says she is clean and working a legitimate job." Unpleasant conversations. She hated the recriminations that her mother heaped on her head.

"When was the last time you saw her?"

"Three months ago. I took her out to dinner for her birthday."

"You didn't notice anything unusual when you talked to her?"

She shrugged. "Same as always. She was clean and sober, working at the diner. She missed me. Why didn't I love her enough to come home more often? And my personal favorite, could I give her money?"

"Ouch."

"Yeah. Mom has guilt trips down to an art form."

"Does she hit you up for money often?"

"Every time I talk to her or see her.

"I'm sorry." He wrapped his hand around hers. "That must hurt."

"More than I'll tell her."

"Does she know what you're saving the money for?"

Laughter slipped out. "I don't dare tell her I have any savings. Otherwise, the pressure to share my money with her would never let up."

"Did you tell her you want to be a doctor?"

She watched citizens of Winston hurry by the shop on their way to their first appointments for the day, to work, or school, and thought about the conversation two years ago. Her cheeks burned even now thinking of her mother's scorn.

"Lacey?"

She turned, lifted her chin as she stared into his eyes. "Mom laughed and said I wasn't smart enough to be a doctor."

Another hand squeeze. "She's wrong."

Such simple words, yet his belief in her ability to learn and persevere soothed some of the ragged edges of hurt her mother had inflicted. "Thank you."

Jake finished the last bite of his sandwich. "You need a coffee refill before we go to your mother's?"

Lacey grimaced. "I'll pass."

He chuckled and policed their trash. In the SUV, he said, "Which way?"

"Right at the next corner. Go six blocks, then turn left on Orlando Drive. Mom's house is at the end of the street."

Jake followed her directions without comment although he kept glancing in the mirrors.

She twisted to look out the back window and scowled. "Don't they ever give up?"

"You have more than one cop keeping an eye on you?"

"Told you. Most of the men in town know my mother very well."

"Including the police?"

"Especially the police. My mother may not be turning tricks, but that doesn't mean she isn't playing musical beds. She never figured out how to be herself without a man in her life. She feels incomplete and is sure she's missing the man of her dreams."

"Dangerous lifestyle."

"Tell me something I don't know."

"Do you have a key to your mother's house?"

"I do. Why?"

"Can't exactly pick the lock with a cop watching every move."

She burst into laughter. "I guess not. Puts a crimp in your style, doesn't it?"

"If you only knew."

More laughter, then, "Can you really pick a lock?"

"In a few seconds, depending on the lock."

"Where did you learn to do that?"

He slid her a glance. "I was in the Army, Special Forces. I learned a lot of skills that aren't legal."

"You any good at these skills?"

"One of the best."

Of course. Why would she think otherwise? There was something about Jake that spoke of quiet confidence and skill. "Were you in the same unit as Durango?"

"No. Durango is Delta Force. I'm a Ranger, like Ethan Blackhawk."

Her mouth gaped. "The Otter Creek police chief was an Army Ranger?"

"That's right. He's still talked about in the Special Forces community, and he's the first port of call for those who need help tracking suspects, fugitives, and missing people. He doesn't take as many cases since he married Serena and especially since his son was born, but he never turns down a case involving children. Brent's been known to tap him for his tracking skills as well."

"I've heard Brent and the others talk about him. Why don't you tell people that you're a military hero, Jake?"

He snorted. "Because I'm not. I was a soldier and medic for eight years. I followed orders and patched up wounds."

"Don't sell yourself short. Adam and the others talk about how many people's lives you've saved with your medical skills."

"I was doing my job."

"An important one."

Jake parked in her mother's driveway. "The job you will train for soon is an important one as well."

"I don't know how soon that will be. My savings account isn't healthy enough to sign up for classes yet."

The medic pointed a finger at her. "Fortress will help. Even if they don't, you'll be able to get a student loan. Once you start working as a doctor, you can repay the loans."

There was no point in arguing with him. The problem was she couldn't stop working full time. She couldn't afford to pay her bills if she worked less than 40 hours a week. Even then, it was tight. How would she have time for classes, complete assignments, and study for tests? She needed terrific grades to have a chance to get into medical school. Hard to do that when she would be short on sleep and facing long work days.

She opened the door and hopped out. Jake met her on the walkway to the front door. As they approached the bright red door, the police cruiser pulled up behind them.

"What do you think you're doing?" The burly policeman stalked after them, his face red.

Lacey looked over her shoulder. "Going into the house, Will. Got a problem with that?"

"Yeah, actually I do." An ugly smile curved his mouth. "Unless you don't mind spending some quality time in the Winston jail. Breaking and entering is against the law." He slid a pointed glance at Jake before spearing her again with his glare.

Lacey grabbed her keys from her purse and found the key to her mother's house. "Can't be breaking and entering if I have a key."

"You don't have permission to be inside the house. It's private property." His right hand fondled the grip of his gun. "Do it, Lacey. I dare you. Nothing would make me happier than to arrest you. It's no less than you deserve since you haven't outgrown your criminal past."

Beside her, Jake stilled. Figuring the medic would object to Will's words and attitude, she wrapped her hand around his and squeezed. "Sorry to disappoint you, Will, but I'm not breaking and entering when I have a key and it's my house."

"Excuse me?"

"You heard me. This is my house. My name is on the mortgage agreement and I've been paying the payments for years."

CHAPTER NINE

Jake's expression impassive despite shock ricocheting through his body. Lacey owned the house her mother lived in? No wonder she didn't have enough money to start college. With her salary, her dollars must be stretched thin to cover her mother's mortgage and Lacey's rent plus her other bills.

Will Beckett sneered at Lacey. "You're a liar, baby." He reached for her. "You're coming with me."

Jake stepped between the cop and Lacey. "Hands off."

"Get out of my way, Davenport. I'm taking her into custody until I confirm she's blowing smoke, then I'll arrest her and talk with the judge about losing her cell key."

"That's not the way it works. Confirm if she's telling the truth. We're going inside. You know where to find us. If you arrest Lacey, her lawyer will sue you and the Winston PD for false arrest and harassment." A teeth-baring smile. "The lawyer is very good."

The door opened behind him. Jake backed inside, his gaze on the red-faced cop. He locked the door as soon as Beckett stomped off the porch and stalked to the cruiser.

He turned, almost plowing into Lacey. Alert for a problem, Jake didn't see anything out of place. In fact, the living room was tastefully decorated with a leather couch and throw pillows, a recliner he'd love to nap in, two end tables with lamps, a gorgeous coffee table. His mother would have been comfortable in this room. "What's wrong?"

"The furniture."

He looked at the room again, puzzled. "What's wrong with it?"

"Where did she get the money for this?"

He stilled. "You don't recognize the furniture?"

She swung around. "Three months ago, the living room was filled with thrift store bargains. You know, the typical ugly brown sofa, a lime green recliner, and a beat-up coffee table with condensation rings over the surface."

"Is it possible someone gave her the furniture?"

"I doubt it. She doesn't inspire that kind of favor in people." Lacey drew in a careful breath. "We should look at the rest of the house before we search for clues to where Mom might have gone."

"Let me check the house before you walk through."

"Why?"

"In case someone is hiding." He also wanted to be sure Lacey didn't stumble onto anything unpleasant without preparation. Doubtful a dead body was in the house. Didn't mean that someone with nefarious intentions hadn't left an ugly surprise for Lacey.

Although she looked skeptical, the coffee shop manager nodded.

"I won't be long." After Jake cleared the three bedrooms, two baths, and kitchen, he opened the door to the garage, turned on the light, and peered inside. Empty except for boxes stacked against the walls. A grease spot stained the center of the concrete floor where evidence indicated Yvonne normally parked her vehicle.

He started to close the door when he noticed another stain. Dread coiling in the pit of his stomach, he crossed the concrete expanse. Jake dropped to his haunches, opened his flashlight app, and focused the light on the stain. Rust colored.

Oh, man. He didn't want to show Lacey this. He followed a trail of rust brown drops a few feet to where they abruptly ended. He ran scenarios through his mind, figured the most likely was the truth.

Returning to the kitchen, he found a plastic sandwich bag and retraced his steps to the garage. Jake unsheathed his knife and scraped a sample of blood off the floor and dumped it into the bag. He shoved the bag into his pocket and called Zane. "Need a favor."

"Name it."

"Do we have a lab we use in this area?"

"Hold." A moment later, Zane said, "No lab. However, we have an operative in your vicinity. I'll have him stop to pick up whatever you need analyzed."

"Who's the operative?"

"Cade Ramsey. What's going on, Jake?"

"I'm standing in Yvonne Coleman's garage, staring at a trail of blood that disappears at about the cargo area of an SUV. The amount of blood isn't enough to be dangerous, but it does indicate to me Yvonne didn't leave under her own steam."

"Not what we wanted to hear."

"Beckett followed us to Yvonne's house and threatened to arrest Lacey for B & E. Lacey's name is on the mortgage. She's been paying to keep a roof over her mother's head."

"On her salary?" Zane whistled. "No wonder she asks Rowan for more shifts."

"Tell Maddox I need to talk to him about Lacey."

"Is she all right?"

"Lacey's fine. She wants to go to med school to be a trauma surgeon."

"She interested in working for us?"

"The idea intrigues her."

"He'll be expecting your call."

"Thanks."

"Jake, is it safe for me to look around?" Lacey called.

"I have to go, Z."

"When you get a chance, check your email for info I sent on the Becketts."

"Copy that."

Jake returned to the living room where Lacey waited.

"Is everything okay?"

"The house is clear, but the garage isn't."

All color drained from Lacey's face.

He mentally berated himself as he gripped her upper arms. "Sit." In seconds, he nudged her down to the leather sofa. She obeyed his order without a protest which told him how upset she was. Hurrying to the kitchen, he checked the refrigerator for cold water and found only beer.

With a scowl, Jake filled a glass with cold water from the tap. He sat beside her and pressed the glass into her hand. When she'd consumed half, Jake set the glass on the coffee table and turned Lacey's face toward his. "I'm sorry. I didn't mean to scare you. I found a trail of blood in the garage. The volume wasn't enough to indicate a grievous wound. The injury indicates your mother didn't leave of her own accord."

"What has she gotten herself into?"

"We'll find her." He cupped her cheeks, brushing his thumbs gently over the velvety texture of her skin. His gaze dipped to her lips. If he moved just a fraction of an inch closer, he could taste her as he'd longed to do for months. The timing was lousy, though. He'd just confirmed her mother was in serious trouble. This wasn't the time to capture the kiss he ached for. Soon, he hoped.

One last butterfly touch, and he dropped his hands. "Do you want to see what I found?" When she nodded, Jake led her to the garage.

Lacey stopped short in the doorway. "That's the cleanest I've seen this garage in years."

"Looks like she cleared space for her SUV." He wrapped his arm around her waist and urged her toward the first blood drops. Crouching, he pointed at the rust-colored stains. "I think your mother was attacked as she approached her SUV. She fell here at the larger stain, then she was carried to the back of the SUV. That's why the trail disappears there."

"Is she dead?" she asked, her voice soft.

"Based on the evidence, she was alive when she left this garage." Whether she was still alive was anyone's guess. Given that she hadn't been seen or heard from in days, the likelihood of finding her alive diminished with each passing day.

"Is there any chance to find her alive?"

He didn't want to lie to her. "We need to move fast."

"Let's walk through the house."

She went to the kitchen. "Mom keeps a notepad on the counter to write messages from her answering machine." Lacey grabbed the pad of paper. "Blank."

Jake studied the paper for a few seconds, then grabbed a pencil from a nearby coffee cup filled with writing implements. He used the side of the pencil lead to rub across the paper's surface. Yvonne's last markings on the pad showed up white against a field of gray. "*Eleven o'clock, M.* Any idea what that means?"

She shook her head, frowning. "I'll keep trying to figure it out."

"Let's search the rest of the house. Tell me if you notice anything missing or out of place."

They went to the master bedroom next. Lacey drew in a sharp breath. "New bedroom furniture, too? Where did she get the money for this?"

"Ask your mother when we find her. Look for anything out of the ordinary aside from new furniture."

Jake stayed out of the way as she searched through the closet and under the bed. She went to the dresser, pulling out drawers, searching the contents. When Lacey turned to him, her expression made him straighten from the wall. "What's wrong?"

"Mom was seeing someone."

"How do you know?"

She gestured toward the dresser, her cheeks pink. "She buys new underwear when she gets involved with someone."

"Since you haven't been inside the house in months, how do you know this is new?"

The color in her cheeks deepened. "I priced new underwear for myself and had to mark this line off my list. It's too expensive for my budget."

But Yvonne Coleman didn't have a problem spending all this money on herself and begging her daughter for more. "Did she do the same when she was working the streets?"

A snort. "You better believe it. That's one thing she never skimps on. When I lived at home, I had to do the laundry. Mom insisted on special laundry detergent and hanging her delicates to dry."

"We need to check the master bath and nightstands. Which do you want?"

"Bathroom." She went into the bathroom and soon she was rummaging through the drawers in the vanity.

Jake turned his attention to the nightstands. He opened the drawer of the nearest one and riffled through the contents. The loose paper and condoms didn't raise an eyebrow. The pile of cash did surprise him. He did a quick count and blew out a breath. No way Yvonne earned that much in tips from a dive.

Lacey returned to the bedroom. "Nothing in the bathroom that I didn't expect. What about you?"

He turned, the stack of cash in his hand.

Her jaw dropped. "Are you kidding me? How much is this?"

"Ten thousand dollars."

CHAPTER TEN

Lacey cupped trembling hands around the white coffee mug. Trail End, the diner where her mother worked, still hopped at ten o'clock. Wouldn't be long before the lunch crowd filled the shop.

Her gaze locked with Jake's. "My mother didn't make that much money in tips from this place." One glance at the cracked red vinyl seats and booths, peeling black-and-white linoleum, faded paint, and blue-collar workers was enough to convince Lacey that Yvonne Coleman didn't make a bundle with her salary or tips.

"No, she didn't," Jake agreed.

She leaned closer. "When Mom drinks, she blows through cash. At least I know she hasn't fallen off the wagon."

Loretta White, her mother's friend, bustled to the table with a coffee carafe. "Refill, sugar?"

"Please. This coffee is much better than the sludge they serve at the coffee shop across the street."

She snorted. "Been telling Dorothy, the owner of the coffee shop, that she needs to train her workers better. They aren't bringing in near the profit they should because the brew they serve is so bad."

"The place was busy earlier this morning despite the lousy joe," Jake said.

"That's because people stopped on the way to work, short on time, and didn't want to fight the crowd in here."

True enough. Lacey hadn't wanted to deal with the crowd of neighbors and acquaintances herself. That's why she'd suggested the coffee shop. Turned out to be a bad decision, one she wouldn't repeat.

"When will you have a break, Loretta?"

The waitress peeked at the clock on the wall. "Fifteen minutes."

"Would you join us on your break?"

"Sure. Been ages since I've had a chance to catch up with you."

"Not much to tell. Work and more work. The update will take all of two minutes, maybe less. I wanted to talk to you about Mom."

Sympathy filled the older woman's gaze. "I won't be much help, but I'll be back in a few."

Jake studied Lacey's face. "What are you thinking?"

"Mom got in over her head and now she's in deep trouble, the kind I may not be able to help with."

"How long have you been paying for her house?"

She lifted her chin. "Since I started working a full-time job. I may not be able to live in the same house or town with her, but I still love Mom. I didn't want her to end up without a roof over her head, and she can't afford the payments on what she makes here." Her lips quirked. "At least I didn't think she could. Turns out the laugh is on me."

"You're a good daughter, Lacey."

She sipped her coffee, proud of the fact her hand almost didn't tremble this time. "She would disagree with you."

"She's wrong, something I'll point out to her when I have the chance."

If he got the chance. Lacey's stomach lurched, thinking of the blood on the garage floor. She was afraid for her mother. If she went off with a boyfriend, why hadn't anyone heard from her? Yvonne Coleman wasn't shy about sharing news with her friends. Maybe Loretta would shed some light on the situation or point them in the right direction. If her mother was seeing a man, Loretta would know. Whether she knew if Mom was turning tricks again was another question.

Jake covered her hand with his. "We'll find the answers you need."

"But will it be fast enough?"

He squeezed. "I hope so."

She turned her hand over and laced their fingers together. At least he hadn't given her false hope. She'd prefer honesty over a lie to spare her feelings any day. "Mom's laptop is missing."

"You sure?"

"Positive. She keeps it on the breakfast bar in the kitchen."

"She might have moved it."

"We searched the rest of the house, Jake. There are only two other places she leaves that computer. It wasn't in either place. Someone took her computer." But why? What motive prompted the theft of the laptop but left everything else in the house untouched?

"Another puzzle to solve." He hesitated. "This isn't the right time, but I want to ask you a question."

Her stomach knotted. She'd never seen him unsure of himself. That alone made her dread the question. "Ask."

"Have you been seeing anyone lately?"

Lacey blinked. "Seeing anyone?"

"Dating someone," he clarified.

She shook her head. "Why?" Was Jake working up to asking her for a date? Nothing would make her happier although she couldn't believe he'd choose to be with her.

Although the men from Fortress Security were in and out of the shop all the time and were unfailingly polite, none of them hinted they were interested in anything more than their next cup of coffee and a pastry from one of their favorite baristas.

"Would you be interested in going to dinner with me?"

Lacey's heart skipped a beat before surging ahead at breakneck speed. "You're asking me to go on a date?"

"You're an attractive woman and I enjoy your company. If you need it spelled out, yes, I'm asking you on a date. Will you go with me?"

A date. Jake Davenport, the man she'd dreamed about for months, was asking her for a date. "I'd like that." Like it? Lame word for the geyser of joy exploding inside her.

A smile curved his lips.

Loretta returned to the table, this time with three pieces of apple pie. She placed two in front of Lacey and Jake, then pulled out one of the chairs and sat, keeping the third piece for herself. "It's a little early for dessert, but I felt like making an exception today."

A snort from Jake. "It's never too early to eat apple pie."

Now it was Lacey's turn to stare. "You're a medic. Shouldn't you be telling us to eat an apple instead?"

"I run five miles or more every day plus whatever grueling workout Adam devises. I can afford a piece of pie once in a while."

"Who do you work for, Jake?" Loretta forked a bite of pie into her mouth.

"I'm with Fortress Security, a private security firm."

She frowned. "Lacey said you're a medic."

He inclined his head in agreement. "You never know when a good medic will come in handy."

Based on what Rowan shared with her over the past few months, Jake was highly skilled, in great demand, and had recently been assigned to Adam Walker's team.

Her mother's friend looked skeptical, but didn't argue the point. She turned to Lacey. "What do you want to know, hon?"

"Is my mother has been seeing anyone?" When she realized she'd chosen the same turn of phrase that Jake had used, she flicked a glance at the dark-haired man. Her cheeks burned at his wink.

"Your mom has a string of men vying for her attention, Lace. You know that. However, the only man she pays attention to is Harley Owens."

"The guy who owns the garage on Mayes Street?"

"That's the one. He comes in when Yvonne works and sits in her section. He's crazy about her."

"How long has this been going on?" Jake asked.

"About four months." Loretta cast a questioning glance at Lacey. "You didn't know?"

"Mom didn't tell me."

"Well, it sure is the talk of Winston. He treats her like a princess. Harley's been worried sick about Yvonne."

Jake sipped his coffee. "Why didn't he file the missing person report?"

"I beat him to it. He'd been trying to reach her for two days and planned to file the report when he closed the shop. I worked the early shift that day and went over to the police department to file the report. Figured if I got them going, they'd find Yvonne sooner." Disgust filled her eyes. "Lot of good that did me. Those yahoos over there think your mom took off with another guy and didn't tell anybody. Can't convince them otherwise."

She patted Lacey's hand. "Don't you believe what they tell you, honey. Yvonne's not the same woman since she's been with Harley. She's not doing what she did before."

Even though her heart ached, Lacey smiled. "It's okay, Loretta. You can use the term. You're sure she wasn't earning money as a prostitute?"

"I'm positive. Yvonne is head-over-heels in love with Harley. She wouldn't run off with some other man. Now, if the man she'd run off with was Harley, I wouldn't have a problem believing that because he's been after her to marry him for weeks."

Tears stung Lacey's eyes. She wanted her mother to be happy. Was it possible that she'd found the man of her dreams in Harley?

Jake scooted his chair closer to hers and wrapped his arm around her shoulders. "Would Harley talk to us, Loretta?"

"I don't see why not. He's as worried over Yvonne's disappearance as I am, maybe more."

"Did you notice anything different with her in the past few months?"

Loretta finished her last bite of pie before answering. "Now that you mention it, Yvonne has been secretive, almost smug. I thought the change in attitude was because of Harley."

He frowned. "Did she explain?"

The waitress snorted. "Are you kidding? When I asked, she said she'd tell me later. She disappeared right after that."

"Have you been in her house recently?" Lacey asked.

"Oh, yeah. I couldn't believe it when I saw all the new stuff in her place."

"Did she tell you how she managed to buy a whole house full of new furniture?"

Loretta shook her head. "From the way she was acting, I figured Harley bought it."

Something to ask Harley when she and Jake went to the garage.

"Tell me about you, Lacey." Loretta leaned closer. "What's going on with you? You promised me an update."

"Told you. Not much to tell. I've been working a lot of hours at Coffee House."

She shifted her curious gaze to Jake. “And what about this handsome man? What’s the story there?”

Lacey glanced at Jake. How did she explain her relationship with him? They’d been friends for a few months, but they didn’t have one date to talk about. Soon though, she hoped.

“Lacey and I are dating,” Jake explained. “We’ve been friends a while, but I just convinced her to give me a chance to win her heart.”

Her head whipped his direction. Win her heart? Did he mean that or was the phrase for Loretta’s benefit?

“Oh, my. How sweet.” Loretta sighed. “Yvonne didn’t mention Jake.”

“She doesn’t know about him.”

“Well, when you tell her, she’ll be thrilled.”

Lacey wasn’t convinced. She’d have to make sure her mother didn’t have Jake’s phone number. The last thing Lacey wanted was for her to hit up Jake for money. She didn’t know how much the operatives from Fortress made, but she knew Brent paid his people well.

Loretta stood. “I’ve got to get back to work, honey. Jake, it was good to meet you. Take care of our girl.”

“Count on it. Do you have the check ready?”

She waved that aside. “Coffee and pie are on the house. You can pick up the tab next time you’re in here.” With that, she left to wait tables again.

Jake fished out his wallet and dropped a twenty-dollar bill on the table. “Come on. Let’s talk to Harley.”

CHAPTER ELEVEN

Jake opened the passenger-side door for Lacey and surveyed the building. Harley's Repair Shop was a large cinder-block building painted white with blue trim. Five bays were open, vehicles on a lift in each with a parking lot at the back filled with trucks, SUVs, and cars already repaired or waiting to be worked on.

A mechanic with the name Mike embroidered on his grease-stained shirt approached them. "Help you?"

"Harley around?"

"In the office." Mike pointed to the dirty gray door at the side of the closest bay. "In that door, turn right. Go straight back."

"Thanks." Jake laid his hand against Lacey's lower back and urged her toward the door. They followed Mike's directions to an office with a door open. Inside, a ginger-haired burly man pecked at a computer, scowling at the screen in front of him.

Jake knocked on the door. "Harley?"

"Yeah. Have a seat. Be with you in a sec." He jabbed a few more keys before shoving away from the computer. His eyes widened when he recognized Lacey. The garage owner rose and planted his hands on the desk, his expression hopeful. "Have you heard from Yvonne?"

She shook her head. "I'm worried about her."

Hope faded in his eyes and he dropped heavily into his seat, motioning for them to sit in the chairs in front of his desk. "So am I. This isn't like her. She never goes this long without contacting me." He stopped abruptly, realizing he'd revealed his relationship with her mother. "Uh, we're friends you know."

"Loretta told me. Mom's been keeping you a secret, Harley."

"Yvonne wanted to wait until you came home for the holidays. Said the news would be a nice surprise for you."

"She's right. I'm happy for both of you."

Relief flooded his face. "I'm planning to marry her as soon as I convince her to say yes."

Lacey smiled. "That's great. This is Jake."

After the men shook hands, Jake said, "When was the last time you saw Yvonne?"

"The night she disappeared." A quick look at Lacey had him clearing his throat, face flushing. "We had a disagreement."

"About what?"

"She'd been keeping secrets the past few weeks, something she hasn't done since we first started going out. She told me she had a meeting that night and had to go. I didn't want her to leave. What kind of fool meeting happens at that time of night? I told Yvonne it wasn't safe. Women have been disappearing around here for the last six years, and I didn't want her to be one of them."

Jake stilled. "How many women?" Had Lacey known about the disappearances? One look at her shocked face gave him his answer.

"Not that many, I guess. A couple a year."

"In a town the size of Winston, that's a lot. Did law enforcement contact the FBI?"

Harley shrugged. “No clue.”

“I doubt it. Chief Beckett is arrogant enough to believe he can figure out the person taking the women himself,” Lacey said. “If he calls in the federal cops, he can’t claim responsibility for the arrest.”

“Loretta said she filed the missing person report on Yvonne.” Jake watched Harley for signs of deceit.

“That’s right. I reported her missing by eight the next morning after she disappeared, but the cops refused to look for her.”

Jake nodded. “They have to wait 48 hours to take action.”

“Seems to me with those missing women the Winston PD would have been more inclined to break the rules. I don’t care what they say. Yvonne didn’t run off with some other man.”

Wishful thinking on Harley’s part or did he know Yvonne well enough to accurately judge her feelings for him?

“You said you had a fight with Mom.”

“I didn’t want her going out that late at night. I didn’t think it was safe. Unfortunately for all of us, I was right.”

“You sure that’s the only reason you and Mom fought?”

Harley stared. “Are you accusing me of hurting the woman I love?”

“I’m asking if there was a reason Mom would have left under her own steam and not returned.”

“To get away from me, you mean.” The mechanic scowled. “The only other disagreement is Yvonne holding off on marrying me.”

“Is there a reason for that?” Jake asked.

“Besides stubbornness? Not a good reason.” He shifted his gaze back to Lacey, his eyes pleading for understanding. “Your mother was concerned that people in town would look down on me for marrying her, afraid it might affect my business."

"You have the only garage and body shop in town."

"Told her that. She still circled back to her past. Yvonne hasn't plied her trade since you left town, Lacey. She wanted to make you proud of her. She said she couldn't do that if she returned to that lifestyle. If things were tight and she needed extra money, she picked up another shift or two to help with expenses."

Jake frowned. What expenses? Lacey had been paying for the house. Utilities couldn't be that much for one person. Until recently, Yvonne didn't have a vehicle. Maybe Harley lied, but Jake hadn't seen signs of it. "How did she purchase the new furniture for the house?"

"Said it was a gift."

"It wasn't from you," Lacey said, her voice flat.

"No and she wouldn't tell me who it was, either. I hoped it was you."

She gave a huff of laughter. "I can't afford new furniture for my own place much less Mom's."

Jake withdrew the paper with the cryptic message from his pocket and showed it to Harley. "Does this make any sense to you?"

He took the paper, studied it a moment. "That's the time of Yvonne's meeting the night she disappeared."

"Do you know what the M stands for?"

"Could be anything. Maybe it stood for the name of the person she was meeting or a meeting place."

"Did she mention a name or a place?"

"If she had, I would have told the cops. Even the bumbling Winston police would have checked it out after Loretta filed the missing person report."

A knock on the door and Mike popped his head in the office. "Hey, sorry to interrupt. Mr. Foster is here about his car. Gave him the bad news and now he insists on speaking only to you."

Harley grimaced. "Be right there." He handed the piece of paper to Jake. "I'll keep thinking about that and let you know if I come up with something. If you need anything to help find Yvonne, tell me and I'll do my best to see that you get it. I love her, Lacey."

"Mom's lucky to have you in her life."

Jake drew Lacey to her feet. "Thanks for your time." He escorted her from the shop, frowning when he saw the Winston PD prowl car idling in the space next to his SUV.

He unlocked his vehicle and made sure his body was between Lacey and the cop watching with cold eyes. Once she was safely inside, Jake turned. "Looking tired, Will. Aren't you going home to take a nap before your next shift?"

Beckett sneered. "Didn't know you cared, Davenport."

"I don't. Doesn't mean I want you plowing into the back of my vehicle because you fell asleep at the wheel. Since I don't want you to get lost on the way to our next stop, I figured I'd tell you we're headed to the station."

The other man looked uneasy. "What for?"

Jake didn't bother to answer. He circled the hood and climbed into the driver's seat.

"What was that about?" Lacey demanded.

"Yanking his chain."

"It's not smart to antagonize Will."

"Somebody needs to. We're going to the police station."

"Why? They won't be any help."

"Maybe not. We'll still talk to the detective in charge of your mother's case." He hoped the cop had some insight into what happened to Yvonne. He was also interested in the detective's thoughts of the missing women in the area and if he thought Yvonne's disappearance was connected.

Fifteen minutes later, Jake parked in front of the police station with Beckett swinging into a space six spaces away. Although it made him twitchy to be unarmed, he unloaded his weapons and locked them in the weapon safe installed in all Fortress SUVs. He couldn't protect Lacey if he was twiddling his thumbs behind bars. They walked into the double doors and approached the desk sergeant.

The grizzled cop sized Jake up as a potential threat and scowled before sliding his gaze to the woman at Jake's side. He nodded. "Lacey. Been a while."

"Yes, sir. How are you, Sergeant Holland?"

He squinted at the calendar. "Looking forward to retirement in five months, six days, and four hours. The wife and I are moving to Florida the minute I walk out of here for the last time. Already got the purchase of a condo on the beach in the works."

"Congratulations. That sounds wonderful. I want to talk to the detective in charge of my mother's case."

"That would be Detective Jones."

"I don't think I know him."

"You went to school with Todd Jones."

A smile appeared on her face. "Todd is a detective now? That's great. Is it possible for us to talk to him?"

The door opened behind them and Beckett stalked inside. As he stomped past Jake, the cop shoulder checked him and kept going through a set of double doors.

"I'll check with Jones, see if he's available," the desk sergeant muttered. "Have a seat."

Jake led Lacey to a row of chairs shoved against the wall. He wrapped his arm around her shoulders and drew her against his side. "Do you believe what Harley told us?" he murmured.

"I do. I think he's devastated by Mom's disappearance. We've got to find her, Jake. I want my mother to have a life with a man who loves her."

The double doors opened again. This time, a dark-haired, dark-eyed man strode into the lobby and headed straight for them. "Lacey." He shook her hand, then Jake's. "Todd Jones."

"Jake Davenport. I'm Lacey's boyfriend." With his arm still around her shoulders, Jake felt Lacey startle at his claim. Yeah, it was a little soon considering they hadn't been on a date yet. However, he wanted word to spread that he was looking out for her. Besides, if he had his way, he would be Lacey's boyfriend. He intended to romance the woman who had haunted his dreams for months.

In all the time he'd been slowly building a friendship with the beautiful barista, Jake had heard rumors about Frank's treatment of her. From all accounts, the abusive jerk hadn't appreciated her. No one had mentioned flowers, dinner dates, picnics in the park, concerts, movies, nothing except sports events because that was Frank's interest. The ex had insisted Lacey run his errands and prepare his meals. Jake looked forward to showing Lacey how real men treated their women.

"Come on back." As soon as Todd opened the double doors again, the raucous noise of phones ringing, perps yelling and cursing at officers, and various conversations around the room assaulted Jake's ears. "It's a zoo in here today. Let's find an empty office or an interrogation room."

The detective led them down a long, narrow hall, glancing into rooms as he passed. Finally, he stopped and motioned for them to precede him inside the room to the left.

Jake and Lacey sat on one side of the wooden table, Todd on the other. Jake scrutinized the room, noting the two-way mirror and camera secured in the corner of the ceiling. Definitely an interrogation room.

"How have you been, Lacey?"

"Busy."

"Haven't seen you since I left town after high school. What have you been up to?"

"Managing a coffee shop outside Nashville."

"Like it?"

"It's fun."

"Want to own your own shop one day?"

She shook her head. "I'd like to go to school to be a doctor."

"Wow. That's great. I hope you succeed. You always were the smart one of our class."

Lacey blinked. "You think I'm smart?"

The detective snorted. "I remember you're smarter than me. You killed the curve on tests."

"That was a long time ago."

Todd shifted his gaze to Jake. "What about you? What do you do for a living?"

"I'm a medic with Fortress Security."

The other man straightened. "I've heard of your group."

Interesting. Fortress didn't advertise. They didn't have to. Business came looking for them. "Where?"

"Military. I served a tour in the Sandbox before I mustered out and came home. The guys in my unit were hot to get on with Brent Maddox."

"But not you?"

"Nope. I wanted to marry my high school girlfriend. We'd been saving every spare dollar since I enlisted. I had no interest in signing on with a private outfit no matter how good they were supposed to be. All I wanted was to come home and start a life with Maryanne, and she was tired of being afraid for me all the time." He grinned, cheeks flushing. "She wanted a husband to keep her warm at night. Now, what can I do for you, Lacey?"

"We want to know everything you know about my mother's disappearance."

Jake squeezed her hand. "We also want to know about the women who disappeared in and around Winston, and whether you believe the disappearances are connected to Yvonne."

Todd massaged the back of his neck. "You want the truth?"

"Of course."

He leaned closer to them, cast a quick glance at the two-way mirror behind him before he murmured, "The truth is we've got nothing."

CHAPTER TWELVE

Lacey stared at her former classmate, stunned by his words. "You don't have anything to tell me?"

"A whole lot of nothing. Your mom walked out of her house at 10:45 the night she disappeared, drove off to some mysterious meeting, and never returned."

"Have you found her SUV?"

Todd shook his head. "We have a lot of rural areas around Winston. There are any number of places to hide a vehicle. We searched, but came up empty. We talked to her friends, and no one seems to know where she might have gone."

"Did you talk to Harley?"

"Yeah. He says he and Yvonne are in love and he's doing his best to convince her to marry him. From what I saw, he's pretty broken up about your mother's disappearance. There's no indication from their friends or neighbors of disputes between the two, and we haven't answered any domestics from either address."

Lacey noticed Jake staring at the mirror. From his intent expression, he saw more than their reflection in the glass. What did he see?

When Todd opened his mouth to speak, Jake held up his hand. He leaned forward. "Check the observation room," he murmured.

The detective stood. "I need some water. May I bring some for you and Lacey?"

"Please." When Todd left the room, Jake turned and wrapped his arms around Lacey, burying his face in her hair. "Someone is watching from the other room. Be careful what you say until I'm sure it's safe to share information."

Lacey wrapped her arms around his neck to add to Jake's projection of unaware lovebirds. She breathed deep. Man, Jake Davenport had the best aftershave lotion ever invented. She pressed her lips to his jaw. "How did you know?" she asked, her lips still against his skin.

"I was watching the mirror and caught a shadow of movement when someone from the hallway looked into the room."

Raised voices could be heard from outside the door. "Sounds like Todd caught someone spying on us."

"My guess is he caught Beckett." Jake trailed his lips from her neck to the corner of her mouth. He lingered, planting a light kiss. "You have no idea how much I want to kiss you."

Why was he stopping? She'd dreamed about a kiss from Jake for months. "Why don't you?"

"I'm afraid I won't stop at one kiss. More important, I don't want our first kiss witnessed by a voyeur. It's a special, private moment I refuse to share with anyone but you."

She placed a series of soft kisses at the corners of his mouth. "Soon?" she whispered.

A soft groan rumbled in his chest. "A long wait for that kiss might kill me."

Lacey's heart beat hard enough she thought it might fly out of her chest. She brushed her lips across his in a whisper-light caress.

Jake's arms tightened around her. "You're playing with fire."

"Funny. I thought I was playing with you."

He uttered a choked laugh. "I'm going to pay you back for this."

"Something tells me I won't mind paying the price."

The door to their room opened, and Wayne Beckett lumbered in with Todd following close behind, three bottles of water in his hands. He didn't look happy to have the chief of police in the room. That made three of them because Jake's eyes were narrowed at the interruption from the policeman.

"What are you doing here, Lacey?" Beckett demanded.

Jake released Lacey. "Who are you?"

"Wayne Beckett, chief of police here in Winston. I already know who you are, Davenport, and what you represent."

"I'm here to support my girlfriend."

He sneered. "Is that what they call it these days?"

The man who still had one arm around her stiffened.

Under cover of the table, Lacey squeezed his knee. She didn't want Jake arrested, and Beckett waited for an excuse to toss both of them in jail. For some reason, the chief hated her and her mother. Tossing her 'boyfriend' in jail would give the man a great deal of satisfaction.

The medic glanced at her, his jaw tight. He covered her hand with his and held it captive against his knee, then gave her a barely perceptible nod.

Relieved he'd let her handle this encounter for now, she turned her attention to the police chief watching their interaction with avid interest. "I came home to look for answers."

Beckett scowled. "I already gave you all the information we had. Yvonne is back to her old trade and she took off with some john. She'll come back when she's good and ready."

Lacey's cheeks burned. "My mother hasn't been in the business in six years."

"You ain't lived here in a long time, and you hardly ever visit, girl. You don't know what she's been up to."

"I know you need to keep looking for her. I don't believe Mom slid into prostitution again and neither does Harley."

"You're wasting my detective's time. He's busy, got several open cases without having to hold your hand over nothing." The chief of police shot a glare at his detective. "Finish up with them and get back to work." He jabbed a finger at Jake. "You stay out of trouble. Interfere in police business, and you'll be spending your time in Winston behind bars." With that threat, he left the room.

Todd dropped into the chair he'd vacated minutes before. "Sorry," he murmured. "I tried to head him off, but he was determined to poke his nose into my case." He slid the water across the table.

"Thanks." Jake broke the seal on one bottle and handed it to Lacey. "Who was in the other room?"

"Chief's son." Todd guzzled part of his water, then sat back in his chair, arms folded across his chest. "What did you do to tick off Will?"

"Told him to take his hands off my woman."

The detective scowled, his gaze shifting to Lacey. "He hurt you?"

She thought about the bruises she'd discovered on her arms this morning in the shower and knew if Jake hadn't showed up when he did, Will would have done more. She'd seen it in the cop's eyes, recognized the cruelty in his gaze. It was the same look Frank had every time he'd used her as his punching bag. She flinched. In the past, she reminded herself. She'd walked away from Frank and the poisonous relationship.

"Lacey." Jake cupped her chin in the palm of his hand and turned her face toward him. "He hurt you, didn't he? You should have told me."

"I didn't want him to arrest you, and I've had worse injuries. This was nothing." After Frank laid into her the first time, Lacey had been in the hospital for days. She'd been so stupid. That was the perfect time to kick the loser out of her life. Instead, she had given him a series of second chances until Adam and Brent had chased Frank off and had a serious talk with Lacey. She spent several hours talking to one of the counselors from Fortress after that. In fact, Marcus Lang had decided their sessions could be reduced to once a month with the stipulation that Lacey call if she needed to talk sooner.

"Can you show me where you're hurt?"

Thankful she'd worn layers today, Lacey shrugged out of the tailored button-up black shirt she'd paired with an emerald tank top. She sat still while Jake examined her arms, his touch gentle.

He leaned down and pressed a soft kiss to each arm. "Any other injuries?"

She shook her head. "I'm sorry, Jake. I didn't want to worry you over something as minor as a bruise."

"If there is a next time, tell me. I'll take care of you after I take out whoever hurt you." He helped her slip back into her shirt, then reached for her hand. "What do you know about the women who disappeared, Jones? Was there any connection between them?"

"Aside from living in and around Winston or visiting, they were all ages, from 16 to 35 with the exception of Yvonne. They were all attractive women, slender in build. A few were friends, several others visitors to the area. Many of the women disappeared before I came on board, but I pulled all the case files to look for patterns. There aren't any aside from their appearance."

"Bodies?"

"Nothing so far." He dragged one hand down his face. "It's only a matter of time. Bodies are hard to hide."

"Have you stopped looking for my mother?" Lacey asked.

"No. I will find her, Lacey."

"But will it be in time?"

"I hope so."

"The Becketts believe Mom ran off with a john."

"There's no evidence to indicate that was the case, but the story is spreading through town. Is there anything you can tell me to help me find her?"

"I doubt it. I know some things aren't adding up."

"Like?"

"Mom isn't stupid. She doesn't go out at night after ten. She told me nothing good happens after midnight." Ironic considering what she used to do for a living. Maybe of all people, her mother knew the truth of that statement.

"If that's true, why would she leave to meet someone at eleven?"

"That's the question, isn't it? Another oddity is her house. She has a house full of new furniture. Mom works at the diner. She doesn't make enough tip money to pay for that much new furniture in such a short period of time."

"Huh. When did she buy the furniture?"

"Sometime in the last three months. That's the last time I was in the house. Unless Mom's tastes have changed, she bought the new stuff at Riley's Furniture Emporium. They can probably narrow down the time line for you."

"That's great. Thanks, Lacey."

Jake pressed Lacey's hand tighter. "With rumors flying around town that Yvonne was plying her trade again, is there any proof to back that up?"

Todd hesitated, his gaze darting toward her.

"Look, whether it hurts me or not, we need to know the truth." And hearing that her mother had lied to her and everyone else, especially Harley, would gut her. Better to know the truth than not.

"While I interviewed Yvonne's neighbors, Nora Chesterfield claimed that your mother was sleeping with her husband."

"She thinks every woman is sleeping with her husband. She even accused me of the same thing right before I graduated from high school." The whole incident had sickened her and made her even more determined to put Winston behind her.

"Nora says she found your mother's underwear in her bed."

"I don't doubt she found another woman's underwear, but it wasn't Mom's. She values good underwear plus she wouldn't touch Paul for any amount of money. She loathed the man and says he's the scum of the earth."

"Can't argue with that. The guy's a louse."

She hoped she wasn't about to make a major mistake. "When we were inside the house, I noticed Mom's laptop is missing. Did you take it, Todd?"

The detective frowned. "I didn't know she had one. Yvonne might have taken it with her."

To a meeting late at night? What would be the point of that?

"Did you ping her cell phone?" Jake asked.

"No luck on that."

"Whatever you find out as you look into the disappearance, we want to know," Jake said. "We'll return the favor."

A sharp glance from the detective. "You're investigating. You heard the chief. He won't tolerate any interference."

"How can it be interference when we're sharing information and cooperating with you?"

Thirty minutes later, Jake and Lacey walked out of the police station. Back in the SUV, Jake cranked the engine. "You up for talking to Nora Chesterfield?"

Lacey twisted in her seat. "That can wait. I think I know where Mom might have gone for her meeting."

CHAPTER THIRTEEN

Jake turned right toward the Martin farm and winced as the SUV bounced along the rutted gravel road. "How long has this place been vacant?" he asked Lacey as he steered around another crater.

"At least ten years. Old man Martin passed away when I was a freshman. Because he and his wife didn't have children, he named a distant relative as his heir. We expected the heir to either move to Winston or sell the property, but he didn't."

"Why are we driving out here?"

"A caretaker's cabin sits at the back of the property. Mom used to entertain her johns there." She slid him a look. "I don't know if you noticed last night, but Winston shuts down at 8:00. If Mom wanted to meet men without the whole town knowing, she needed a place away from town. Everybody knows everybody in Winston, and there's one flea-bag, no-tell motel in town that would let her ply her trade. The place is on the main drag at the outskirts of the business district in the middle of town."

"Not the best place for customers if they want an anonymous hookup. Can't hide what you're doing from the town gossips and your loved ones. I'd say the men didn't want their names linked with your mother."

"Not if they wanted their private lives left off the gossip circuit."

He drove around a long curve and parked a distance from the cabin. If Lacey's mother was inside along with her captor, Jake didn't want to alert them to his presence. "Wait here."

"Why?"

He leaned over and captured her lips in a light kiss. A mistake on his part. The quick touch of his lips to hers made him want more, a lot more. He growled. "Not the time for this."

"You sure you won't make an exception?" She leaned closer.

He held her off. "Lacey. That's two real kisses you owe me. Our first kiss shouldn't be inside my SUV. You deserve better treatment from me." Jake was tempted to break his own decree. She had no idea how hard she was to resist. "Wait here. I want to make sure it's safe." And no bodies.

Lacey didn't look happy, but she nodded her agreement.

"I won't be long."

He left the vehicle, easing the door closed with a quiet snick. He approached the cabin at an angle to stay out of sight from the windows even though the place appeared deserted.

Jake walked to the front window with noiseless steps, his back to the wall. He quartered the surrounding area before he peered through the glass. The living room was empty. Making his way around the sides and back of the structure, he checked for occupants and found none. He retraced his steps to Lacey.

When he opened the passenger door, she climbed down.

"What did you see?"

"Dirt and dust."

"No bodies?"

He smiled. Smart lady. While he'd been scouting the cabin, she worked out for herself that he was protecting her. "No bodies."

"If Mom was here recently, maybe she left a clue to tell us where to look next."

"I thought you might want to look around. In case the police decide to come here and investigate, I have latex gloves in my pocket. We don't want the cops to find your fingerprints inside the cabin."

She blinked. "You came prepared for anything."

"In my line of work, being unprepared is deadly." He led her to the front door and tugged on a pair of gloves. With one last look around, he tried the doorknob. Locked. "Turn around."

"Why?"

"You don't want to know."

A smile curved her lips. "Let me guess. You plan to use more questionable skills to get us inside."

He tapped her nose. "Turn around."

"Will you show me sometime? I'd like to learn the skill. It might come in handy."

He chuckled. "Sure. Now, turn around. And no peeking."

When Lacey's back was to him, Jake reached into the pocket of his cargo pants and pulled out his lock picks. Highly illegal and very effective in the hands of someone trained. He and his fellow operatives were very well trained. He'd learned many things in Special Forces. Fortress had honed all of his skills and taught him more. Maddox didn't mess around when it came to equipping his operatives for every eventuality. Within seconds, the knob turned under his hand. "You can turn around now."

Lacey smiled on seeing the open door. "A useful skill if I lock myself out of the apartment."

"When we're home, I'll teach you how to pick locks as long as you promise not to embark on a life of crime." Jake reached into his pocket and pulled out a second pair of gloves. "Put these on." When her hands were covered, he followed her inside the cabin. A leather couch, loveseat, and recliner sat in the living room atop an area rug that had seen better days. The leather was split in places. An end table had layers of dust on the surface. Tattered magazines littered the coffee table.

"Jake!"

Sig in hand, he ran toward the master bedroom. After a quick check, he holstered his weapon. "What is it?" When he drew in a deep breath, the smell hit him. Blood and death. Nothing good had happened in this room.

Lacey threw herself into his arms. "The walls. Look at the walls."

His arms tight around her back, he scanned the room. Oh, man. Not good. Brown spots dotted the surface of the walls. He cupped the back of Lacey's head with his hand.

"It's blood, isn't it?"

"No way to be sure without testing it, but this looks like blood splatter to me." He examined the walls again and realized something that made ice water run through his veins. "Too much blood to be from one person."

"How do you know?"

He hesitated. "Lacey…"

"No, don't try to protect me. Just tell me how you know."

"When you first cut someone's throat, blood sprays from the wound. But the pressure eases off with blood loss. This is too much blood to be from one person."

"Do you think some is Mom's?" she whispered.

"I don't know. It's possible." He released her and examined one of the walls close up. Although he touched his finger to the surface, his fingertip came away clean. Not too recent at any rate. Didn't mean much, though. Yvonne had been missing for four days. Too much blood to justify taking samples.

The skin on his nape prickled. Jake needed to get Lacey out of this cabin. They had stumbled on a crime scene. If the killer claimed this place as his own, he would return. Worse, he'd want to protect his little kingdom.

He perused the room again. Nothing out of the ordinary aside from the blood splatter. Jake turned his attention to the mattress covered by a large quilt. That quilt didn't look ten years old. In fact, the covering seemed fairly new.

Jake strode to the bed, yanked back the quilt, and froze. Through a clear plastic covering, Jake saw a brownish-red stain soiled the bare mattress. "We need to leave." He tugged her from the room, not giving her a chance to argue. His instinct screamed at him to spirit his girlfriend from this cabin.

In the living room, Lacey yanked her hand from his. "Wait." She raced to the couch and dropped to her knees.

A flash of red caught Jake's attention. One glance and bone-deep fear exploded in his gut. He scooped Lacey into his arms as she snagged something pink from under the couch. He sprinted from the cabin.

"Put me down. I can run."

Without breaking stride, Jake let her feet drop, holding onto her until she was running flat out beside him. The countdown clock ticked down in his head. At the last second, he shoved Lacey to the ground and dived on top of her.

An explosion rocked the ground. Blistering heat rolled over them.

CHAPTER FOURTEEN

Jake hissed as burning debris from the cabin landed on his arm. He flicked the piece of wood from his bicep and rolled off Lacey. "You okay?" No response. "Lacey." When she still didn't move, he ran his hands along her arms and legs, then her torso. No breaks.

Heart racing, he rolled Lacey to her back. Blood dripped from her upper arm, and a goose egg was forming on her forehead. Though reluctant to move her further, he feared more for her safety. Whoever set the bomb would know soon it had detonated. He or she would check to see who was caught in the trap.

Praying he didn't hurt his girlfriend, he grabbed the pink purse and lifted Lacey. He covered the final thirty feet to his SUV in seconds. Maneuvering her into the passenger seat, he belted her in and hurried around the hood. After cranking the engine, he sped from the cabin. Sirens sounded in the distance. Since the fire department would come from town, Jake turned in the opposite direction at the road.

He forced himself to drive the speed limit. He couldn't afford to be pulled over. One look at Lacey, and a cop would think the worst of Jake. He didn't have time to explain himself. He needed a safe place to examine Lacey and treat the cut on her arm.

A soft moan reached his ears a moment later. He stole a glance at her, ripped the rubber gloves from his hands, and trailed the backs of his fingers over her cheek. "Lacey, can you hear me?"

"Jake?"

"Yeah, it's me. Tell me what hurts."

"Everything. I feel like a truck hit me."

Guilt spiraled through him. "That was me. I'm sorry."

"What happened?"

"The cabin was wired for explosives. We triggered the timer when we went inside. The place is in a million burning pieces now."

"How did you know it would explode?"

"I spotted the countdown clock when you grabbed that purse from the floor."

"Thank you."

He snorted. "For what? Throwing you to the ground and causing a concussion?"

"For saving my life. Wait." She struggled to sit up. "Are you hurt?"

"Couple of minor burns. I've had far worse and survived."

"I want to see."

"When we're safe and after I've taken care of your arm."

"My arm?" Lacey examined her arm. "Oh, boy. No wonder it hurts."

"Anything else hurt?"

"My head aches. Considering the alternative, I'm lucky to be alive."

"Wish I could have executed that rescue without hurting you."

"Are we going back to the hotel?"

"Yes, but I turned a different direction because the fire engine was coming down the lane. I didn't want someone remembering a vehicle fleeing from the scene of a fire at an abandoned cabin."

"When you reach the highway, turn left. That will take us back into town. The hotel will be on our right."

Jake parked at the back of the hotel fifteen minutes later and opened Lacey's door. "Easy," he murmured as he helped her to the asphalt. "I would carry you, but we'd draw attention. I'll wrap my arm around your waist. I won't let you fall. If you anyone approaches us, turn your face toward me. Your forehead needs an ice pack."

"Does it look bad?"

"Bad enough to prompt questions we don't want to answer."

Jake scanned their surroundings as he walked to the hotel with Lacey. He used his key card to open the door to the first floor and guided her to the bank of elevators.

As they waited for the silver doors to open, he noticed another hotel patron approaching. "Company," he whispered to Lacey. She leaned against his chest, her injury hidden from prying eyes. Her black shirt would disguise the blood seeping from her arm.

He palmed the back of her head with his hand and, when they entered the elevator car, nudged her to the back corner away from the businessman paying more attention to his cell phone screen than them. Jake also made sure Lacey's face was hidden from the security camera. The businessman exited on the second floor without glancing their way.

When Lacey started to move, he held her still. "Camera."

She relaxed in his arms. "Did that man notice us?"

"I don't think so."

The elevator dinged as the car reached the third floor. They walked down the hall to their rooms. "The mike bag is in my room."

"Mike bag?"

"Medical supplies."

"Do you always travel with it?"

"Yep. Actually, all Fortress operatives travel with a large medical kit although theirs isn't as extensive as mine." He unlocked his room and ushered her inside where he secured the door.

Jake led her to the second double bed and urged her to sit on the edge. "The black shirt comes off. I need to see the damage to your arm."

"Bad enough I probably need a doctor." Her head raised. "Unless you take care of it."

"I treat team injuries in the field. However, if you want a doctor, I'll have someone brought in from out of town. If we go to the hospital or a doctor here, all of Winston will know about your injuries by the end of the day."

She gave a light laugh. "You don't give the gossips enough credit. The whole town will know within an hour. I trust you, Jake. I'd rather you take care of me."

Jake's tension eased at her words. At least she trusted him that much. He'd vowed to himself to protect her, but had been the cause of her injuries. He helped her remove the shirt and lay back with her head on the pillow. Grabbing his mike bag, Jake found the supplies he needed to clean her cut. He thrust his hand back in the bag and snatched a chemically-activated ice pack.

After gently cleaning the goose egg, Jake shook the ice pack and laid in on her forehead. "How is your vision?"

"Fine. My biggest problems are the headache and my arm."

"Once I treat your arm, I'll give you something mild for pain."

She smiled. "It's nice to have my own medic."

He chuckled and turned his attention to her arm. "I have to clean the cut and it will hurt." Jake tore open antiseptic pads and cleaned her arm. Looked like she'd fallen on a stick or a sharp rock. Dirt had lodged deep in the wound, a wound needing several stitches to close. She'd probably have a scar to show for the incident at the cabin. At least she'd be alive to show off her war wound.

Reluctant to hurt her more than necessary, Jake held up a vial of lidocaine he used to numb wounds when he had to work in the field. "You have debris in the wound, deep enough that I want to numb your arm before I clean and stitch the cut."

"Stitches?" Her voice sounded faint.

"You're not going to pass out on me, are you?"

"Not a chance. I wouldn't miss watching you work for anything."

"Yeah, you say that now. You might change your mind when I start stitching."

"Can you give me serious biceps like Lily Doucet?"

He laughed. His ripped teammate was married to a former NYPD homicide detective. Both of them were good friends. "I'm afraid that's not going to happen. I can tell Lily you'd like to work out with her."

"As long as it's a baby workout routine. She could work me into the ground without breaking a sweat."

She probably could. Lily was one tough woman. "I'll tell her to go easy on you." Jake filled a syringe with the liquid from the vial. "You ready?" When she nodded, he murmured, "A little stick."

Once he finished, he sat back to wait for the medicine to take effect. "Where do you want to go for our first date?"

"I've been thinking about that."

"What have you come up with?" he asked, pleased she'd been thinking about them as a couple.

"I've never been to The Hermitage. I'd love to explore the house and grounds with you."

Huh. Never would have guessed she'd choose visiting the home of President Andrew Jackson as a first date. Then again, Lacey was not typical of the women he'd dated in recent years. They were nice, but none were interested in anything but entertainment on dates. He'd seen more movies, musicals, operas, symphony and ballet performances than he cared to count. This request was a refreshing change of pace. "You like history?"

"Although I don't have much time, I like to read biographies and history, especially the presidents and their wives. Their lives fascinate me."

"Have you ever been to Mt. Vernon?"

Her eyes lit. "George Washington's house? No, but I'd love to visit."

"Fortress teams go to Washington, D.C. occasionally. Next time we're sent, I'll ask Maddox about taking you. We'll visit Mt. Vernon."

"I'd love to as long as I won't be in the way."

He smiled. "It's a date. Another one."

"Did you mean what you said about dating me?"

"Every word. I wanted to ask you out for months. I held off so you would be comfortable with me before I approached you."

"Months?"

"From the first moment I saw you behind the counter at Coffee House I wanted to ask you to dinner. Since you had just broken up with Frank, I made myself wait."

Jake touched her arm. "Feel that?"

"Pressure. No pain."

"Perfect. If you feel discomfort, tell me and I'll give you more medicine."

He worked in silence for a few minutes, cleaning and stitching the wound. He glanced at her face a few times, checking that she was all right. Each time he caught her watching his hands, utter fascination in her gaze. Yeah, definitely future doctor material. He hoped she followed through on her plans. He intended to encourage her when the opportunity arose.

Thirty minutes after he started, he bandaged the now cleaned and closed wound. Jake reached into his mike bag again and pulled out two packets. "The blue pills are a mild pain killer. The numbness will wear off in two hours and you'll need the relief. The capsules are an antibiotic to prevent infection."

A knock sounded on his door. Jake signaled Lacey to remain silent as he freed the Sig from his holster. He approached the door with noiseless steps, ready to deal with a probable threat.

CHAPTER FIFTEEN

Lacey removed the ice pack and swung her feet over the side of the bed. The room spun. Oh, man. She felt terrible. Must be the headache. She didn't know who was at the door, but she wanted to be ready in case Jake needed her.

She wanted to laugh at herself. Jake was a highly trained black ops soldier. He didn't need her for anything. Just look at the way he'd handled her injuries. Watching him stitch her cut was an amazing experience and reawakened a deep longing to go to college. Lacey wanted to have the skills to treat injuries. The only way to do that was to go to school and obtain the medical training necessary.

Jake peered through the peephole and slid his gun away. He unlocked the door and motioned for the man in the hallway to enter.

"Took you long enough," Jake said. "I expected you hours ago."

"Got delayed. Z sent me to another meet-and-greet first." The stranger's gaze shifted to Lacey. "I'm Cade

Ramsey, with one of the Otter Creek based Fortress team. You must be Lacey Coleman."

"That's right. How did you know?"

"Zane told me Jake was with you. I'm sorry to hear about your mother's disappearance. Anything new, Jake?"

He snorted. "Not unless you count nearly being blown up in a deserted cabin almost an hour ago."

Cade stiffened. "Remote detonation?"

"We tripped a sensor and started a countdown. We made it out of the cabin with seconds to spare." He inclined his head to Lacey. "I just finished putting twelve stitches in her arm."

"That might explain the police presence at the front of the hotel. I hear you're already on the local cops' radar."

"One of them put his hands on Lacey."

A scowl. "You deck him?"

"Warned him off. I won't be so nice if he touches her again."

While the two men talked, Lacey's mind raced. If the goose egg on her forehead was as noticeable as Jake said, she needed to do something fast to cover it. She was sure the ice pack had helped, but there hadn't been enough time for her forehead to return to normal. "Jake, do you have scissors in your mike bag?"

He stopped mid-sentence, his eyebrows soaring at her question. "Sure. Why?"

"Camouflage. Beckett or Jones will be banging on the door any minute. If I'm not finished, hold them off." Lacey snatched the scissors from his hand and hurried to her bathroom. She needed to do this fast, then change her shirt at least. She had to cover up the bandage on her arm. Seeing that would raise questions she and Jake didn't want to answer.

In front of the bathroom mirror, Lacey grabbed a comb from her makeup bag and set to work. Within two minutes, she had changed her hairstyle to create long bangs, covering the injury to her forehead. She gathered the remnants of her hair from the sink and flushed it. Can't have Beckett or his buddies realizing she had given herself a new hairstyle in the past two minutes.

When she heard a pounding on Jake's door, Lacey ran to her suitcase and grabbed another shirt, this one a long-sleeved black t-shirt. She retreated to the bathroom as a rumble of male voices reached her ears. She changed her shirt and checked her hair again to be sure her handiwork was still in place. After a quick spritz of hair spray, Lacey returned to Jake's room. To his credit, he'd held the cops in the hallway despite their obvious frustration and increasing ire. She walked further into the room and noticed all signs of him treating her injuries had vanished. The two operatives had cleared away everything that might generate questions, including her torn and bloody shirt.

Cade turned, stared a moment, and nodded in approval. He coughed softly.

"You either let us in, Davenport, or we'll just haul you and your buddy down to the station along with Lacey. It's where you all belong anyway."

Will Beckett. Of course. Who else would enjoy flaunting his authority more than the chief's son?

Jake spread his hands and stepped back. Will surged into the room, followed by two more officers, all with weapons drawn.

Todd Jones brought up the rear. He scanned the room, his gaze landing on Lacey. Although he narrowed his eyes, he didn't comment on her change in appearance.

Will's gaze slowly dropped from her head to her feet, a gleam growing as his attention lingered on certain places. "Looking good, baby," he said, his voice deeper than normal. "You should keep better company than these two yahoos."

"You don't have the right to call me that," she snapped. "I don't want anything to do with you, and you mean nothing to me."

Anger flared in his eyes. His hands fisted as he lunged toward her.

Cade moved in front of her, and before his coworkers could react to stop whatever he planned to do, Jake collared the belligerent cop and shoved him against the wall, arm pressed against Will's throat.

When the others moved to intervene, Todd ordered them to stand down.

"You already laid hands on my woman once. You will not touch her again. Do I make myself clear, Beckett?" Jake's voice was pitched low, but every word could be heard by all the room's occupants.

"You're under arrest for assaulting an officer," he croaked.

"No, he's not," Todd said. "When Jake lets you go, you're walking out of here without another word."

"He assaulted me."

"He protected his girlfriend from an abusive cop. I know what he's capable of, Beckett. You're lucky you're still breathing. You want to try and press charges against Davenport? There are six people in this room who will swear Lacey was afraid and her boyfriend neutralized the threat to her safety." He tapped Jake on the shoulder. "Let him go. Beckett's going back on patrol."

Another minute passed with Will's face growing redder by the second before Jake stepped back.

"You'll pay for that," the furious cop muttered and shoved past Jake. A moment later, the elevator signal indicated Will had left the floor.

Jake signaled Cade and his fellow operative slipped from the room.

"Where's he going?" Todd asked.

"To make sure Beckett leaves the premises." Jake walked to Lacey's side and brushed her lips with his.

She smiled. "That's three," Lacey whispered.

"Keeping count, are you?"

"You bet. I'm looking forward to the real thing."

His eyes glittered. "So am I. More than you know."

Todd cleared his throat. "Can we sit down, please? I have to ask you where you've been since you left the police station."

Jake wrapped his arm around her waist and led her to one of the two chairs in the room. "Why?"

The detective ignored his question. "Have you been to your mother's place, Lacey?" His eyes held a silent warning to be careful what she said.

He already knew she and Jake had been at the house. They had told him earlier in the interrogation room. Her mother's neighbors had been at work so that left Will Beckett as the one who was pointing fingers at her. But what was he accusing her of?

"Jake and I went to Mom's right after we left the coffee shop this morning. The coffee was horrible, in case you were wondering."

One of the cops at the door grinned. "Ain't that the truth? Tastes like runoff from the city dump."

Cade returned to the room, key card in his hand. He looked at Jake and nodded.

Good. At least one of their problems was out of the way for now. She was sure Will would pop up again when they least wanted him as was his habit of late.

"Why were you at Yvonne's place?"

"As I told Officer Beckett at the time, I own the house. I let Mom stay there so that it's occupied, but she's not paying the mortgage or the utilities. I do. Jake and I went to house to see if we could find anything to indicate where she might have gone. Most people think she took off with a john. I don't believe that for one minute."

The uniformed cops shifted their weight.

"Did you find anything to indicate where she went?"

Lacey was careful not to look at Jake. What could she say? She was a terrible liar and under most circumstances, that was a good thing. Now, though, she didn't need to incriminate either of them. Jake had found the paper with the mysterious notation on it, but they didn't know if the notation meant anything. It might be for a different appointment reminder, one on a later date. Her mother had a habit of forgetting appointments so she routinely made notes like that ahead of time to remind herself of what was coming. "If we had, we would have called you."

"Officer Beckett believes you removed something from the house that belonged to your mother."

"Really? Did he say what he thinks I took?"

"Will you give me permission to look through your belongings?"

"Hold up," Jake said. "I think Lacey should call her lawyer."

Todd inclined his head. "That's up to you. I don't have a warrant at this time, but I won't have a problem obtaining one."

Cade snorted. "I'll bet," he murmured.

Thankful for Jake's forethought in preparing her for this eventuality, Lacey said, "You have my permission as long as you search my bags in my presence."

He nodded in agreement and looked at Jake, shifting his inquiry to the Fortress operative without verbalizing the question again. "Only if I unload the bags. You can watch, but no touching my supplies."

"Unusual restriction, but I agree to your terms. Let's start with your bags, Lacey."

She led Todd into her room with Jake following a step behind. Motioning to the detective to go ahead, Lacey sat on the opposite bed while the policeman pawed through her suitcase. Jake sat beside her, his hand wrapped around hers.

"Is this the only bag you have?"

"Aside from my purse."

"May I search that?"

"Go ahead."

Todd dumped the contents of her purse on the bed and sifted through everything. "Thank you. Jake, you're next."

Cade, who had remained in the other room with the two uniformed officers, moved away from Jake's bags at their approach. The medic hauled his bags to the bed and systematically unpacked everything, starting with his mike bag.

Lacey was astonished at the amount of medical supplies Jake hauled around. That bag must weigh a ton and she knew he also carried heavy weaponry as well.

"Incredible." Todd stared at all the medical supplies. "This is your normal stash?"

Jake grinned as he repacked. "This is a scaled down version. If I was going on deployment, there would be more."

"Why did you insist on unpacking that yourself?" One of the cops by the door asked. "Looks like a bunch of bandages and stuff."

"I have to be able to put my hands on these supplies in seconds. In the field, I don't have time to hunt for the right bandage or a suture kit."

"You actually stitch people up in the field?"

"Some of our missions are in remote locations. If injuries are severe enough, a teammate could die before we reach medical help. Fortress medics are almost as well trained as doctors."

"Impressive." Todd indicated the next large bag. "What's in that one?"

The medic unzipped his black bag and started pulling guns and knives from the darkened interior until there was a pile on the bed.

CHAPTER SIXTEEN

Jake stood back as the three cops surrounded the bed, shock and envy in their gazes as they stared at his weapons stash. He smiled. "This is also a scaled down version of what I carry on deployment."

"What else would you pack?" Todd asked.

"RPG plus several grenades, more ammunition, a rifle, C-4, detonator, flashbangs, concussion grenades."

A soft whistle from the detective. "Nice. Must weigh a ton."

Cade leaned one shoulder against the wall, seeming at ease. Lacey didn't buy the illusion for one minute. She had a feeling the operative could react to a threat in a split second.

"Easily fifty pounds or more." Jake started to repack his bag. "Depending on where we're deployed, my teammates and I carry as much as 100 pounds of gear."

"Man, you guys must train like demons to carry out maneuvers with that much added weight."

"It pays to be in better shape than the terrorists," Cade said. "Keeps us alive."

"In our business, being fit saves our hide, too." When the bag was secured again, Todd nodded at the third bag on the bed. "What's in there?"

"Clothes and shaving kit." He went through the same routine, unpacking the contents and spreading it out on the bed for the officers to see, then stored his gear again.

"Know anything about an explosion and fire at the Martin place?"

And there it was. The real reason for this friendly visit. Todd was fishing for information. "Why would I?"

"If there was something that incriminated your girlfriend in that old cabin, you might be inclined to set a bomb to destroy the evidence."

He reconsidered the idea of fishing. Maybe a witness had spotted them in the area. "I'm a medic, not an EOD guy, and as you've seen I'm also not carrying C-4."

"If you were carrying, I doubt you would have agreed to the search of your belongings so easily. Mind if we search your rooms?" Todd asked.

"Knock yourselves out. Same stipulation applies. We have to be in the room to watch." Prevented the possibility of one of the cops planting evidence, a less likely occurrence now that Beckett was out of the room.

The search took a matter of minutes since neither he nor Lacey had stored anything outside their luggage. Finally, Todd held out his hand. "I appreciate your cooperation. We'll get out of your way."

Jake shook the detective's hand, then shoved his hand in his pocket. "We want to hear the minute you find out anything about Yvonne."

"I'll be in touch." After a brief handclasp with Lacey, he and the other policemen left.

Cade eased the door open an inch and watched through the opening. A moment later, he secured the door. "You think Beckett put them up to this stunt?"

"I'd bet on it."

Lacey sat on the edge of the bed. "How did Will know we took something from the house?"

"He'll be disappointed Todd didn't find anything incriminating in our possession." Could be the surly cop just took a shot in the dark to see if he hit anything.

Cade returned to his position against the wall. "What did you take?"

"Ten thousand dollars in cash and a piece of paper with a meeting time and the letter M on it."

He frowned. "Does your mother routinely keep that much cash on hand, Lacey?"

"She works in a diner. Mom never had that much money on hand in her life. She also has a house full of new furniture that I can't explain either."

"Cops have an explanation?"

She sighed. "Mom's past is colorful, to say the least. She was arrested several times for public intoxication and prostitution."

"Ah. The cops think she's gone back to her old habits."

"That's the prevailing theory." Jake grabbed a few dollars from his wallet and handed them to Cade. "Vending machine is down the hall to the left."

"What do you want?"

"Three bottles of water and a soft drink. Lacey needs to take pain meds and replenish her fluid level."

"I'll be back in a minute."

Jake crouched in front of his girl. "I like the haircut." He brushed back her bangs to check her forehead. "Smart move. Hides your bruise and helps us avoid scrutiny. Headache worse?"

She laughed softly. "How did you know?"

"I can see it in your eyes."

"Sounds like the lyrics to a love song."

"It also happens to be true. You handled yourself like a pro with the police, Lacey." He trailed his fingertips down her cheek. "Did I scare you?"

"When?"

"The confrontation with Will."

"Of course not."

"Good. I don't want to do that. I would never hurt you."

"I know, Jake."

"Do you? Frank was a poor excuse for a man. I don't want you to lump me in with him as a lout who can't control himself or his temper."

"Never." She entwined their fingers. "You don't have to convince me. Besides, if you ever touched me in anger, Brent and Adam would tear you apart."

Oh, yeah. Should Jake ever hurt Lacey, he wouldn't live to regret such a boneheaded move. His boss and his team leader had a soft spot for Lacey Coleman. The truth was, though, their affection for the lady was mild compared to the depth of emotion he felt. He was just beginning to realize how much he cared about her. "I want a promise from you."

"What kind?"

"If I ever do anything that scares you or makes you uncomfortable, tell me so we can talk about it."

"I promise."

"Lacey, you'll have some bad moments when memories of what you went through with Frank will surface."

Her cheeks flushed. "They told you."

Jake squeezed her fingers. "Not directly. I heard enough to put the pieces together for myself. When we're alone and you're ready, I'd like you to tell me about Frank and your relationship with him. In the meantime, when those bad moments come, we'll handle them together."

"Okay. When do I get the first of those kisses you owe me?"

He chuckled. "Patience. Soon."

Cade returned with water and soft drinks. His eyebrows raised. "Should I come back later?"

Jake kissed the back of Lacey's hand and rose. "Not necessary. When do you have to leave?"

"I'm not. I talked to Z, told him we would overnight the blood sample to the lab. You need someone to watch your back."

"Appreciate it, Cade."

"Yep. Okay if I bunk in here with you?"

"Sure."

The other operative dropped onto the first bed and propped himself against the headboard. "We didn't have much time before the cops interrupted the party. Bring me up to speed."

Between them, he and Lacey gave Cade the information they cobbled together since arriving in town, precious little in light of what they needed to know to find Yvonne.

Cade scowled. "You're telling me there's a serial killer on the loose in Winston and the local cops haven't called in outside help?"

"No bodies according to the detective, but that's the gist of it."

"How many years has this guy been hunting?"

"Todd didn't say anything about the women being taken by a man," Lacey pointed out. "And there's no proof the women are dead."

"The first woman taken still hasn't been found. Odds are she and the rest are dead. Statistics say most serial killers are men. I just can't see a woman being guilty of the crime."

Lacey stared at Cade. "You think my mother is dead?"

Jake shot his coworker a warning look. He didn't disagree with Cade's assumption, but wanted to spare Lacey the anguish of believing something that hadn't yet been proved.

"Every hour she's gone makes the chance of finding her alive more remote."

Another glare at Cade. "The point is, Lacey, we need to find your mother, fast."

"But how? We don't have anything to go on."

"I wouldn't say that. We have the injuries to prove we stumbled onto a kill house."

Lacey straightened. "Your burns. Let me see."

Cade straightened. "You're hurt, Jake?"

"It's nothing."

"I want to see," Lacey insisted. "You took great care of me. Let me help you."

He started to refuse and reconsidered. His girlfriend needed this, he realized, and reached for the hem of his black t-shirt. While Jake yanked his shirt over his head, Cade opened the mike bag.

"Turn around so I can look at your back." Lacey's soft hands gripped his upper arms and exerted pressure. She drew in a ragged breath. "Oh, Jake. You have several burns back here and a couple on your arms."

Yeah, now that she mentioned them, he could feel the ache and constant throbbing. Amazing what symptoms adrenaline dump masked. "I have burn ointment in the mike bag."

Cade unzipped the bag and peered inside. "White tube?"

He nodded. "Lacey, if the burns are clean, smooth the ointment on in a thin layer." Minutes later, he was much more comfortable although shirtless. He twisted to face Lacey. "You need to take your meds now. Drink some of the soda to help the pain killer dissolve faster, then start on the water."

"Bossy, much?"

"When it comes to your safety and health. Other than that, you're free to get in my face about anything you don't like."

A quick grin. "I'll remind you of that at the appropriate time." She swallowed one pill from each packet he'd given her.

He stared pointedly at the water bottle near her hand.

With a roll of her eyes, she started sipping on the liquid.

"I don't know about you kids, but I'm hungry." Cade scanned the room service options. "Anyone interested in ordering burgers and fries?"

Lacey grimaced. "Pass."

"I'm in," Jake said. "Find something lighter for Lacey that she can heat up when she's ready." The room came equipped with a small microwave and four-cup coffee maker.

With a nod, Cade called room service and placed an order. "Forty-five minutes," he said. "I'd like to shower before the food arrives."

Jake held out his hand to Lacey. "Grab your water and come with me. You look like you're ready to drop."

"I'm so tired I can hardly keep my eyes open."

"Adrenaline dump. It will pass." He led her back to her room. "If I promise to keep the connecting doors open, would you mind if I stretched out on the other bed? I need to let the ointment on my back dry before I pull on another shirt." He also wanted to keep an eye on her, just in case she had a flashback or the pain level cranked higher.

"I don't mind."

"Rest a few minutes and let the pain meds work. I'll be here if you need me."

On the opposite bed, Lacey curled up on her uninjured side and closed her eyes. Within minutes, she was sound asleep.

Jake watched her for a while. Lacey had grown into an amazing woman despite her rough childhood. Her life in Nashville showed grit and hard work. The more he knew about her, the more Jake admired Lacey and longed to introduce her to his family. They would love her.

Would she have a problem with them? She came from humble beginnings. Many people with that background were uncomfortable around him and his family. That was one reason he chose not to share his background with most people. Only Brent and Adam knew he was connected to Davenport Enterprises, a multibillion dollar tech company.

Cade appeared in the doorway, freshly showered and shaved. Expression grim, he waggled his phone and signaled that he needed to talk to Jake.

Maybe Zane had shared information with him. Couldn't be good news. After a glance at Lacey, Jake pushed up from the bed and padded out of the room on silent feet. He partially closed the door. "Tell me."

"Zane hacked into the detective's computer files."

"And?"

"He sent a copy of the photos of the women who have gone missing from Winston in the past six years to my phone and yours. You need to look at them, Jake."

A ball of ice formed in his stomach. He grabbed his phone and clicked on the email from Zane. Jake scrolled through the pictures, stunned at what he was seeing. "I don't believe this."

All the women had the same physical appearance as Lacey Coleman.

CHAPTER SEVENTEEN

Jake dropped onto the bed, his hand clenched around the hard plastic of his cell phone. "Jones didn't mention the victims' resemblance to Lacey." A point he would be making to the detective the next time he talked to him.

This was a vital piece of information in protecting his girlfriend from the guy hunting in this Alabama town. "Why hasn't anyone noticed this before now, especially Yvonne?"

"According to Z, the computer files indicated the local cops felt it was a coincidence, that the women had left of their own free will and they all happened to be blond. No bodies so they must be alive, just somewhere else."

"Right. Looks like I brought Lacey into the line of fire. Much as I hate dealing with the feds, Chief Beckett should have contacted the FBI."

"The other detective who had the previous cases suggested just that to the police chief. Beckett blew him off, told him the feds didn't know the locals like he did. If anyone could find the women, it would be him, not some agent from an alphabet agency."

"For all their grandstanding, the Federal Bureau of Investigation has resources the Winston PD desperately needs. If Beckett hadn't been so arrogant, he might have found the guy responsible for the disappearances."

"Unless he has a suspicion about who the guilty party is and wants to handle it his own way."

"Or he doesn't want to handle it at all." Jake dragged a hand down his face. He frowned, thrust his hand into his pocket, and grasped the business card Todd had slipped him when they shook hands.

"What's that?"

"The detective gave me his card when he shook my hand." He turned the card over. On the back, Todd had scrawled his cell phone number in bold black strokes along with a message telling Jake to call him.

He checked on Lacey again before he placed the call. "Can you talk?"

"Hold on." A muffled conversation later, the sound of a car engine cranking came over the speaker. "Lacey okay?"

Jake's eyes narrowed. "She's sleeping."

Silence, then, "We left your hotel room less than twenty minutes ago. She didn't look tired to me."

That observation just proved the detective didn't know Lacey. "She hasn't slept well since she learned her mother is missing. Why did you ask me to call?"

"Look, I'm in the car. No one is with me. It's just you and me, and I'm considering myself off the clock. Level with me. Did you and Lacey take anything from the house?"

"You don't want to know."

A loud sigh. "I'll take that as a yes. Is it something that would shed light on my case?"

"Unconfirmed."

"Nothing like being vague to frustrate an overworked, underpaid detective. Let's try this. If you knew whatever you took had bearing on my case, would you tell me?"

"I would find a way to give you the information you need. Answer a question for me?"

"Shoot."

"Who suggested that we removed something from Yvonne's place?"

"I'm sure you can figure it out without me getting myself into trouble."

Beckett. What was his stake in this? Jake didn't believe the belligerent cop cared about anything but himself. "Same person who put you up to the search of our belongings?"

Silence.

He chuckled. "I'll take that as a yes."

"I won't apologize for doing my job, Jake."

"Same here. Lacey is my priority. I'll do whatever is necessary to keep her safe."

"I don't know what you did that ticked off Beckett so much, but he's gunning for you."

He snorted. "The only thing I've done is gotten in his face about my girlfriend. Maybe you can find out why Beckett has it in for her."

"You should look to Lacey for that answer, buddy. I think there's some history between the two."

Jake stilled. Should have thought of that for himself. Yeah, the lady was a serious distraction. He needed to get his head screwed on straight or Lacey would be the one to pay for his inattention, and that was unacceptable. "You noticed anything interesting about the missing women?"

"They're all blonds like Lacey."

"They also have similar features and build."

"Do I even want to know how you learned that?"

"No. You should have told me when we were at the station, Jones."

"I'm not supposed to talk about open cases, and you didn't need to know."

"Lacey is a prime target in this town. How is that not my business? If the situation was reversed and your wife was in danger, you would have been all over my back for not warning you. Now that I know, I'll be even more vigilant."

Todd gave a huff of wry laughter. "Come on. You're more aware of everything than any cops or military personnel I've ever worked with."

"I came here to support my girlfriend and lend a hand if she needed it. Now I know she needs protection, Lacey has just become my principal as well." A problem, for sure. Until they returned home, his attention would be split between getting to know the lady herself and keeping her safe.

Long seconds passed before Todd said, "If you're in love with her, you need to hand off her protection to someone else. Your objectivity is compromised."

"Would you hand off the protection detail if this was your wife?" he countered.

"No." A firm, quick response.

"Why haven't you called in the feds?"

"Not my call to make. If I go over the chief's head, I'll lose my job. My parents and my wife's folks are older and not in the best of health. We can't leave the area, and all I'm trained to do is be a cop."

"There are other law enforcement jobs available. You might want to consider applying for a position with the state cops."

"Maybe."

"From what I've observed so far, you're going nowhere in the Winston PD. Although I can't prove it, I think there's some corruption in your department."

No response.

Jake didn't blame him. Although his phone was secure thanks to Zane's handiwork, the same couldn't be said for Todd's. "You're not calling the feds?"

"No."

"Don't be surprised if they show up on your doorstep anyway."

"I didn't hear you say that, but thanks for the heads up. Later."

A knock sounded on the door. Weapon in hand, Cade checked the peephole and slid his weapon into the holster at his back. "Room service," he murmured.

Perfect. He was starving. Unlike Lacey, the adrenaline surge hadn't dampened his appetite. A couple minutes later, he and Cade started devouring their hamburgers and fries. Jake sighed. Cooked exactly the way he liked them.

They were almost finished with their meals when Lacey pushed open the door between the two rooms. Jake walked to her and cupped her cheek. "How do you feel?" He studied her face, not liking the pallor of her complexion.

"My arm hurts," she admitted.

"And your head?"

"Better."

"Hungry?" Cade asked.

"I'm getting there. What did you order for me?"

"Grilled chicken sandwich. It was the most neutral thing on the menu." Cade removed the covering from her meal, and motioned for her to take his chair. "I'm finished, and I need to send that blood sample to the lab."

Jake retrieved the plastic bag with the blood scraping from his mike bag and handed it to Cade. "Make sure Beckett doesn't follow you."

"No problem."

After Cade left, Jake sat across from Lacey and started talking about some of the more humorous things that had happened to him over the years in the military and his time with Fortress. Before long, her plate was empty and she had a smile on her face.

"Did all that really happen?"

"Every bit." He rubbed his neck, remembering the embarrassment he'd suffered over the years at the hands of pranksters in his unit and the various teams from Fortress he'd gone on missions with. The pranks were ways to relieve stress, and he was as guilty as anyone of pulling a good joke on a teammate. Didn't mean he liked baring his experience as the butt of jokes for Lacey's enjoyment.

"Bet you don't like camels."

He grinned. "You would be right. No matter where I work in the Sandbox, I always seem to run into one."

"I guess it's true they spit."

"Oh, yeah. They definitely do." He'd washed several uniforms after an encounter with the brown, shaggy, ornery creatures. "Need anything else to eat?"

She shook her head. "I enjoyed hearing the stories, Jake. Thanks for sharing part of your work life with me."

"I can't tell you mission specifics, Lacey." Wouldn't even if he was allowed to talk. Some things shouldn't be in her head. He didn't want Lacey touched by the ugliness he encountered.

"I understand. If I ask something you're not allowed to talk about, tell me. Were you distracting me so I could eat?"

"Caught that, did you? That was part of the reason. I want you to know the real Jake Davenport. The operative and Army medic are only one side of me. The truth is you matter to me, Lacey. More than I ever thought possible in the few months we've known each other."

A table and chair, and a loveseat were on the balcony. "Want to sit outside for a few minutes?" He had to talk to Lacey about the similarity between the missing women and her, and he didn't want to have that conversation unless he was holding her. The information would upset her, and he wanted his hands on her. He hoped the embrace would comfort both of them.

She sobered. “I’d like that.”

Jake led Lacey to the loveseat and gathered her close, urging her to lay her head against his chest. He didn’t say anything for a few minutes, giving her a chance to relax in the peace of the waning afternoon light.

“Are you going to tell me what’s wrong?” she asked.

“Detective Jones has been holding back on us.” When Lacey started to sit up, Jake palmed the back of her head and held her still with gentle pressure. “Stay. Please. Zane did some digging into the Winston PD files. I asked him to look into the disappearance of the women. He sent me pictures of each woman. You look remarkably like your mother, by the way.”

“I’ve been told that since I turned twelve. What is Todd holding back?”

“The women who are missing look similar to you. The resemblance is enough to convince me you’re a potential target of this kidnapper.”

She drew in a careful breath. “Okay.”

“I will protect you, Lacey. No matter what it takes. I won’t allow anyone to hurt you.” He wouldn’t feel a moment’s regret if he had to kill to keep her safe. He hoped Lacey could accept that.

CHAPTER EIGHTEEN

Lacey didn't say anything for a few moments, trying to wrap her head around the fact she might be in danger by coming home to look for her mother. "May I see the pictures of the women?"

Jake brought up an email and handed her his phone.

She stared at the first picture, dismay filling her. She knew this woman. "That's Jade Appleton." One by one, she examined the pictures, identifying each woman.

The last picture made her breath catch. "That's a new picture of my mother. I wonder where the police got this photo." She looked so young, happy, as though all the hard living she had subjected herself to in the past had been wiped away.

Lacey's eyes stung. Where was her mother? Dread coiled in her gut. She and her mother had their differences, but Lacey didn't want to lose her.

"Are you okay?"

Tears spilled over as she shook her head.

Jake tightened his hold. "We'll find her."

"I'm afraid it won't be in time. If Cade is right, this man has hunted in and around Winston for six years and no one has a clue to his identity. How did she come to his attention? She's not the right age."

"It's possible her only connection is she's your mother."

"The police won't look for her."

"Jones will."

"It's not enough. The department doesn't believe she's missing and won't support Todd's efforts. Chief Beckett will tell Todd to move on to his other cases soon. If that happens, no one will search for her."

"Fortress doesn't have to follow the chief's orders. Our priority is finding your mother followed by building a case against the man abducting women. We'll stop him. The cops can claim the victory, even if they don't deserve the credit."

"I don't want to lose her."

"Don't lose hope."

"What are we going to do?"

"Search, follow where the trail leads, and call in the big guns."

She wiped the tears from her face with a strangled laugh. "I brought you with me. What bigger guns are we talking about?"

He chuckled. "Brent and possibly the FBI."

"Chief Beckett plans to bring in the feds?" She found that difficult to believe. He wasn't the type to allow strangers to play in his sandbox.

"You know the answer to that. Brent has contacts everywhere. I think he has a SEAL teammate who works for the FBI. My guess is he'll call his friend and ask for an assist."

"Must be nice to have influential friends."

He cupped her chin with the palm of his hand and lifted her face toward his. "You have influential friends." His gaze dipped from her eyes to her mouth.

She couldn't help but smile a little. For a second, Lacey felt guilty for experiencing joy with her mother missing. Taking a minute to enjoy Jake Davenport wasn't wrong. "Please say you're thinking about kissing me."

His gaze flew back to hers. "Thinking, but not acting."

"Why not?"

"Cade will be back soon."

Lacey wrapped her arms around his neck. "I don't think he'll mind." Instead of waiting for him to grab the initiative, she took the decision out of his hands by pressing her lips to his.

The impressions flew past her in a blazing rush. Heat. Softness. The unique taste of Jake. Addicting. She could kiss Jake Davenport for hours.

With a soft groan, the medic ran the tip of his tongue across her bottom lip, silently asking permission to deepen the kiss. When she complied, he spent several minutes learning what she liked and what she didn't.

Amazing. Frank had been concerned with what he wanted. Jake was attuned to her response. While he was learning her preferences, Lacey used the time to find out what caused Jake's breath to catch or made a growl of approval rumble in his chest, and in doing so, imprinted his responses, wiping out Frank's preferences. The thought of anyone but Jake kissing her made Lacey's skin crawl.

Minutes or hours later, Jake eased away from her, his breathing accelerated, lips swollen from her kisses, and cheeks flushed. "That nearly got out of hand, Lacey Coleman. You go straight to my head."

She dragged in a shuddering breath. "That's good, right?"

"It's excellent." Heat lingered in his gaze. "I had a feeling the chemistry was there." He brushed his thumbs across her cheeks. "No bad moments?"

"If you couldn't tell, I didn't do something right," she teased, then laid her hand over his still-racing heart. "No flashbacks."

Satisfaction filled his expression. "I'm glad." He peered into the hotel room. "Cade's back."

She looked over Jake's shoulder. The other operative was ensconced on the bed, laptop perched on his thighs, his gaze glued to the screen. "He looks busy. I doubt he'd notice if I collected my second kiss."

Jake laughed. "Trust me, he didn't miss anything we were doing. My control can't take another dynamite kiss. You'll have to wait for the second installment."

"A good night kiss?"

"If you want one."

"Oh, I do."

Jake stood and pulled Lacey to her feet. "Come on. I want to know if Cade encountered a problem while he was gone."

Cade tore his gaze away from the computer when they entered.

"Any trouble?" Jake asked.

"Not after I ditched the tail. Child's play. The Winston PD isn't well trained."

"Beckett?"

"Nope. Some green rookie who didn't look old enough to drive."

Will's absence made Lacey uneasy. She didn't like Will, but preferred him in her sight. His father made her feel the same. Maybe the feeling was a leftover from years ago when the police rousted her mother on a regular basis unless she provided a freebie for the arresting officer. Charges would then mysteriously drop.

"News from Zane?" Jake asked.

"He sent us files for each missing woman. I checked the dates when the women disappeared."

"Notice anything?"

"The pattern's weird. The women disappeared about every three to six months."

Lacey frowned. Every three to six months? No. It was just a coincidence. Wasn't it? She dropped onto the edge of the opposite bed.

"Lacey?" Concern filled Jake's voice. "Do you feel all right?"

"It can't be," she murmured.

"What can't be?"

"Remember how often I said I visited Mom?"

Her boyfriend stilled. "Every three to four months."

"The disappearances are connected to you," Cade said.

Lacey's stomach knotted. "It must be a coincidence. Right?"

Jake wrapped his arm around her shoulders, and drew her against him. "Do you remember the dates when you visited your mother in the past year?"

"Pretty close."

"We need to confirm or disprove our theory. What were the dates?"

"December 24, the last week in March, the middle of June."

They were silent a moment while Cade worked on the computer. He looked up, his expression grim. "With the exception of Yvonne, each of the last three women disappeared within a few days of Lacey returning to Nashville."

Jake pressed a kiss to her temple. "You're the key to the disappearances. If we figure out why, we'll know who. The answer to everything concerns your past in Winston. Who wants you so bad he kidnaps substitutes when you leave?"

CHAPTER NINETEEN

Jake's arms tightened around his trembling girlfriend as he waited for her response to Cade's revelation. Whoever this clown was, he wouldn't touch Lacey.

"That's not possible. I didn't date much when I lived here. The boys weren't interested in dating the daughter of the town street walker."

"The facts speak for themselves."

"There must be another explanation. I'm telling you, no man cared enough to do something like that because of me."

"What about Paul Chesterfield?"

Lacey stiffened. "He's a grumpy old codger who hits on attractive females when he isn't with Nora."

Jake scowled. "Tell me he at least waited until you were 18 before targeting you."

She remained silent.

Guess that answered one question. "How young were you the first time?" Chesterfield hitting on Lacey wouldn't be a one-time deal. She was a beautiful woman.

"Fourteen."

"He's a pervert, Lacey," Cade said. "Did he touch you?"

Jake clenched his teeth. No. If that old man had molested Lacey, he would be in Chesterfield's face.

"He kissed me. It was disgusting and I made sure he knew."

"Did you tell Yvonne?"

"She was drunk when those incidents happened. I didn't bother to tell her. She wouldn't have remembered me telling her about the incidents much less done anything about it."

Jake's gut clenched at the thought of Lacey alone and vulnerable, fending for herself. She didn't have anyone in those days, definitely not the case now. Even if she wasn't a favorite at the coffee shop with the Fortress operatives, Lacey had him now. "We'll look into Chesterfield, see if anything pops. Who else comes to mind?"

"What about that cop, Beckett?" Cade asked.

"What about him?" Lacey walked to the table where Cade had set an extra bottle of water for her. She broke the seal and sipped the liquid before returning to Jake. "I never dated him. He was two years ahead of me in school. We didn't run with the same crowd. He and Noah Holt, another jerk, were in the groups of popular kids. I was on the outside looking in. I ran into Will all the time. In a town the size of a postage stamp, I couldn't help but see him everywhere."

"Did he strike up conversations with you?" Jake asked.

"If you call asking who my mother was banging lately conversation, then sure, he talked to me. Same with his wealthy buddy, Noah." She shuddered. "Noah was the worst, wanting to know the price Mom and I charged for a double booking."

"Will never asked you on a date?"

Her cheeks flushed.

"He must have. I take it you turned him down."

Another sip of water. "I didn't want anything to do with him, his buddies, or his father."

"His father? What does Chief Beckett have to do with this?"

"If you and Cade dig deep enough, you'll discover Wayne Beckett was one of Mom's johns along with most of Winston's police force."

"Are you serious?" Cade's eyebrows shot up. "He never got caught?"

"Are you kidding? The whole town knew. No one spoke about it because they didn't want to be on the chief's bad side. He makes a great friend and a terrible enemy. He has wealthy, influential friends and would do anything to stay in their good graces."

"No one called his hand on it." Jake rubbed the back of his neck. "Unbelievable. Chief Beckett knew you were aware of his visits to Yvonne?"

"He never said so specifically, but he kept close tabs on me. He seemed to be everywhere I went in those days, too." She scowled. "And so was Noah."

"Want me to check into the Becketts?" Cade asked.

"I asked Zane to look into them."

The other operative turned his attention to Lacey. "Since Z is tearing apart the Becketts' lives, I can try tracking your mom's cell phone."

"Todd said he tried that with no luck."

A shrug. "Won't hurt to give it a shot now."

Lacey told Cade the number. Her eyes widened, and she clamped her hand over Jake's. "The purse. Where's the purse I grabbed from the floor of the cabin?"

"My SUV. I was more worried about you than the handbag. Why?"

"I think it belongs to Mom."

Jake stood. "I'll get it."

"I'm going with you. I'm too antsy to wait here."

"Back in a few, Cade." He made sure the hallway was clear before he escorted Lacey from the room. Minutes later, he unlocked his SUV and reached under the passenger seat for the pink purse.

Jake urged her toward the elevator. "Wait until we're in the room before you look inside the purse," he murmured, scanning the concrete structure. "We don't want to give the police anything to see if they pull the surveillance footage."

"I didn't think about security cameras."

"It's my job to think about those things."

The elevator doors slid open. Knowing the risk of observation held true in the car, he blocked the camera's view of her with his body. Jake wrapped his arms around her and said softly into her ear, "Don't look at it, but there's a camera in the upper left corner. Keep the purse between our bodies."

"How do I do that when we arrive on our floor?"

He kissed her ear, smiling when she shivered in reaction. "Easy. Keep your attention focused on me as though you are under my spell."

"How will that help?"

"I'll be doing the same because I'm fascinated with you. I'm your boyfriend, after all. I should be crazy about you."

The bell dinged to indicate they'd reached their floor.

"Are you crazy about me?" Lacey asked.

"Can't you tell?" He walked off the elevator with her. "I'll have to do better the next time I kiss you."

"If you do any better, I might melt onto the floor," she muttered.

Jake burst into laughter. "You saying I have skills, Lacey?"

"I think you're lethal in more ways than one."

Still chuckling, he unlocked the door to his room and nudged Lacey inside. She hurried to the second bed and dumped the contents of the purse on the spread.

She gave a watery laugh as six tubes of lip balm rolled away from the pile. "Mom loves different flavored lip balm. Her lips are always dry. She also claims the men she dates love to kiss her to see what flavor she's wearing."

Incredible. "How many flavors does she have?"

"Thirty, maybe more. She buys new flavors when she runs across them at the store or online." Lacey shrugged. "I don't say anything to her. I'd rather she buy lip balm than waste her money on an addiction that might kill her."

"That's nothing," Cade said. "The head of Personal Security International is married to the owner of Otter Creek Books. She has hundreds of books in their home. Josh says they'll have to move to a bigger house soon because there won't be room for them plus the books and his weapons stash."

"No cell phone in the purse?" Jake asked her.

She thrust her hand back into the bag and unzipped an inner pocket. "Nothing. Mom always drops the phone in this pocket. She hates having to sift through the contents of her purse to find it."

"Cade?"

"I don't know why the Winston PD couldn't find anything, but the Fortress program is triangulating Yvonne's cell phone's signal. So far, I can tell the phone is still in the Winston area."

"How long will it take to narrow down the location?" Lacey asked Cade.

"A few more minutes." He glanced at Jake. "Call the boss."

He dropped a soft kiss on Lacey's lips before he called Maddox and placed it on speaker.

"Yeah, Maddox."

"It's Jake. You're on speaker with Lacey and Cade."

"You're still there, Ramsey?"

"Yes, sir. Jake and Lacey ran into trouble. Thought I should stick around."

"What happened, Jake?"

"Had a couple run-ins with local cops, searched Yvonne Coleman's house, and drove to an abandoned cabin she used for meeting men." He felt Lacey flinch. "Sorry," he murmured to her before continuing to speak in a normal voice to Brent. "The cabin was wired for explosives."

"You or Lacey hurt?"

"Minor burns for me, bruises and a deep cut for her."

"Do I need to squash a hospital report?"

"Jake treated me." She sipped more water. "Now I know why you hired him. He's excellent at his job."

"He's one of the most requested medics in Fortress. Anything more, Jake?"

"Lacey found her mother's purse in the cabin. She scooped it up seconds before the place blew up. Unfortunately, that's not the worst of it." He explained about the missing women who were close to Lacey's age with similar features, hair and eye color, and body type.

"You're telling me my wife's best friend has caught the attention of a serial killer?" Ice cold rage filled Brent's voice.

"Yes, sir. Another woman goes missing within days of Lacey leaving Winston and returning to Nashville."

"The local cops called in the feds yet?"

"The police chief refuses to bring them in. He says he has a better chance of finding the culprit than a stranger."

"Any bodies turn up yet?"

"Negative."

"Do you need your team?"

"I don't think so. I wouldn't be opposed to a fed poking around, though, if it's one you trust."

"I have a friend who works for the FBI. I'll see if he's free. If not, I'll work out something else. Be expecting someone to arrive by tomorrow at the latest."

"Thanks, boss."

"Lacey, how are you holding up?"

"I'm worried about Mom."

"We'll find her. In the meantime, stay with either Jake or Cade. Don't go off on your own for any reason. If this guy is taking substitutes for you, let's not give him the opportunity to take the real deal. Keep your cell phone charged and with you at all times. Jake, do you have an extra tracker in your equipment bag?"

"I'd already planned to use it with Lacey."

"Good. Make sure it's something she wears all the time, something inconspicuous."

"Copy that."

"Zane will be sending a report on the Becketts. I take it these are the cops giving you grief?"

"Police chief and his son."

"What's the connection with Lacey?"

"The father was a customer of Yvonne's." He scowled, remembering the way Will Beckett had looked at Lacey. "The son doesn't know how to keep his hands to himself."

Silence, then, "He hurt you, sugar?" Brent's words came out very soft.

Jake winced. He'd hate to be on the receiving end of the boss's anger.

"Not really."

"Lacey."

"Jake arrived before things got out of hand. I have a few bruises. They'll fade."

"Did you take care of him, Davenport?"

"Warned him off last night, and slammed him against a wall a little while ago when he tried to put his hands on her again."

A sigh. “All right. Watch your back. He sounds vindictive. I want another update in four hours. Anything changes, I want to know immediately.”

“Yes, sir.” He ended the call.

“Got it,” Cade said, glancing up from his computer screen. He twisted the laptop around so Jake could see the map where he’d plotted the coordinates.

Jake studied the map and stilled. Oh, man.

“I’m not great at reading maps. Where is she?” Lacey’s hand clamped on his.

He didn’t want to tell her. Had he missed Yvonne? Searching the cabin had revealed no one, including Yvonne. “The Martin cabin.”

“No,” she whispered. “We didn’t see her. With the explosion…” Her voice choked off.

“Her cell phone signal is still strong. If the phone had been inside the cabin, the explosion and fire would have destroyed it. The phone is outside the burn zone. Does Yvonne silence her phone?”

“I’ve never known her to do that.” Hope lit her eyes. “Maybe she’s near the cabin.”

He raised their clasped hands and kissed the back of hers. “If we’re lucky, we might be able to track her phone’s ring tone.” Hopefully, they would find Yvonne alive.

CHAPTER TWENTY

Jake clasped Lacey's hand as he led her toward the woods at the cabin's back property line. He and Cade had checked the area around the burn site before allowing Lacey to leave the safety of the SUV, but they couldn't check the surrounding forest without leaving her vulnerable.

He wished his teammates were here. Jake had a bad feeling about taking her to find the phone. He'd never forgive himself if they stumbled upon Yvonne's body. However, short of handcuffing her to the steering wheel, he couldn't stop her from coming with them. Truthfully, if it was his mother, he'd be out here looking for her no matter what anyone advised him. He'd go through any obstacle in his way.

"If I tell you to drop, do it without question, Lacey," he murmured.

"I will, I promise."

He hoped he didn't regret his decision to let her accompany them. More important, he hoped Lacey didn't regret it.

They walked in silence, the night air brisk, woods utterly still as they journeyed deeper into the trees. Jake's skin prickled. Wildlife should have been stirring. Lacey wasn't quiet trekking through the area, but that didn't explain his gut-deep feeling they weren't alone out here.

A limb cracked, sounding almost like a rifle shot. Cade crouched, quartering the area with his weapon. Jake pushed Lacey against a tree, signaled her to go to the ground, and positioned himself between her and a potential threat, Sig in his hand, tracking as his gaze scoured the trees and shrubs for signs of a two-legged predator stalking them.

A rustle to his left drew his attention. Animal or person? Cade had heard the noise and moved to intercept. Though he longed to follow, Jake refrained. He wouldn't leave Lacey alone and unprotected.

They waited for tense moments until Cade reappeared, his expression grim. "I have something you need to see." His gaze slid to Lacey. "Might be best to stay here, Lacey."

"No. The worst thing about this whole situation with my mother is not knowing the truth."

He was silent a moment, then shook his head. "The nightmare is knowing the truth and not being able to change it." The operative turned away after a warning glance at Jake.

Oh, man. Had he found Yvonne? Whatever it was, Jake wanted to spare his girl more pain than she'd already suffered. Unfortunately, he no longer believed that was possible.

"Don't say it." Lacey looked at him. "You won't convince me to stay safe in whatever cocoon you find for me. I have to see for myself."

"I care about you and don't want you hurt."

"Life is full of bumps and bruises. You can't protect me from life. Please, don't try. Just be there if I need you."

An invisible band tightened around his chest. Although she appeared fragile, Lacey was anything but delicate. She might be the strongest woman he'd met, and he was falling in love with her. He accepted the truth, and prayed her feelings for him would grow as deep. Otherwise, he was destined for a broken heart in the near future.

He brushed his lips across hers. "Come on." Jake clasped her hand and followed Cade deeper into the woods. Ahead, the operative's flashlight shone, a beacon leading them to his location.

Cade waited where the tree and vegetation cover thinned. "She shouldn't be here, man."

"She's not a hothouse flower. Lacey can handle it." His girl squeezed his hand in appreciation for his belief. Hoping his confidence in her wasn't misguided, Jake shifted his attention to the area in front of them. "What am I looking at?"

"You tell me. This is more your area than mine."

Jake frowned and played the beam of his flashlight over the ground. What were those odd black lumps on the dirt? Jake released Lacey's hand. "Stay here." He looked back at her. "Please."

She gave him a short nod.

He moved closer to the nearest black mass and crouched, balancing on the balls of his feet. He ran the light over the oddly-shaped lump. Metal gleamed in the center. Jake drew in a sharp breath. No. Dread coiling in his gut, he stood and carefully walked around the edges of the area, choosing his steps carefully to avoid leaving traces of his passage. As he walked, Jake did a quick tally in his head.

He had to call Jones, but his priority was locating Yvonne's cell phone. Retracing his steps, Jake stopped in front of Lacey.

"Jake?"

"Come here." He drew her into his arms.

"You're scaring me. What did you see?"

"There's no easy way to say this."

"Fast. Tell me fast."

His admiration for her grew stronger. “The black objects on the ground are body bags, baby.” Although she didn’t make a sound, Lacey’s knees buckled. Jake tightened his hold on her, easily taking his girlfriend’s weight. “Call your mother’s phone.”

“What’s the point?” Lacey’s voice broke. “So I can identify which bag is hers?”

“There are fifteen body bags, not sixteen. Call her phone.”

Lacey stayed in the circle of his arms while she retrieved her cell phone. She shoved the instrument into Jake’s hand. “My hands are shaking too hard. You do it.”

“Code to unlock your phone?” Once she’d given the information, he brought up her contact list. Scrolling down, he found Yvonne’s name and called.

Within seconds, a phone’s ring tone broke the silence of the woods. Cade skirted the dump site and followed the sound of the phone, followed by Jake and Lacey.

He gripped Lacey’s hand, catching her when she stumbled on an exposed tree root or a rock difficult to see in the inky darkness. When the ring tone stopped, Jake initiated another call.

Cade raced toward the left and plunged through a thick stand of bushes. A moment later, he called back, “Jake, over here.”

The medic found a gap in the brush and tugged Lacey into the opening with him. On the other side, he pulled up short as he almost ran into Cade.

“Careful.” The other operative directed his flashlight beam toward the ground.

Jake eased closer to the edge, his own light flashing over the gaping chasm in front of them. A ravine, a deep one. “Where’s the phone?”

Cade tipped his chin toward the embankment. “Down there.”

“Heard any movement?”

"Not yet. Haven't tried calling out. Figured if Yvonne is down there and able to respond, she'll be more inclined to respond to her daughter than a stranger, especially a man."

Jake lay on the ground and scooted to the edge, directing his beam along the side and as much of the bottom as he could see from this angle. "Only one way to find out if she's down there with the phone. One of us needs to rappel to the bottom."

A nod. "I'll get the gear."

"Lacey, lay flat and ease to the edge of the ravine." When she was in place, he said, "Call out to your mother. If she's down there, let's see if she'll respond to you."

"Mom?" Lacey called. "It's Lacey. Are you down there?"

Nothing.

"Mom. Please, answer me or make some noise."

Was she afraid? The night was quiet. If Yvonne was still alive, maybe she'd heard unfamiliar male voices and decided to remain silent.

"I'm here with friends from Nashville. They're good men here to help you. You can trust them."

Still nothing.

Jake eased back from the edge and urged Lacey to do the same. His heart clenched when he noticed the wet streaks on her cheeks. "We don't know that she's down there."

"If she is, she's hurt. She has to be. She's been missing for days."

He wrapped his arms around her and pressed a kiss to her temple. "I know."

Cade jogged back to the ravine, slid a pack off his back, and handed Jake his mike bag. "Rappelling gear. You going down?"

He bent and started pulling on the safety equipment. “If Yvonne is down there, she’ll need medical help.” If it wasn’t already too late.

“Figured. I’ll keep an eye on Lacey and call the police.”

Jake sent a text to his Cade. “That’s Jones’s cell phone number. Don’t talk to anyone but him.”

“Roger that.”

With the safety harness in place and double checked, Cade tied off the other end to a tree. “There’s an outcropping of sharp rocks to your right. Watch yourself.”

With a nod, Jake squeezed Lacey’s hand.

“Be careful, Jake.” She pressed her hand against his cheek for a moment, then stepped back.

He eased his body over the side of the ravine and controlled his descent. He learned to rappel while in the military, but all Fortress operatives were trained to handle rugged terrain rescues as well.

Rappelling in the dark in unfamiliar terrain was different, though. He wasn’t a fan of heights and doing this without good light asked for injuries. Finally, Jake reached the bottom of the ravine. “On the ground,” he called.

“Keep the rigging on in case I have to haul you up in a hurry.”

“Keep your eyes on Lacey. She’s your priority.” He adjusted his mike bag and freed his flashlight. Sweeping the light along the ground, he hunted for any sign of Yvonne or her cell phone. “Call the phone,” he said to Lacey.

A moment later, a ring tone started again, this time to his right. He tracked the sound through the ravine. “Again,” he said when the phone went silent.

He scowled. Where was the phone? He should be right on top of it based on the sound. Slowly sweeping the light along the ground, he caught a metallic gleam. Easing over a fallen tree limb, Jake squatted on the uneven, rocky terrain.

A cell phone. He pulled a pair of rubber gloves from his pocket and tugged them on his hands. Jake didn't know if there were any fingerprints besides Yvonne's on the phone casing, but Jones wouldn't be happy if he contaminated any evidence. "Call the phone again."

Seconds later, the phone in his hand lit up and a ring tone sang out. Guess that answered the question of whether or not this was Yvonne's. He silenced the ring tone. "Got the phone."

"Do you see Mom?"

"Not yet." Sliding the phone into a pocket of his mike bag, Jake refocused the beam of his flashlight and swept the ground in a grid pattern. "Yvonne? My name's Jake. I'm Lacey's boyfriend. I'm here to help."

Silence.

He moved further up the ravine. As he was about to turn and go back the way he'd come, he noticed drag marks in the dirt. He followed the snaking trail fifty yards before he spotted the sole of a tennis shoe.

Jake's heart sped up as he hurried over to investigate. His light revealed a jeans-clad leg. "Yvonne?" A soft moan reached his ears. He swept the light over the figure lying prone on the ground. Although her face was battered and bruised, Jake recognized Lacey's mother.

"Cade, we need an ambulance."

"Copy that."

"Did you find Mom?" Lacey sounded frantic. "Is she all right?"

"I found her. Not sure how bad she's hurt." Jake shrugged off his mike bag and grabbed his Mylar blanket. He draped the cover over Lacey's mother. "Yvonne, can you hear me?" Another moan. "I need you to talk to me and tell me where you're hurt."

The woman dragged in a painful breath. "Dreaming?"

"You're not dreaming. I'm here with your daughter. We'll get you to the hospital." While he talked to her, trying to keep her grounded and conscious, Jake checked her vitals, then felt for broken bones. When he reached Yvonne's ribs, she cried out.

Definite broken ribs. They'd have to be careful when they moved her or the jagged edge of the bone could puncture her lung. Broken wrist, probably from trying to break her fall. Several cuts and abrasions. She also had quite a lump on her head.

"Lacey?" she whispered.

"She's up top, waiting for you. She's anxious to talk to you." He moved to her legs. "Lacey, say hi to your mom."

"I'm here, Mom. I've been worried about you. Jake and I talked to Harley. He's been worried sick about you, too."

"Harley."

"We met him earlier today. He's an interesting guy." Another groan when Jake examined her right ankle. "Hate to tell you this, Yvonne, but you won't be waitressing for a while. You have broken ribs, a broken wrist, and a broken ankle." He was also worried about internal injuries. Nothing he could do about those except transport her to the hospital as soon as possible. Unfortunately, he'd have to wait for the EMTs and the basket to hoist Yvonne out of here without further injuring her.

"Who?"

He studied her face a moment. She was trying to focus her gaze on him. He found two vacuum splints in his mike bag and worked to stabilize her wrist and ankle. "Try not to move, okay? My name is Jake. I'm Lacey's boyfriend."

"Doctor?"

"Medic." Once the temporary splints were in place, he thrust his hand back into the mike bag and grabbed the supplies for an IV. Yvonne needed fluids, fast.

As he worked, the sound of multiple sirens grew louder. "Hear that, Yvonne? Once the ambulance arrives, we'll free you from the ravine. How did you end up down here?"

She frowned. "Don't remember."

Though he hated to press, his time alone with her was short. "Harley said you had a late meeting with someone four nights ago. Who did you meet?"

"Don't know."

Once the IV was taped in place, Jake gently felt around her head, praying he didn't find anything serious. A couple of good-sized lumps. Might account for the memory loss.

Yvonne's uninjured hand moved toward his. He sandwiched her hand between his own. "I'm right here."

"Don't leave me. He'll kill me."

CHAPTER TWENTY-ONE

Jake pressed her hand. "Who wants to kill you, Yvonne?"

Confusion filled her gaze. "I don't know. Why can't I remember?"

"You've suffered trauma, including blows to your head. Temporary memory loss is normal."

"How will I protect myself?"

"I'm employed by Fortress Security. We'll make sure you're safe." Her protection was a job for more than two operatives. He needed to call Adam and Brent. Jake wanted Remy and Lily Doucet in Winston. Yvonne and Lacey would be well covered with four Fortress operatives. He hadn't forgotten the serial killer's ultimate prize was Lacey.

"Lacey, too?"

"No one will touch Lacey on my watch." He ignored the fact he'd already given Beckett an opening to bruise Lacey's arms. Wouldn't happen again.

Relief smoothed the worry lines from Yvonne's forehead.

"Davenport."

Jake twisted to shine his flashlight for Jones to pinpoint his location. "Where's that ambulance?"

"EMTs are two minutes behind me."

Yvonne gripped Jake's wrist with surprising strength. "Who?"

"Todd Jones, a Winston police detective. He's been looking for you."

A fierce squeeze. "What if he's the one?"

"You won't be alone with anyone except me or my teammates. No one will hurt you again. You have my word."

After a moment, she gave a short nod.

He turned to look back at the ledge. "Have you seen the bags?"

"Yeah," came the grim response. "Our crime scene team could use help."

"Tomorrow." Maybe sooner when he called Brent. The crime scene was too large for a small police department to process alone.

"I'll deny any knowledge of that, but thanks."

Shouts and running feet interrupted the exchange between Jake and the detective. Klieg lights were set up and the shadows receded in the ravine as the beams illuminated a broad swath of the terrain.

Two members of the fire department rappelled down the steep ravine wall. When they were on the ground, their medical equipment and the basket to extract Yvonne were lowered.

"I'm Nolan. I hear you're a medic," one man said.

"Jake. First in the Army, now with a private security firm."

"What do we have?" The second man gawked at Yvonne. "Man, am I glad to see you. How you doing, hon?"

"Hurts."

"The doc at the hospital will fix you right up, although it looks like Jake here has given you an IV."

"Saline. She's dehydrated."

"What do we have?" Nolan asked.

"Broken ribs, wrist, ankle. Couple good bumps on her head. Some memory loss. Possible internal injuries. You bring a back board and neck brace?"

"Yep. Left them up top until we knew if we needed them." Nolan swiveled on one foot. "Hey, Cliff, send down the board and brace."

"Coming down," came the muffled response.

Kevin, the second EMT, untied both items and carted them to Yvonne.

Between the three of them, they strapped on the neck brace and secured Lacey's mother to the back board, then moved her to the basket.

"Helo?" Jake murmured. He hadn't heard the rotors of a chopper hovering nearby.

"Transporting two critical accident victims," Nolan said. "Ready for transport. Bring her up, nice and slow. Possible back and neck injuries."

"Jake," Yvonne said.

"I'll be right behind you. My teammate, Cade, is up top with Lacey."

"You'll go to the hospital with me?"

"Yes, ma'am. I won't leave unless someone I trust is with you." He squeezed her fingers and stepped back. "Pull her up," he ordered the firefighters at the top.

Using a pulley system with multiple ropes to keep Yvonne from bumping against the ravine wall, the basket began a slow ascent. Jake policed the trash from the medical supplies he'd used, then closed his mike bag. After shrugging into his pack, he climbed from the ravine.

He crested the edge to see Lacey gripping her mother's uninjured hand, smiling despite tears rolling down her cheeks. As soon as Jake unhooked his rappelling equipment, Cade said, "I'll take care of the gear. Go with your patient. I'll come to the hospital when I shake free."

Might be a while from the looks of things. He nodded and followed the EMTs, Lacey, and Yvonne. Jake caught up with Lacey and hooked his arm around her waist.

"How can I ever thank you?"

He urged her closer to his side. "Not necessary. I'm glad we found her."

"Was it in time?"

"She's a tough lady. To have survived alone and injured this long, she's a fighter. Your mother won't be able to work for several weeks. She has a broken wrist, ankle, and ribs, memory loss, probable concussion, and maybe internal injuries." He squeezed her waist. "She's strong, like her beautiful daughter."

Lacey's breath caught. "Beautiful?"

"You haven't looked in the mirror lately if you don't believe me."

"I know I'm not a troll or anything."

A snort. "Not even close."

"Jake?" Yvonne called.

"Right here, Yvonne." He moved close enough for Lacey's mother to see him. The relief on her face was obvious. "Focus on yourself. Let me worry about everything else."

Although it took a little persuasion, he and Lacey rode in the back with Yvonne and one of the EMTs. Minutes later, the ambulance stopped outside the emergency entrance, and hospital personnel rushed Yvonne into an exam room. Jake and Lacey stayed with Yvonne until the doctor entered the room. "We'll be in the hall," Jake assured Lacey's mother.

He escorted Lacey to the hallway and the door closed behind them. "Do you want to go to the waiting room?" he asked, already knowing her answer.

Lacey shook her head. “I don’t want to be far in case she needs me.”

Jake slid the mike bag off his shoulders and set it by Lacey’s feet. “I’ll find two chairs.” At least they’d be comfortable while they waited. He grabbed two chairs from the waiting room and carried them to Lacey.

Once they sat, she leaned close and asked, “Did Mom tell you anything? Does she know who is responsible for this?”

“She doesn’t remember the meeting or how she landed in the ravine.”

She moaned, voice soft. “We’re still short on facts and long on speculation.”

“Unfortunately.”

“Will she regain her memory?”

“Maybe.” He wouldn’t hold his breath, though. “It’s also possible she won’t ever remember. Sometimes your brain protects you from shock or trauma by hiding the truth.”

Lacey rested her head against the wall. “I was sure if we found Mom, we’d have the answers we needed.”

Knowing a cop would arrive soon, Jake pulled out his phone. He needed backup to aid him and Cade in protecting Lacey and Yvonne.

His call was answered on the first ring. Shouldn’t have surprised him, but he thought his boss would be asleep at this hour. “It’s Jake.”

“Hold” A rustle of movement, then a door shut softly. “Talk to me. What’s the latest?”

“We found Yvonne at the bottom of a ravine near the cabin that exploded.”

“She alive?”

“A few broken bones, memory loss, dehydration, a couple good bumps on the head. For the amount of time she spent untreated and exposed to the elements, she’s in remarkably good shape.”

"Survival chances?"

Mindful of Lacey's presence, he said, "Unknown. I'll let you know what the ER doc says."

"What else?"

Yeah, Brent Maddox always knew when there was more to the story. "While we searched for Yvonne, we stumbled across fifteen body bags."

"The missing women."

"That would be my guess. I left the confirmation to Todd Jones, the detective assigned to Yvonne's case. With that many bodies, he'll need fed help sooner rather than later. They're not equipped to handle the volume or the circumstances." Serial killers weren't the norm in small towns. Based on what Jones revealed in the interrogation room, the detective didn't have law enforcement experience on a larger police force.

"En route. Rafe Torres should arrive in town within two hours. I gave him your number. He'll contact you as soon as he arrives."

"Thanks, Brent."

"What do you need from me?"

"Remy and Lily. Cade and I need assistance with Yvonne and Lacey."

"Done. Adam and Veronica might come along. They are your teammates."

Jake sighed. He hadn't wanted to ask Adam and Vonnie for help. They were newlyweds, and Vonnie was recovering from her recent injuries. "I'll call Adam and Remy myself. Tell Rowan Lacey may be out of pocket for a while. Her mother will need help while she recovers."

"Believe me, she'll be glad for the inconvenience because it means Yvonne is alive and healing. We thought you would find Yvonne's body."

"So did I."

After Brent gave him a few last instructions, he insisted on talking to Lacey. Moments later, she ended the call and handed Jake his phone.

Despite the late hour, Jake called Adam Walker, his team leader. "Sorry to wake you, Adam."

"What do you need?" came the gravelly response.

"The team in Winston, Alabama."

"Sit rep."

In a quiet voice, Jake brought Adam up to date on events since he and Lacey arrived in her hometown. "I need more boots on the ground to protect Yvonne and Lacey."

"Expect us in town by nine o'clock."

"Thanks, Adam."

"Where are you staying?"

He gave the name of the hotel. "Lacey, Cade and I have two connecting rooms on the third floor."

"I'll call Remy. We'll be in touch as soon as we're on the road. Any place in town with good coffee?"

Jake smiled. "The diner. Avoid the coffee shop or you'll regret it."

"Interesting. See you in a few hours, Jake."

He slid his phone into his pocket. "My teammates will be here soon."

"I'll be glad to see them, but why do you need help? Mom won't be going anywhere for a day or two."

Longer, by Jake's estimation. "I want two people with Yvonne at all times. We don't know who we can trust. Someone in this town is a killer and he's already attempted to kill your mother once."

"By throwing her into the ravine?"

"Did you notice the bruises on her throat?"

She frowned. "I thought they were from her fall."

"Those bruises are from a man's hands. The killer tried to strangle your mother."

CHAPTER TWENTY-TWO

"Strangled?" Lacey's stomach clenched at the horrible visual images. Memories of her own brush with death at Frank's hands swelled to the forefront.

Jake cupped her chin with the palm of his hand and turned her face toward him. "I'm sorry. I should have found a better way to tell you. You've already had more than one shock tonight."

"No, it's not what you think." How did she explain in a way that wouldn't incite him to hunt down Frank? Jake's protective streak was a mile wide and their new relationship would push him further along that path.

"Tell me."

"The last time Frank attacked me, he strangled me until I passed out, then revived me."

Jake shifted his hold from her chin to wrap an arm around her shoulders and draw her close to his side. "One time?"

"No. Over and over."

A growl rumbled deep in his chest. "You're lucky he didn't kill you."

"I had bruises on my throat for weeks after that incident."

"If he touches you again, he's a dead man."

"Frank hasn't bothered me in months. Adam and Brent scared him."

"I want to know if he shows his face anywhere near you."

"He won't. Frank's a coward."

He flashed her a heated look. "I expect a phone call or text if you see him again. You matter to me, Lacey. I need to know you're safe."

There was some undefinable emotion behind those words, a hidden message in there, an important one. "I promise to tell you."

They sat in silence for a time, hospital personnel hurrying along the hall. She and Jake garnered a few sideways glances, but no one objected to their vigil outside the exam room.

The door swung open and the doctor walked out with bunched plastic in his hand. "I'm Dr. Royce. Are you Ms. Coleman?"

"Yes. I'm Lacey. How is Mom?"

"We're taking her for x-rays, then the operating room for surgery. She has bad breaks in her wrist and ankle. The good news is Yvonne is doing well considering what she's been through."

The doctor turned to Jake. "You must be the medic."

"That's right." He held out a hand. "Jake Davenport."

"Here are the vacuum splints you used on Yvonne. What branch of the military?"

"Army Rangers," he answered as he placed the splints in his mike bag.

Royce's eyebrows winged upward. "Special Forces. I served in the Air Force."

Jake grinned. "A fly boy."

"Eight years. You?"

"Ten."

"Good work out there, Davenport." The doctor moved away from the door as two orderlies approached. "If you want to relocate to this part of the country, I'll put in a good word for you with the fire department. They could use more qualified EMTs."

"I love my job, but thanks."

The orderlies guided the bed bearing Yvonne from the room. Jake held out a hand to Lacey. "We need to stay with her," he murmured to the doctor. "She's not safe."

"I understand. Lacey, I'll keep you updated on your mother's condition."

Once the surgeon studied the x-rays, Yvonne was prepped and wheeled to the operating room.

"Come on." Jake clasped Lacey's hand. "The waiting room is down the hall so we'll know if there's trouble in the OR."

He was right, but Lacey hated to be far. She'd come so close to losing her mother she wasn't comfortable with distance between them. Soon, though, she would be anxious to return home. She missed her job at the coffee shop already, but Mom would need help while she recovered. The thought of remaining in this town for several weeks wasn't appealing.

An hour later, Cade strode into the waiting room. "How's Yvonne?"

"In surgery," Jake answered. "How soon can we expect the police?"

"Within the hour. Jones has his hands full so I'm not sure who will question us."

"Hopefully not the Becketts." Lacey sipped the water Jake bought for her. "I've had enough of them to last a lifetime."

"How bad is it out there?" Jake asked.

"As bad as it gets. This is rough on the cops working the scene. Some of the women were friends and neighbors, and a sick creep killed them for no good reason."

"Have they positively identified the remains in any of the bags?"

Cade shook his head. "The coroner arrived a few minutes before I left. Once he does his thing, they'll start the transport. With that many bodies, it's going to take a while to move them to the morgue and identify them all."

A nod. "Adam and the others will be here in a few hours."

"Figured. You still need me?"

"Stay if you can. I'd like to put my teammates on a round-the-clock protection detail for Yvonne. You and I can cover Lacey."

"Fine with me. I talked to St. Claire on my way here. He said we're not due for deployment for another month."

"We won't be in Winston that long. If we haven't run the killer to ground by that point, we'll either move Yvonne to Nashville temporarily or have Brent assign a team of bodyguards to keep an eye on her."

Lacey's eyes misted as she caught the extent of the plans Jake had already put together to protect her mother.

Cade settled into the vacant seat beside Lacey. "How are you?"

"I'll be better when I'm sure Mom will recover and is safe." She sat up. "Harley. We need to call Harley." Lacey shoved a hand through her hair. "I don't know his number. Wait. Never mind. Winston is a small town. I can ask someone."

"I'll go to the nurses' desk and ask. Do you need a snack?"

She shook her head.

"Be back in a minute." With a glance a Cade, he left the room.

"Why does he do that?"

The operative looked puzzled. "Do what?"

"Every time he leaves me, he looks at you. Why?"

"He's handing off your protection to me until he returns."

Lacey frowned. Really? "We're in the middle of a hospital. What could possibly happen here?"

"Too many exits to cover. We can't control who comes or goes. The hospital is a security nightmare. Jake needs someone he trusts to pull a trigger if necessary to keep you safe. Otherwise, his attention will be divided between you and whatever task he needs to complete."

Her stomach lurched. That explained a few things. "That's why he's bringing in Adam and the others, isn't it?" He'd explained his reasoning earlier, but she didn't truly understand how dangerous this situation was at the hospital. She'd been so focused on finding her mother that she hadn't considered the continuing danger as Yvonne received medical treatment.

Cade inclined his head in silent agreement. "He's a good man, Lacey."

"Yes, he is. Are you worried I'll hurt him?"

"No." No hesitation. "The career we chose isn't easy for loved ones who spend their lives waiting for our return from deployment. We have high-risk jobs."

"Sounds like you're warning me off."

"Never, but you should know what to expect before you go deeper into this relationship."

She pressed his hand. "Thanks."

Jake returned, his eyebrows raising when he caught sight of her hand on Cade's. "Harley's on his way."

His cell phone rang. Jake checked the screen and answered the call. "Davenport." He was silent a moment, then told the caller they were at the hospital. When he conversation ended, he returned to his seat on the other side of Lacey. "That was Rafe Torres, Brent's friend in the FBI. He'll be here in a few minutes."

Several policemen strode into view, including the Becketts.

"Torres will arrive in time for the circus," Cade murmured.

Lacey's stomach knotted. How could he joke at a time like this? The last thing she wanted to do was spend time with the police chief and his son.

Wayne Beckett came to a halt in front of Lacey, eyes hot, face flushed. "Where is your mother?"

"Surgery."

A scowl. "I need to question her."

"The questions will have to wait," Jake said, wrapping his hand around Lacey's. "Yvonne's been in surgery for an hour. When the surgeon is finished, she'll be in recovery. You can talk to her when she's been assigned a room."

"She has answers to my questions. I have a field full of dead women who deserve justice."

"You won't get answers by sacrificing her health."

What would the police chief say when he realized Mom didn't remember anything? Knowing Beckett, he would probably accuse her of obstructing justice.

"You don't tell me how to conduct police business, Davenport. You're a gun for hire, nothing more."

"Where is Detective Jones?" Lacey asked. "I thought he would be here by now since this is his case." Might as well distract the chief while they waited for Brent's friend to arrive at the hospital.

"Still at the scene," he answered curtly. "You and your boyfriend interfered in my investigation."

What investigation? From what she'd gathered, the police chief hadn't lifted a finger to solve any of the cases, including her mother's.

A dark-haired, dark-eyed man walked into the waiting room dressed in a black suit, white shirt, black tie, polished shoes. With his close-cut hair plus his bearing, something about him screamed military. She'd bet this was Brent's friend.

"Wayne Beckett?"

The chief swung around to glare at the newcomer. "Who wants to know?"

The stranger flipped open the small wallet in his hand to reveal a badge. "Rafe Torres, FBI."

He sneered. "A fed? What are you doing here?"

Torres stared at the police chief. "The better question is why didn't you call in federal help? You have a serial killer using your town as a hunting ground."

"Didn't need no outside help."

"Really? You should have contacted us after the first three or four women went missing. Because you couldn't swallow your pride, fifteen women have died and another woman is fighting for her life."

"There's no proof the Coleman woman's case is connected to the other deaths."

"Keep telling yourself that. In the meantime, the FBI will be lending your detective a hand."

A muscle in Beckett's jaw twitched. "I told him not to call you boys. We handle our own cases in my town."

"Not very well from what I can see. However, no one from your police department contacted us."

The police chief turned to stare at Jake, eyes narrowed. "I've got you to thank for this interference?"

Jake smiled.

"I'll expect your full cooperation, Chief Beckett. You owe it to your citizens to give us as much help as possible."

"You're taking over, then?"

"No. We're using our resources to aid your detective in solving the case."

A snort. "Right."

"You going to let them just take over, Pop?" Will swaggered to his father's side.

"Don't have much choice, do I?" He swung around to glare at Lacey. "Your mother say anything we can use before she went under the knife?"

Nice way to put it. "No."

"No, as in she didn't say anything or what she said wasn't useful?"

Jake squeezed her hand and Rafe Torres shot her a warning glance.

Yeah, Lacey knew she had to be careful. They couldn't really trust anyone in this town with her mother's safety. "She said very little. She was in shock and a great deal of pain. Instead of prodding her with questions, Jake gave her medical aid until the EMTs arrived, then we brought her here."

Beckett's expression was one of pure disgust. He turned back to the FBI agent. "I expect updates every step of the way."

Torres just stared at him, his expression giving nothing away.

"Let's go, boys. Now that the feebs are here, we can get on with our jobs."

Will's gaze crawled over Lacey, giving her the creeps. Jake must have sensed how uncomfortable she was because he stood and stepped in front of her, blocking Will's view.

Once Will was gone, Jake walked toward Torres. "Jake Davenport," he said, holding out his hand.

"Rafe Torres. Commander Maddox sent me to look into the murders."

"Thanks for coming at short notice." He nodded at Cade. "Cade Ramsey, also with Fortress. He's on Lacey's security detail." Jake turned and held out his hand to Lacey.

She rose and walked to his side.

"This is my girlfriend, Lacey Coleman. Her mother is the woman in surgery."

Rafe shook her hand briefly. "I'm glad you and Jake found your mom. Let's sit down while we talk. I need to know everything." An hour later, he shook his head. "I can't believe Beckett or his detective didn't call the feds. More important, I think you know the danger is not over. Lacey and Yvonne are the key to this killer."

CHAPTER TWENTY-THREE

Jake locked his gaze with Rafe's. "Trust me, that's not something I'd miss. I saw the resemblance between the victims, and Lacey and Yvonne. The killer is fixated on Lacey. The timing of the disappearances can't be a coincidence."

"Given the eerie similarities between Lacey and the murder victims, I'd say you're right. How does Yvonne play into this?"

"I'm not sure if Yvonne knew what was going on and who was doing it, or just suspected. It's also possible the only connection is that Yvonne is Lacey's mother. Whatever the reason, she caught the attention of the killer. Based on the bruises to Yvonne's neck, I think he believed he'd killed her."

"Or maybe we interrupted him and he couldn't finish the job," Cade put in. "Someone was in those woods when we first arrived tonight."

Jake frowned. He couldn't argue with that. His instincts had warned him they weren't alone in the darkened forest. However, he hadn't seen evidence of someone scrambling from the ravine in a hurry. "Some of the bruises on her neck are several days old."

"He could have kept her prisoner, choked her out a few times before he decided it was time to end things."

When Lacey shuddered, Jake tucked her tighter against his side. "It's not easy to choke someone to death with your bare hands. It's possible the killer thought she was dead and, when he went for a body bag to dump her in the field with the rest of the women, Yvonne regained consciousness and tried to run for help. She might have fallen into the ravine. From the drag marks I found in the dirt, Yvonne was unconscious for a time, then dragged herself to a more hidden location. With her unconscious and motionless, the killer could have believed her dead and he didn't bother to make sure until he knew we were in town."

Cade lifted one shoulder. "Would have been easy to tumble over the edge of the ravine. I almost fell into the blasted thing when I burst through that hedge."

"Tell me where the crime scene is." Rafe stood and stretched. "I need to see the area for myself and find out what Detective Jones has discovered."

Jake told him where to find the cabin and directions to the dumping ground. "Look, Jones is a good man. He wanted to call the FBI. The chief nixed the phone call."

"Not surprising. The feds and locals often clash." He lifted one shoulder. "It's a battle for territory."

After giving him the name of the hotel where they were staying, Jake said, "My teammates will be here in about four more hours. They will be serving as Yvonne's bodyguards. Don't expect to question her without the Fortress operatives present. Brent knows you, but I don't. Yvonne is my girlfriend's mother. By extension, her safety is now a priority to me and my teammates. Your responsibility is broader in scope."

"Understood. As long as your teammates don't interfere, I'm fine with them being in the room. I'll be in touch later this morning after I get a handle on the situation at the crime scene."

Rafe hadn't been gone long when the orthopedic surgeon came into the waiting room. "Coleman family?"

Lacey stood. "I'm Yvonne's daughter, Lacey."

"I'm Dr. Reacher. Your mother did great, Ms. Coleman. The wrist and ankle should heal without a problem, but she won't be able to work for several weeks. I understand she's a waitress."

"That's right."

"She'll return to work in about twelve weeks, depending on how quickly the bones mend. In the meantime, she'll need assistance when she's released."

"We'll take care of her," Jake said.

A nod. "She's in recovery. Don't expect her to be awake much. She may not be coherent for a few hours. If she wants to sleep, let her."

"We won't push her." That would frustrate them and the patient. "Yvonne will have someone with her at all times while she's in the hospital. I'd appreciate it if you would pass the word to the nursing staff and other physicians assigned to her case."

Although he looked surprised, Reacher didn't object to the precaution. "You think that's necessary?"

"No question."

"I'll make sure the right people know." He turned to Lacey. "I'll check on your mother before I finish my shift. If you have questions or concerns, don't hesitate to talk to the nurses." With that, he gave a quick nod and left the waiting room.

Running footsteps had Jake and Cade shifting to stand in front of Lacey. Harley burst into the room, his shirt buttoned wrong, his ginger hair covered in a baseball cap with the name of his garage stitched across the front. "Where is she?"

"Recovery." Jake smiled. "She'll be fine, Harley. Yvonne has broken bones that, once mended, will be good as new. She's a very lucky woman."

The relief was so great, the mechanic staggered. Cade caught him by the shoulders. "You okay, buddy?"

"I will be as soon as I see Yvonne."

"The surgeon just left," Jake said. "We should be able to see her now. She may not respond much because of the anesthesia and pain meds."

"I don't care. I just need to be with her." His voice thickened. "I thought I'd never see her again. Thank God you found her."

"Come on, Harley." Lacey tucked her arm through his. "Let's go see her. Dr. Reacher said to ask the nurses questions if we have concerns. Jake and his friends will provide security for Mom while she's recovers."

He stopped in the middle of the hall. "Security?"

"I'll explain later," Jake said, his voice quiet. "I work for a private security firm and there's a good reason why Yvonne can't be alone."

"I'm not leaving her."

"You don't carry a weapon and you have a full-time job that needs your attention during the day." He didn't intend to leave Yvonne's safety to the grizzled mechanic at night, either, but that would be apparent soon enough. "You focus on supporting Yvonne however you can. Leave the question of security to us."

"You sure you know what you're doing?"

Jake might have been offended if he hadn't understood Harley's concern. The thought of leaving Lacey's security to someone he didn't know made his skin crawl. Yeah, that would never happen as long as he drew breath. No one meant more to him than the woman standing by Harley's side. "I was an Army Ranger, and now I work for the best private security firm in the business. I know what I'm doing. I would trust Lacey's safety to Fortress."

Harley sized up Jake and Cade, and turned to continue down the hall toward the recovery room.

When they reached the right area, a nurse directed them to the last bed in the corner. Excellent. He and Cade could keep an eye on the people coming and going from the room without leaving their back unprotected.

Jake waited a moment, allowing Lacey and Harley time with Yvonne. He half expected the nursing staff to tell them there were too many people around the patient. Thankfully, no one tried to kick them out.

Cade inclined his head toward the mike bag. "Want me to take that to the SUV?"

"Thanks." He slid the pack from his back and handed it over.

"Should I call the boss while I'm out?"

He shook his head. "I'll go to the hall and talk to Brent. I'll be able to keep an eye on Lacey and Yvonne from there, and I won't disturb the other patients." He couldn't afford to be overheard. The conversation might incite a panic in town.

With a nod, the other operative left, Jake's bag hitched over his shoulder.

Jake walked to Lacey's side and smiled at Yvonne. "How do you feel?"

"Tired. Why so sleepy?"

He laid a hand on her shoulder. "The anesthesia takes time to wear off. I'm going to the hall to call my boss. I'll watch over you from there. You'll be able to see me."

"You won't leave?" Anxiety filled her hazy gaze.

"No, ma'am. I made you a promise. I don't break them."

A small smile curved her lips and her eyes closed.

Jake cupped the back of Lacey's neck and kissed her with gentle thoroughness. "I won't be long." In the hall, he called Brent.

"Talk to me."

"Yvonne will be fine. No internal injuries. She needs help for several weeks, but she'll make a full recovery."

"Thank God. Rafe arrived yet?"

"Roger that. He's already gone head-to-head with the police chief and came out on top. Don't know how long that will last. Beckett won't back down easily."

"I scanned through the files Zane prepared for you. When you have a chance, you'll find the Becketts' files in your inbox."

"Give me the short version."

"The son ought to be serving a life sentence for murder, but he got off with a slap on the wrist. The old man has been the police chief a long time and has friends in powerful positions. No evidence, but my gut says the police department in Winston is corrupt. Watch your back, Jake, and keep the lawyer's contact info handy."

Amusement twisted through him. "Copy that."

"You need anything else from me?"

"Not at the moment. Adam texted me a few minutes ago. He and the others are on their way here."

"Good. Keep me updated."

He ended the call with Brent and immediately placed another call, this one to Cade. "Bring my laptop. Z sent files I need to read." That done, he returned to the recovery room to see Harley leaning down to kiss Yvonne's forehead. That action brought a smile to her face. Nice. Maybe the mechanic would have better luck convincing Lacey's mom to marry him now that Lacey knew about their relationship. Didn't take much time in their presence to realize the lovebirds were made for each other.

Lacey smiled at him. "I have a question."

"Shoot."

"What was the contraption the doctor gave you before Mom's surgery?"

"Vacuum splint. You pump the chamber full of air to stabilize broken bones. We use them in the field all the time."

"It's standard equipment?"

"For medics. When deployed, we can't take an injured teammate to a local hospital. We carry everything we need on our backs until we transport them to safety."

She gestured to the metal brace on either side of her mother's wrist. "And that?"

"Pins to hold your mother's wrist in place while the bones mend."

"Jake."

He turned his attention to Yvonne. "What do you need?"

"Thank you. You saved my life."

"It was a team effort." To get the attention off himself, he said, "Harley says he wants to marry you."

A ghost of a smile appeared. "He's persistent. I wanted to tell Lacey before I gave him an answer."

"I know now, Mom." Lacey brushed a strand of hair off her mother's forehead. "You deserve to be happy."

"You won't mind?"

"As long as he promises to take good care of you and let me visit every now and then, I can't think of anything I'd like more than to see you married to the love of your life."

Tears trickled from the corners of Yvonne's eyes. "He's my soul mate."

"Sounds like you should take him up on his offer before some other woman nabs him."

Harley kissed the knuckles of her uninjured hand. "What do you say, Yvonne? Will you marry me?"

She smiled. "Yes. Can't figure out now why I waited so long."

Harley leaned down and kissed her gently. "I'll bring your ring tomorrow. Guess it's a good thing you broke your right wrist instead of your left. I want every man in town to know you're mine."

As they talked, Lacey turned into Jake's arms and wrapped her arms tight around his waist.

"Happy?" he murmured.

"So much I can't express it properly." She lifted her tear-filled gaze to him. "Thank you for bringing my mother back to me."

He tightened his hold on her. "I'm glad I was able to help."

During the next hour, Yvonne drifted in and out of sleep. Finally, the orderlies moved her to a room. Once she was settled and asleep, Jake took Lacey to the cafeteria to purchase coffee for everyone but Yvonne.

When they returned and distributed the steaming beverage-filled cups, he brought in two extra chairs.

Harley's eyebrows rose. "You and the other don't have to stay, Jake. I'm not leaving the woman I love."

"Yvonne was targeted by the man who abducted all those women."

His mouth gaped. "But she's safe now."

Jake made sure Yvonne was still asleep. "Harley, you need to keep this information to yourself until it's been released publicly, but the abductor killed the women. We found their remains near where we found Yvonne. When the killer realizes she's still alive, he'll want to finish the job."

CHAPTER TWENTY-FOUR

Lacey watched her mother sleep, grateful for the opportunity. Oh, she knew soon enough her mom would start in on her again about finding a real job. Maybe when she married Harley, Yvonne would stop pushing Lacey to send money.

She frowned. Where had the money in her mother's house come from? With Yvonne's amnesia, Lacey wondered if her mother remembered or if she would share the information.

Based on the interactions between Harley and her mother, she didn't believe Yvonne returned to prostitution. She wouldn't want to lose the love of her life.

Lacey's gaze shifted to the medic beside her. His laptop was open, the light from the screen illuminating his handsome face. Jake Davenport was a good friend and she found herself more enthralled by him each passing moment.

Watching Jake and interacting with him in the months since Rowan met Brent had caused her to "crush" on the medic essential to Fortress missions in country and abroad.

After spending time in his company, Lacey's infatuation was changing at light speed to something deeper and hotter.

She considered the information she knew about him. It wasn't much. Lacey had answered his questions, but he hadn't shared information. Not much time for her to ask, either. Perhaps the information was classified information. How could she know the man she was fast falling in love with if most of his life was classified?

Jake looked up. "Something on your mind?" he whispered.

Honesty was always the best policy, right? "You."

He smiled. "Good thoughts, I hope."

Would he consider Lacey falling in love with him good? Her stomach pitched. What if Jake viewed this relationship as friends only? She breathed away welling devastation. If true, that would rip her to shreds inside. "I don't know as much about you as I want."

"Ask. If I can't tell you something, I'll let you know."

Lacey peeked at her mother and Harley. Yvonne was sound asleep. The nurses came in every two hours to check on her, but otherwise left her alone. Harley slept in a chair next to the bed, his hand wrapped tight around her mother's. His soft snoring indicated that he, too, was asleep.

"They're out, and Cade will stay in the hall until Adam and Veronica relieve us," Jake murmured. "Ask your questions."

"Do you have family?"

He closed the lid on his laptop, sheathing his face in shadow. "Mom, Dad, three siblings."

"Brothers, sisters?"

"A combo. Two younger sisters, one older brother."

"Are you close to your family?"

He grinned. "They're nosy and constantly nagging me to come home for a visit."

"You love them."

"Fiercely. They're amazing, and I wouldn't be what I am today without them."

She smiled, wistful. That had been the family life she'd always dreamed of. "They sound wonderful."

"The Davenport clan is loud and boisterous, and I can't wait to introduce you to them."

Lacey stared. Introduce her? He couldn't be serious. They'd officially changed their relationship yesterday. By his expression, though, she saw Jake was serious. "Why?"

The medic set the computer on the floor and turned back to cup her face between his warm palms. "You matter to me, honey. I want my family to know you. I want you to be comfortable with them."

She studied his face a moment. "Why wouldn't I be comfortable?"

After placing a series of soft kisses on her lips, he drew back. "My background is very different from yours."

That much was more than obvious from the simple statements he'd offered. "I don't think anyone's background is like mine. You had a good childhood in a loving family."

"That's true. But it's more than that. My parents own Davenport Electronics."

Lacey froze. "That's a huge corporation."

"DE has subsidiaries all over the globe, most recently in Tokyo. My whole family works for the corporation. Dad's the CEO and Mom's in research and development. Bruce works in the finance division, Alyssa in marketing, and Susan in human resources."

She paid close attention to what he said and what he didn't. "You're the black sheep. Why didn't you enter the family business?"

He shrugged. "My heart wasn't in it. I asked myself if I would be happy working for DE until I retired. I couldn't see it. The military drew me from the time I was five years old. Most boys asked for toy cars, trucks, and footballs for birthdays and Christmas. Not me. I asked for toy soldiers, tanks, and Army Jeeps."

"Your parents didn't mind that you went your own way?"

"They want me happy. The Army fulfilled a need and allowed me to protect my family and country. I'm built to protect. The Army taught me how to provide medical care to injured soldiers. Now Fortress provides me a place to share my skills and abilities to help others. My teammates depend on me."

"I've heard the operatives talk about you."

"Yeah?"

"More than one said they wouldn't have come home alive without you. What you do matters, Jake."

"My job can be dangerous. We do our best to prepare for every scenario, but it's impossible to plan for every contingency. If my job will be a problem for us, you need to tell me now before…"

She held her breath, waiting for him to finish. When he remained stubbornly silent, she prompted, "Before what?"

"Before it's too late to walk away with my heart in one piece."

Was he saying he was falling in love with her? Lacey's heart almost leaped from her chest. "What do you mean by that?"

"What does it sound like?"

Did he want her to spell it out? Could she? What if he didn't feel the same as she did? Only one way to find out. "Sounds like you're falling in love with me."

"Does that scare you?" His thumbs gently stroked her cheeks.

He didn't deny her statement. Could she trust that he knew his heart? "Maybe I should ask you the same question."

Jake froze, his gaze locked on hers. "Nothing would make me happier than if you were falling in love with me."

He placed a hard kiss on her mouth. "Falling hard and fast for someone alone is scary."

Lacey inched closer until her mouth brushed against his as she spoke. "You're not in this alone, Jake."

He pressed his forehead to hers. "Thank God. You're okay with my job?"

"You could be a cop and face as much danger on the streets as you do on missions."

"I would have a set time to work and return home. I don't have that luxury with Fortress. My team can be deployed at any moment, and I don't know how long we'll be gone. There's no guarantee I'll be home for holidays, birthdays, or anniversaries. A lot of women can't deal with the uncertainty in their lives."

"I'm not most women."

A smile curved his mouth. "No, you aren't."

"When will I meet the rest of the Davenports?"

"After your mother is able to fend for herself and Rowan can spare you at the shop."

"I'm looking forward to meeting your nosy, boisterous family. They sound like fun."

"I hope you still say that when they tease you unmercifully for being with me."

"I'll handle it." Lacey cast him an uncertain glance. "Is this too fast? We haven't been on a date yet."

"Not from my perspective. I've been slowly working my way into your life for months, hoping not to spook you." He squeezed her hand. "Your ex did a number on you, and I didn't want you to run from me. I would never hurt you."

"I didn't think you would."

Jake shook his head. "That's not good enough. You have to know that truth deep down or you won't trust me enough to let me close. And I want to be close to you. I want to be an important part of your life."

He already was, a truth rocking Lacey to her core. Time to change the subject for a while. She motioned to the computer. "What have you been working on?"

"Reading the report Zane put together on the Becketts."

Lacey wrinkled her nose. "Can't be good."

"It's not."

"What did he find?"

"Will should be rotting in prison."

Her breath caught. "Why?"

"He was on a date with a girl several years ago. The girl, fifteen, died. Will was two days shy of turning 18. Otherwise, he'd be in prison, not tormenting you."

Lacey threaded her fingers through Jake's. "How did the girl die?"

"Some kind of sex game gone wrong. The details aren't in the police report. Z is working on hacking into the medical examiner's records."

"You don't think he'll be able to break the cybersecurity?"

A soft snort. "Child's play to Zane. No, I'm more concerned that good old Wayne squashed the details in the report."

"How? He doesn't have control of the medical examiner's office."

"Maybe not, but he knows powerful people who do. Grease a few palms with enough cash, and things disappear."

Somehow, that didn't surprise her. After all, Wayne Beckett managed to keep himself out of police records for years. Although her mother had been his main source of sex outside his marriage for years, he'd never been arrested. "Zane said Will killed this girl. I don't remember his name being associated with another teenager's death."

"The incident occurred in Florida while the Becketts were on vacation the summer before his senior year."

“I would have been a freshman.”

Jake was silent a moment. “Are you going to tell me about what happened between you and Will?”

The muscles in her back tensed. “I told you. I didn’t hold anything back.”

His gaze dropped to her upper arm.

Lacey scowled. “Okay, I deserved that. Aside from the bruises, I didn’t keep anything from you.”

“Good to know. But I’m not talking about the incident in the hotel parking lot.”

Blood drained from her face. Jake knew.

CHAPTER TWENTY-FIVE

Lacey looked away from Jake, her face devoid of all expression. His heart skipped a beat, and a depth of anger he'd never known simmered in his gut. What had Will Beckett done to the woman sliding under Jake's defenses?

He cupped her cheek and turned her face back toward him. "Lacey."

She shook her head. "I can't," she whispered. "Not here." Her gaze darted to her mother.

"At the hotel, we'll talk. I need to know." Her answer would determine how he moved forward with her and whether he needed to pound the pathetic excuse for a cop into the ground for hurting Jake's woman.

A light tap sounded on the door. Jake positioned himself between the women and the door, hand resting on the grip of his Sig. He relaxed when Cade slipped inside the door.

"Jones and Torres are here. They want to talk to Yvonne."

"No." Lacey stood. "They can wait."

On this, Jake agreed. A few more hours wouldn't make a difference to the case, but would give Lacey's mother aid in healing. The doctors had done all they could. Now Yvonne had to rest and let her body mend. If they were lucky, she would remember part of what happened since she was taken. Any clue at this point would be better than what they had discovered so far. He motioned for Lacey to follow him out to the hall.

The detective's back was pressed against the wall, his eyes closed, exhaustion in every line of his body. Torres, on the other hand, stood straight and tall, sipping from a large to-go cup. Must be cafeteria coffee since nothing was open this time of morning in Winston.

"How is Ms. Coleman?" Torres asked.

"Sleeping." Lacey folded her arms across her chest. "You're going to leave her alone until she wakes up on her own or a nurse disturbs her."

Jones stirred. "We need to talk to her, Lacey. It's important."

"I get that. You're still going to wait. Mom almost died out there. You can give her a chance to rest for a few hours."

"Every minute we delay, the trail grows colder."

"It's already ice cold." Jake wrapped his arm around his girl's shoulders and tucked her against his side. Cognizant of the foot traffic near Yvonne's room, he moved two steps closer to the cops. "Unless something has changed in the past few hours, Yvonne doesn't remember what happened."

Torres' eyebrow rose. "You asked?"

"My girlfriend's safety is at stake."

"What did Yvonne say?" Jones demanded.

"She didn't remember who she was meeting or who hurt her. She mentioned being afraid that 'he' would kill her. She's afraid he'll find her and finish what he started. Yvonne panics unless I'm within sight or Cade."

"She has good reason to be worried," the agent murmured.

"Why do you say that?" Lacey edged closer to Jake.

"Your mother was strangled repeatedly, yet the man didn't kill her."

"Not for lack of trying," Jones muttered.

Torres inclined his head in agreement. "The medical examiner started on causes of death for the women found in the woods. With that many victims, working through all the autopsies is going to take a while. The FBI is sending in a team later today to lend a hand. Meanwhile, the ME's done enough preliminary work on two of the victims to determine their hyoid bones were broken."

"What does that mean?" Lacey asked Jake.

"They were strangled to death."

"Like Mom's abductor tried to do to her."

"Now you see why it's so important we talk to your mother," Jones said.

"What if she can't tell you anything?"

"You might be surprised what she does remember when she feels safe and her body is healing." Torres lifted one shoulder. "We know she's fragile right now, Lacey. Although we won't push her too hard, every piece of data she gives us puts us one step closer to finding the man who snuffed out the lives of fifteen innocent women who could be substitutes for you. Are you willing to spare Yvonne and yourself a few minutes of discomfort at the expense of another woman losing her life?"

"That's enough," Jake said, his gaze fixed on Brent's friend. Cade moved into position on Lacey's other side.

Torres' eyes glittered as he took in the united front the three of them presented. "I'll apologize after we put the UNSUB behind bars."

"Question them, but I won't let you badger Yvonne or Lacey."

The door to Yvonne's room opened and Harley lumbered out, eyes hazy with sleep, his hair standing up in crazy tufts. "Yvonne's asking for ice."

"I'll take care of it," Cade said and turned toward the nurses' station.

"We need to talk to her, Harley," Jones said. "It's important."

"I'll ask if she's up to it."

Jake sent a hard glance toward the detective.

Jones held up a hand to Jake. "Thanks. I wouldn't insist if it weren't a matter of life or death."

The mechanic's eyes widened and he hustled back into the hospital room. A moment later, he returned. "Come on in. You go easy on her, Todd. She's been through a lot." Fierce protectiveness gleamed in his gaze. "Cop or not, friend or not, I won't let you upset her."

"I understand. We'll do our best to not traumatize her further."

With a nod, Harley led the way into the room and returned to his seat. "Yvonne, honey? Todd's here."

Lacey's mother opened her eyes and turned her head slowly to her visitors. "Hey, Todd."

Jake nudged Lacey back to their seats, content to allow this interview to play itself out. For now. The moment he believed Yvonne was too distressed to continue the interrogation, he'd step in.

"How are you, Yvonne?"

"Lucky to be alive, I think."

"You are correct," Torres said. "My name is Rafe Torres. I'm with the FBI."

She frowned. "Why do you want to talk to me?"

After a glance at Harley, Jones clasped her uninjured hand. "We need to ask you questions about what happened."

She dropped her gaze to the sheet and blanket covering the lower half of her body. "I don't remember anything."

"Let us ask questions anyway. If you don't remember, say so. We need you to be honest, Yvonne."

"Can't it wait?"

"I'm afraid not," Torres said. "There's a reason why we need to ask now. Let's run through the questions first, then we'll explain the urgency."

Yvonne's gaze darted to Jake, fear evident in her expression even from across the room.

"It's important for your safety and Lacey's. Tell them the truth."

Her eyes widened. "Lacey?"

"She's at risk, too. Your fractured memories might hold the key to protecting your daughter."

"You'll stay?"

"Absolutely."

"I'd prefer to talk to her without an audience," Jones muttered.

"That's not going to happen."

A scowl. "You don't trust me?"

"This is not about you. It's about helping Yvonne feel safe." He glanced at his watch. "And you'd better ask your questions. The nurse will be in soon to administer the next dose of pain meds. Once Yvonne takes those, she'll be out again within minutes and you'll be forced to wait another few hours for answers."

Cade walked into the room at that moment, a plastic pitcher, cup, and a spoon in his hands. He set them on the table beside Harley. "There's more where that came from, Yvonne. Let me know if you need a refill." With that, he left the room to stand watch in the hall.

Harley fed his bride-to-be a couple ice chips and settled back again, his gaze watchful.

"What do you want to know?" Yvonne asked, her gaze shifting to the detective.

"Harley said you left your house Friday night at 10:45 p.m. to meet someone. Who was it?"

She looked at Harley, as though seeking the answer from him.

"Yvonne," Torres said. "Look at me. Any information has to come from you. We need to know what you remember, unprompted by anyone. Who did you meet?"

"I don't know. I can't remember. Why can't I remember?"

"You're still healing. It's normal. You may not remember everything, but you will recall a few things that might be a game changer in our investigation. Let's try this. What was the last thing you remember prior to leaving Harley at your house?"

Yvonne bit her lip, discomfort evident in her expression.

Torres smiled. "Besides spending some personal time with Harley. Start with what you did leading up to going to Harley's the night you were taken."

Immediately, she relaxed. "I went to work first thing that morning. I work the early shift at the diner."

"How long is your shift?"

"From 6:00 in the morning to 2:00 in the afternoon."

"Like working there?"

"I love it. Loretta and I have a great time talking to folks and making sure they enjoy their meal. It's fun."

"Both shifts are busy?"

"Oh, the diner is usually packed except for a lull from 9:30 to 10:30, then the lunch rush starts. The place is a dive, but rich people and poor alike love the food we serve."

"You like working there?"

Yvonne beamed. "We're family. It's like having a family reunion every day with food I don't have to cook."

"Anyone come into the diner who makes you uneasy or afraid?"

Jake had to admire the way Torres circled away from the topic of the abduction although he poked at the edges of what or who made her afraid since that's what she remembered clearly. What were the chances that the person who hurt Yvonne ate in that diner each week?

"I need more ice." She turned to Harley. "My mouth is so dry."

She was also avoiding the question. Jake exchanged glances with the cops. "Yvonne, does the diner have security cameras?"

Lacey's mother took the ice, a thoughtful expression on her face. "We have one pointed at the register and two more pointed at the doors. Why?"

Perfect. Now they had at least something to scan for a starting point, although he figured the net would catch a lot of fish. He'd bet most of the town dropped into the diner during a typical week based on what she'd said earlier. "Information. Who are your standard customers at the diner?"

"You want a list?"

"Not all of them. Who pops in your mind first?"

Her lips curled. "Cops. All of them stop in there at one point or another all day and night."

Jones' eyes narrowed. "During our shifts, for sure. I'm in there several times a week. The diner is close to the station and it's the only place in town with good coffee 24 hours a day."

"What about the coffee shop I saw when I drove into town?" Torres asked.

"Sludge," Harley said, shaking his head. "The coffee in that place reminds me of oil from a past-due oil change."

"Who else comes to mind, Yvonne?" Jake prompted. He recognized the signs of growing fatigue. The window for questions was closing fast.

"Just the usual crowd. People who work in nearby businesses or stop in during the day between appointments or meetings." She shrugged. "Pretty much everybody."

"Anyone hassle you at work?" Jones asked.

"Who doesn't? There's always someone who doesn't like something they order and blame the waitress."

"You're an attractive woman, Yvonne, and pretty waitresses usually get hit on frequently. Do you have a persistent man trying to win a date and won't take no for an answer?"

"Well, sure. But they don't mean anything by it. The guys are just messing with me."

"How do you know they aren't serious?" Torres asked.

"They just aren't."

"Did you know any of the missing women?"

Sadness filled her gaze. "Some of them. This is a small, close-knit community. We know each other. You've got to love small towns. We nose into each other's business. Yeah, I talked to them a few times."

"At the diner?"

"Told you, everyone comes in there, including the girls. I don't want to talk about them. It's too sad."

Jake noted her choice of words. Was talking about the women sad because she believed they were still missing or did she subconsciously know those women were the victims of a serial killer?

CHAPTER TWENTY-SIX

Lacey listened to the rounds of questions from Agent Torres and Todd, confused as to the purpose for all the seeming side trips. She could tell her mother was tired. The police needed to finish the questions or Mom would fade and they would again be waiting for her to wake.

"Who's been asking about Lacey?" Torres asked.

Lacey jerked. What did that have to do with anything? This was her hometown. People talked. They would ask her mother questions about her daughter.

"I talk about her all the time."

She stared at her mother. Since when did Yvonne Coleman brag about her daughter? What happened to the woman who pushed Lacey to send her money and get a real job?

"Anyone ask about her consistently?"

"Paul Chesterfield." She wrinkled her nose. "The police chief and his son. The preacher at the church. Harley, of course. Noah Holt."

Huh. Lacey hadn't talked to Noah for years. Didn't want to, either. He was one of the ring leaders of the teens who lived to torture the daughter of the town's infamous call girl during high school. He was also one of the reasons Lacey had been glad to leave Winston behind in her dust when she left town.

Beside her, Jake stiffened. "What did Chesterfield want to know?"

"The usual. What she's been doing and when she's coming home for good."

Never. Lacey loved her life. She backtracked. Love was too strong a term for a job she enjoyed. Working at the coffee shop, although fun, was not her calling. She didn't want to spend her life serving people coffee. She wanted to make a difference in people's lives, help them in times of crisis. Amusement swept through her. Sounded exactly like what Jake did in his work. Maybe they were a matched pair, after all. She needed to kick college classes to the top of her priority list. She'd never change her career path if she didn't start school. Lacey could almost feel the window of opportunity closing.

However, the stark reality was she didn't make enough money to keep up with the financial expenses, cut back on working to allow adequate time for studying, and handle the added financial strain of school payments. Lacey sighed. She foresaw sleepless nights either studying or working in her future. When would she have time to spend with Jake? She didn't want to give him up. Was it possible to have everything?

"What did you tell him?" Todd asked.

"Same as always. She's working at the coffee shop and I didn't know when or if she would come home to me."

"Is he close to your family?"

"That old buzzard? No way. He's a dirty old man, always on the make."

"He ever target Lacey?"

Lacey clamped her hand over Jake's and squeezed. Her mother didn't know about Chesterfield hassling her. Mom would have gone after with him a baseball bat if she'd known, the only weapon she had for protection over the years. Yvonne was afraid of guns and likely wouldn't have been approved for a permit even if she'd applied. Lacey and her mother had their differences, but she hadn't wanted to see her mother behind bars. So, she'd kept silent.

Her mother turned toward her. "Not that she ever said. Come to think of it, that's strange. Paul went after every female within sight. Did you hold back information, Lace?"

Too much that didn't matter now. "Nothing you needed to worry about. I handled it."

Yvonne struggled to sit up, wincing. "Wait until I leave this hospital. I'll have a talk with that old man."

"Not a good idea, Mom. Besides, I think Jake has first dibs on Mr. Chesterfield."

Her mother shifted her gaze to Jake and, after a long, hard look, relaxed. "Make sure he leaves my daughter alone."

"I'll take care of it."

"You said the Becketts asked you about Lacey," Torres prompted. "Anything odd about their questions?"

"I don't know what you want from me." Yvonne's voice started to rise. "I can't tell you anything."

Lacey analyzed the almost shrill tone to her mother's voice. Yvonne knew something she was afraid to tell. Who was she protecting? Herself or Lacey?

Tears stung her eyes. Her mother hadn't been a model citizen of Winston, but she loved Lacey. Now that she was sober, Yvonne showed that affection more often.

Jake walked to Yvonne's side, his body blocking her sight of the two policemen. "Yvonne, focus on me." When her terror-filled gaze locked with his, he lowered his voice to a husky murmur. "Breathe in. Exhale. Again. Slow. That's it. You're safe. I won't let anyone hurt you."

"You don't know me, what I've done, how I lived in the past," she whispered. "Why would you put yourself in danger because of me?"

"Lacey is important to me, and she loves you. Protecting people is what my team does."

"I don't know why I'm afraid or even who to be afraid of. How can you protect me from a ghost? What if I'm imagining things?"

Jake freed her hand from Jones' hold, and sandwiched it between his palms. "The fear is not your imagination, and your subconscious knows the truth. We don't have to know the identity of the person who took you to keep you safe."

"You don't?"

He shook his head. "We'll stop anyone who threatens you or your daughter."

"I can protect myself. Take care of Lacey."

"I'm protecting you both. To get to you, they'll have to go through me, and I won't go down easily."

Lacey's heart clenched. Her mother might not believe the words, but Lacey knew the truth. Jake would take a bullet to protect them should that be necessary. Please, God, that wouldn't happen. Losing him would break her heart.

"Did the Becketts' questions about Lacey strike you as odd?" Jake asked.

After a beat, she said, "Not odd. Detailed questions."

"Like what?"

"Same as everyone else." Her gaze shifted again, this time to Lacey. "Where you live, where you work, when you're coming home."

"What else, Mom? The information might help."

"They wanted to know if you were seeing anyone." Hurt seeped into her gaze. "I didn't know about Jake. You should have told me."

To lighten the moment, she grinned. "Sounds familiar. You were keeping a big secret, too." An answering smile from her mother made Lacey positive Yvonne and Harley would be good together. They were crazy about each other.

"Have they always wanted to know if Lacey is dating?" Torres asked.

"Will has been asking since Lacey moved to Nashville. The police chief started last year after Christmas."

Lacey's heart skipped a beat. Why? What reason would either have for asking? Not that she'd dated much. She refused to dwell on her disastrous months with Frank. Her other relationships had been few and far between. Lacey had been too focused on survival to spend much time dating.

"You said Noah Holt talked to you about Lacey." Todd frowned. "What did he want to know?"

"It doesn't matter."

"Tell me anyway."

Another glance at Lacey and Jake, then Yvonne sighed. "He wanted to know if she was like me."

"Like you, how?"

Tears streaked her cheeks. "He wanted to know how much she charged for sex."

Lacey hated to see her mother hurting and embarrassed. She'd changed her life, made something of herself. That mattered. "Mom, you don't do that anymore. You haven't for years."

"People have long memories in this town."

A major reason why Lacey left Winston six years earlier. "With Noah, it isn't about a long memory. He deliberately asked to hurt you." He'd enjoyed hurting people in high school as well, something she'd hoped he'd grown out of the last six years. Guess he hadn't. She made it a point to avoid him when she was in town.

"You should have said something, honey." Harley scowled. "I would have set that young buck straight."

And that's why Mom hadn't said a word. Harley had some muscle on him, but Noah was twenty years younger and a gym rat like Frank. His muscles bulged, making him appear strong enough to bench press a car.

"What did you do after you left work the day you were taken, Yvonne?" Torres dropped his empty coffee cup in the trash and returned to the foot of her bed.

Her mother freed her hand from Jake's and brushed away the moisture from her face. "Late lunch with Harley, then home to do laundry."

"After you finished the clothes?"

"Went to Harley's place and let myself in to prepare dinner. He gave me a key to his house."

"Did you go out anywhere, talk to anyone else after Harley arrived?"

She shook her head. "Well, just to head back to my place for the night. Harley followed me over with his truck and stayed.

"You left Harley at what time?"

"A few minutes before 11:00."

"Did you set up the meeting?"

"No."

"Someone called you that night?"

Yvonne frowned. "No."

"Who asked you to meet?" Torres' voice was gentle.

"I can't remember."

"Answer this question without thinking. Just react. Male or female?"

"Male."

"Did you recognize his voice?"

"I must have. I would never meet someone I don't know that late at night."

"Close your eyes." When she complied, Torres continued. "In your mind, look at your kidnapper's feet. What's he wearing?" He took her higher up the kidnapper's body until finally he asked, "Do you see his face?"

Yvonne was silent, eyes still shut. After a moment, her eyelids flew up. “He wore a stocking mask, one with the eyes and mouth cut out. I didn’t see his face.”

CHAPTER TWENTY-SEVEN

Disappointment spiraled through Jake at Yvonne's declaration. "Are you sure?"

"Positive. That's why I can't remember who hurt me. I didn't see his face. I know finding him will be that much harder, but at least I know I'm not crazy. What happens now?"

"We use other methods to nail this creep." He squeezed her hand. "Don't worry. We'll find him." Jones and Torres would do what they could within the confines of the law. Fortress would do the rest. Wouldn't be the first time the company resources had been tapped to track down a perp. Zane and the rest of the tech geeks were excellent at unearthing the deepest kept secrets and nudging law enforcement in the right direction. "Lacey and I found what looks like blood on your garage floor. What happened?"

She blinked. "Blood?"

Her surprise supported his theory that Yvonne had been taken from her home. "Where is your SUV?"

Her jaw dropped. "It's missing? You have to find my Tahoe, Todd."

"We've been looking for it. No luck so far."

"Do you remember what happened during your captivity?" Jake asked.

"I remember pain and the cold." She turned to Jake. "Where did you find me?"

"At the bottom of a ravine near the Martin cabin. Do you remember how you got there?"

"He kept me tied up in this horrible room, choking me again and again until I lost consciousness. I thought I was going to die." She dragged in a shuddering breath. "Anyway, that last time when I woke up, I was outside on the ground in the woods, alone. I was weak, but got up and tried to run. I didn't know where I was. I chose a direction and took off. As I ran, I realized he'd never taken my phone. No point, I guess, since I couldn't free myself to call for help." A wry smile tugged at her lips. "I guess I chose the wrong direction, though. I ran through some bushes and then I fell. When I woke up that time, I couldn't find my phone. It was in my hand when the ground dropped away. I could hear someone stomping around on higher ground and knew I had to hide. That's when I realized I was hurt and couldn't run anymore. I crawled as far as I could and prayed it was far enough."

"You were amazing, Yvonne." Torres reached down and laid his hand on her uninjured foot. "If you weren't a strong, resourceful woman, the kidnapper would have killed you. Good job."

She beamed at him as the night nurse walked into the room.

"Hey, Todd. What are you doing here?"

"Needed to ask Yvonne some questions."

"Hate to cut the party short, but it's time for Ms. Coleman's pain meds."

"We'll clear out, then." Torres stepped back. "Thanks for answering our questions, Yvonne."

"Wait. You didn't tell me the reason you asked them now."

He slid a sideways glance at the nurse checking Yvonne's vitals, then shifted his attention to Jake, eyebrow raised in silent inquiry.

"I'm sure you have other things to do. I'll talk to her."

"Good enough. We'll see you later, Yvonne." With that, the policemen left.

Once the nurse checked Yvonne's vitals and administered pain meds, she left.

"Tell me what's going on," Yvonne demanded.

With her hand still clasped between his, Jake said, "You know about the missing women."

"Of course. Every woman has been talking about the disappearances for years. No one knows what happened to them."

He squeezed her hand. "They do now. The killer left their bodies close to the ravine. We think he's the one who hurt you."

"But why am I still alive?"

That was the question, wasn't it? "I don't know. I'm glad I have a chance to know my girlfriend's mom."

"Why did Todd and the FBI agent ask so many questions about Lacey?"

"Did you notice the women's appearance?"

Yvonne frowned, thought a moment. "They were all blond and slender with beautiful smiles."

He waited in silence, and saw the moment Lacey's mother made the leap and connected their appearance with Lacey.

"Wait. Are you saying he'll go after my daughter?"

"I think she is the ultimate prize."

"Take her home. Now."

"Mom." Lacey hurried to Yvonne's side. "Don't worry. Jake and Cade won't let anything happen to me."

"But they don't know who this guy is. They can't protect you from a killer with no face or name."

She laid her hand on her mother's uninjured leg. "Yes, they can. You don't know them and their coworkers like I do. They are the best."

Jake smiled at her effusive praise. Good to know she felt that way.

"I still want you to go home."

"Not yet. You need help after the doctor releases you."

"Harley and Loretta will pitch in. Go home, honey. I want you safe."

"I trust Jake with my life, Mom. You should, too. I can tell you're getting sleepy again. Jake and I noticed the new furniture at the house. Where did you buy it?"

"Riverton. I love that place."

"Where did you get the money for furniture and the SUV? Your pay at the diner isn't that great unless the tip money has been excellent."

Yvonne cast her a puzzled glance. "I got the money from you."

"Me? I can't afford to buy new furniture and a vehicle for myself much less buy yours. Why did you think the money came from me?"

"The furniture store and the Chevy dealership each called to tell me the furniture and SUV had been paid for by you and was ready for pick up." She yawned widely. "Sorry."

"No, it's fine. Rest now. We'll talk more later."

"You're staying?" she murmured to Jake.

"Until my teammates arrive to take over. I'll make sure Harley is introduced to them before I leave. Until this killer is caught, you won't be alone and vulnerable."

She smiled faintly. "You're a good man. He's a keeper, Lace." And she was out.

Harley stirred, then. "You really didn't send the furniture and vehicle to your mom?" He stared hard at Lacey.

"I was being honest, Harley. I don't have the money for that."

Not since she was saving money for college. Jake wrapped his hand around Lacey's.

"What's going on in this town?" The mechanic scowled. "This killer is taking women who look similar to Lacey. Why take Yvonne? I think she's the most beautiful woman on the planet, but she's not in her twenties like those other women. What did he want with her?"

"That's what we'd like to know. You didn't think the whole setup was strange?" He would have. Then again, he had a cynical view of things. Nothing in life was free. There were always strings if you looked hard enough.

"Yvonne isn't one to question good fortune. She'd longed for those things for a while and asked Lacey for money for months."

Years, more like. Jake imagined Yvonne hadn't wanted to sound too mercenary to the mechanic when they started dating. He hoped things worked out well for Lacey's mother and Harley. Maybe then Yvonne would enjoy the time she had with Lacey instead of trying to guilt her into sending more money.

"Why would someone give Mom the furniture and SUV? It doesn't make sense. Wouldn't they want something in return?"

"Not necessarily." Jake urged Lacey to sit in one of the chairs again. "Some people want to give gifts without attaching their name to the gesture. They don't want the recognition."

A snort from Harley. "Or they don't want to be asked for more gifts."

True enough. Jake's family was very careful about how they gave gifts and money. More often than not, they gave anonymously to prevent an outstretched hand. "I didn't want to alarm Yvonne, especially after the trauma she suffered."

The older man's eyes narrowed. "Spill it, Davenport."

"We've been digging into the women's disappearances. The first one went missing within a few days of Lacey moving away from Winston. If you track the dates, the rest of the women vanished a few days after Lacey returned to Nashville following a visit to her mother."

His brow furrowed. "You're saying he wants Yvonne's daughter and, because he can't have her, he takes substitutes?"

Jake inclined his head. "I don't have proof, but I believe that is what has been happening."

"We're back to my original question. Why take Yvonne?"

He drew Lacey as close to his side as the chair would allow. "To bring Lacey back home."

Lacey twisted to stare at him. "Are you serious?"

"That explanation makes the most sense."

She was silent a moment, her expression pensive. "Is it possible the furniture and vehicle are from the same person?"

Yeah, his girlfriend was a smart woman. "Yes."

"But what purpose would that serve?"

"If your mother had mentioned enjoying your gifts, you would have denied providing the furniture and vehicle. When you didn't get satisfactory answers as to where they came from, you would have come home to look into it."

"And since Mom never mentioned them and I didn't return home, the killer resorted to taking her. He knew I would come home to look for her."

"He planned this out, step by step, didn't he?" Harley scrubbed his stubble-covered jaw with his hand. "Clever." He shot a pointed look at Jake. "When you find the killer, I want five minutes with him."

Jake's lips curved. "I'll see what I can do." Provided he didn't kill the guy first. Right now, the killer's fate was a tossup. The one thing Jake knew for sure? No one would take Lacey Coleman from him.

CHAPTER TWENTY-EIGHT

Two hours later, another tap brought Jake to the door. Weapon in hand, he opened the door. The tension in his muscles eased. "Thanks for coming, Adam."

His team leader frowned. "We're a team. More important, we're friends. We have each other's backs. You helped me and Vonnie out of a jamb in Belize. I'll never forget that."

An experience he would also never forget. His fledgling team had taken down a drug cartel. Jake had lost a cousin to his cocaine addiction when he was a senior in high school. "Where is your wife?"

A shadow of movement from the hall, then Adam's dark-haired wife stepped into view. "Hi, Jake. Where's Lacey?"

Jake moved aside and gestured to the chair where Lacey had been sleeping with her head pillowed on his chest. He could still feel the warmth of her body against his, and his arms ached to hold her once more. Yeah, he was a goner for sure.

Lacey crossed the expanse of the room and gave each of the newcomers a quick hug.

“How’s your mother?” Adam asked.

“Recovering nicely, according to the medical staff. She has a lot of bruises, a broken wrist and ankle plus some knocks to the head. Jake can tell you better than me, though. I just got the basics.”

“Yvonne is banged up, but she will recover. I need you, Remy and Lily to make sure she stays alive while Cade and I protect Lacey and hunt down a serial killer. Where are the Doucets?”

“Hotel, sleeping. They’ll take over the watch later this afternoon. We secured two rooms across the hall from you.”

“Any trouble on the way down?”

A crooked smile curved Adam’s lips. “Aside from the cop tailing us from the county line into town, no.”

Great. Either Jones had a big mouth or he’d slipped the information about Jake’s team coming into his report, and the wrong person accessed it. No other explanation made sense unless law enforcement routinely trailed cars from Tennessee into Winston.

Yvonne moaned. Harley sat up, and leaned close to the love of his life. “Yvonne, what’s wrong, honey?”

“Hurts.”

“Pain meds are wearing off,” Jake said.

“Shouldn’t they last longer?” Lacey asked, concern coloring her voice.

“Yvonne told the doctor she’d had a problem with addiction and didn’t want to become hooked on pain meds. The medicine they’re using is mild and non-habit forming.”

Yvonne’s eyelids raised. She blinked, then froze at the sight of Adam and Veronica Walker.

Jake stepped into her line of sight. “Yvonne, these are my teammates, Adam and Veronica. They’re going to stay with you today. Another couple, Remy and Lily Doucet, will be here this afternoon. They’ll keep you safe while Cade and I are hunting for the killer.”

Adam moved closer, Veronica at his side. "Hello, Yvonne. It's nice to meet you, although I'm sorry about the circumstances."

Though he was careful to keep his voice low and as nonthreatening as he could manage, Adam was still an intimidating figure for any person to see looming over their bed. Jake wasn't surprised when Lacey's mother pressed herself deeper into the mattress in an unconscious effort to put more space between herself and the big man.

"You're friends with Lacey?"

"Yes, ma'am." Veronica smiled. "We stop at Coffee House all the time. We work for Rowan's husband, Brent. Don't worry. We'll take good care of you."

"I don't care about me. I want my daughter safe."

"We'll protect you both," Adam said. He eyed Harley and held out his hand. "Adam Walker. My wife and I are with Fortress Security."

"Harley Jenkins. I'm going to marry this beautiful woman as soon as she'll let me." He wrapped his hand around Yvonne's.

"Congratulations."

Cade poked his head into the room. "Doc's here."

Veronica turned to Adam. "Why don't you and Jake buy coffee. I'll stay with Yvonne and Lacey."

With Cade stationed outside the room, they would be safe. Jake could use the caffeine kick. While Lacey had catnapped for an hour, he'd been on watch inside the room. Thanks to the Army, the coffee wouldn't be a problem when he did sleep for a few hours. "Good idea." He turned. "Do you want coffee, Lacey?"

She though a moment and shook her head. "See if they have hot chocolate. I don't think I can stomach coffee right now."

"If they don't, I'll see if they have hot tea. Come on, Adam."

When they left the room, Dr. Reacher greeted Jake, humor sparkling in his eyes. "I see you've been awake all night."

"I look that bad, huh?"

The doctor chuckled. "Nope. I just recognize the signs. How is my patient?"

"Hurting. Her memory is returning."

"Enough to identify the guy who hurt her?"

"We'll see."

Another smile from the doctor. "In other words, you won't tell me more information."

"Security."

"I understand. Well, I'll take a look at our girl, see how she's progressing."

"Yvonne's daughter and future husband are in the room. So is Veronica Walker. She's my teammate and will be staying with them." Would he understand the unspoken message, that Vonnie was on duty?

A nod, and he slipped into the room with a cheerful greeting for the occupants.

"We'll bring a cup of joe back for you, Cade," Adam said as he and Jake headed for the elevator. "The doctor didn't seem surprised about Vonnie."

"I talked with him before Yvonne went to surgery. He's former Air Force. Reacher knows enough to understand what's happening."

Within minutes, they returned with coffee for the operatives and Harley, and a large hot chocolate with whipped cream for Lacey. "Doc still with Yvonne?"

"Just left." He accepted the large coffee Adam gave him with a nod of thanks.

"Give me a few minutes, and we'll go to the hotel for a few hours." Jake tapped on the door and walked inside.

Lacey's gaze dropped to the large cup in his hand. "Chocolate or tea?"

"Chocolate with whipped cream." After receiving an update on Yvonne's condition and giving Lacey a chance to drink her hot chocolate, he said, "Yvonne, I'm taking Lacey to the hotel. She needs to sleep for a few hours. Veronica and Adam will stay with you. Don't worry about anything except following the orders of the doctors and nurses. We'll be back this afternoon."

"You'll keep Lacey safe?"

"You have my word."

At the hotel, Cade excused himself to take a shower. He gathered his things and shut himself into the bathroom.

"Do you want to finish your drink or go sleep?" Jake palmed the back of Lacey's neck and drew her into his embrace.

"Finish the drink. I'd like to sit on the balcony. Do you mind?"

He led her to the French doors and outside. She settled on the loveseat and patted the space beside her.

"Thank you, Jake."

He wrapped his arm around her shoulders. "For?"

"Being here with me. I don't know what I would have done without you these past few days."

A shoulder squeeze. "You would have handled it, but I'm glad you didn't have to do this alone." Especially now that he knew she was the ultimate prize of a serial killer. Who in this town was obsessed with Lacey?

Will's name popped into his head, followed by the police chief, old man Chesterfield, and Noah Holt. First on his list of things to do this afternoon after a stop by the hospital was talking to the Chesterfields and Holt. He needed to run their names, see if anything turned up in their background checks.

They lapsed into silence while they finished the last of their drinks. Jake took the empty cup from her hand and placed it on the table alongside his. A glance in the window told him Cade was still in the bathroom, so he drew Lacey to her feet. “Did you notice the fountain in the garden?”

She shook her head.

Jake took her to the balcony railing. He pointed to the left. “Over there, in the corner.”

Lacey leaned against the wooden railing to get a better look.

With a crack, the railing gave way.

CHAPTER TWENTY-NINE

One minute Lacey was looking at the ornate concrete fountain with flowing water sparkling in the morning sunshine. The next she was flailing as the balcony rail gave way and the ground rushed up to meet her.

A scream ripped from her throat as she sailed through the air. Her fall came to an abrupt halt as a hard hand clamped around her wrist. Lacey's body swung like pendulum in the air. "Jake!"

"I've got you, baby. You won't fall." His face was a mask of grim determination, one muscular arm wrapped around a wooden post to keep himself grounded on the balcony.

Easy for him to say she wouldn't fall. He wasn't the one dangling in mid-air. She looked down and wished she hadn't. Man, she hated heights. Her stomach pitched and rolled at the thought of Jake losing his grip on her.

Seconds, or maybe hours, later, Cade appeared beside Jake and extended his hand. "Give me your other hand, Lacey. We'll pull you up." When she reached up, he grabbed her wrist and the two of them lifted Lacey until her feet touched the balcony floor.

Jake wrapped his strong arms around her. “Are you okay? Are you injured?”

“Aside from almost having a heart attack from fear, I’m fine.” Her body trembled, ticking her off. Her knees buckled. She would have sunk to the floor if not for Jake’s hold on her.

He scooped her into his arms and carried her inside, his face colorless. He placed her on the side of the bed closest to the balcony and crouched in front of her. “Talk to me. Are you sure you aren’t hurt?”

Since she shook so hard her teeth chattered, she merely nodded.

Jake snatched a blanket from the foot of the bed and draped the warm cover around her body. He shifted Lacey so her back was against the headboard, then crawled onto the bed next to her and gathered her body against his. She turned, pressing her face to his neck.

With one arm wrapped securely around her, Jake coasted his free hand along her back and arm. Although he acted utterly calm, Lacey felt the tremors in his hands and muscles. Guess she’d scared him, too.

Slowly, the shudders wracking her body eased.

Cade strode into the room. “We have a problem.”

Lacey’s lips twitched. “Besides me nearly falling off a balcony three stories off the ground?”

His eyes lit with humor before he sobered again. “Someone tampered with the railing.”

Jake’s arm tightened on her back. “Cut?”

“Sawed nearly clean through. Smooth. No way that was an accident.”

Lacey’s hands knotted in the blanket. “The serial killer who hurt Mom wanted me to fall?”

“He tampered with Jake’s balcony, not yours.”

She jerked. “I thought he was after me. Why kill Jake?”

Jake pressed a kiss to her temple. "Falling from the third floor probably wouldn't kill me, but I would have suffered enough injuries to sideline me. With me out of the way, the killer would have had an easy time grabbing you."

She scowled. "That's crazy. Cade, Adam, and the others would increase their protection."

"My teammates arrived an hour ago. The killer may not know they're here."

"Or he doesn't care whether his balcony accident caught me or Jake." Cade sat on the edge of the second bed. "Taking one of us out of the equation leaves you with less protection. My guess is he never intended for you to be hurt. Why would he hurt you if you are the woman he's been wanting for six years?"

Great. Just what she needed in her life, the attention of an obsessed serial killer. "I'm not going down easy," she vowed.

"You're not going down at all. He chose the wrong target." Jake brushed her mouth with his, then turned to his friend. "Go to Lacey's room and sleep a few hours. I'll notify the hotel manager and check the security footage."

"Call the cops. There is zero chance this was a nasty coincidence."

Jake grimaced. "Yeah, you're right. I'll call Jones, too."

"When will you sleep?" Lacey's body was wracked with another round of shudders. She scowled. When would this stop?

He moved her so the upper half of her body lay against his chest. His body heat helped banish the trembling. "In four hours. That's when Cade will take over the watch."

Four hours? Good grief. How were these guys coherent with that little sleep? Her lips curved. Guess she'd better figure out their secret for med school. She wouldn't be sleeping much, either.

Cade eyed Lacey. "Do you mind if I borrow your spare bed?"

"Of course not."

"Come get me if you need help, Jake." With that, he went to the other room.

"How is your arm?" Jake nudged the blanket aside enough to free her arm. He removed the bandage and examined the stitches. "Good. None of the stitches are broken." He dug another bandage from his mike bag. A moment later, her wound was covered again.

He reached for his cell phone. "No use putting this off." A moment later, he said, "Jones, it's Jake. I need you at the hotel." A pause. "See you in ten minutes." He ended the call on his cell, then picked up the hotel phone and reported the incident. When he'd returned the handset to the stand, Jake settled Lacey against him again.

"I've been in more firefights than I want to count over the years, run into a hail of bullets to aid a fallen soldier or operative, and faced down terrorists with bombs and RPGs." His voice grew thick. "But I've never been as afraid as I was a few minutes ago."

Lacey eased her head back to look him in the face, saw the truth of his words in Jake's eyes. "You didn't show it on the outside."

He gave a soft huff of laughter. "I might not show it, but I'm shaking in my boots on the inside. The person who sabotaged the railing is going to pay for this stunt."

"Scared me, too. Thank you for saving me, again."

He cupped her cheek and pressed a gentle kiss to her mouth. A knock sounded on the door. Jake broke the kiss and released Lacey. He tugged the blanket tighter around her before going to the door and checking the peephole. Hand on his weapon, he unlocked the door.

"Mr. Davenport, I'm Kent Graves, the hotel manager. I can't tell you how sorry I am for this incident. May I come in and inspect the balcony?"

Jake stepped back.

The middle-aged man with salt-and-pepper hair walked into the room. His gaze zeroed in on Lacey. "I apologize for the scare you suffered, Ms. Coleman. Were you injured? We have a doctor on staff who will be happy to come assist you."

She shook her head. "I'm okay thanks to Jake." The thought of letting a stranger poke and prod her made her stomach lurch in protest.

"If you change your mind, call the front desk. I'll leave word that the doctor is to be called immediately if you request one."

"Thanks, Mr. Graves." She'd rather trust her health to her personal medic any day than depend on a doctor provided by the hotel.

He turned back to Jake. "Was the accident from this balcony or Ms. Coleman's?"

"Mine." He strode across the room and unlocked the French doors. The manager followed Jake onto the balcony.

With the conversation in hushed tones, Lacey couldn't hear what was being said. Several times, Jake shook his head. He pointed out the place where Cade indicated someone cut the wood.

While they discussed the incident, another knock sounded at the door. Jake turned, said something over his shoulder to the manager, and retraced his steps to the door. This time, he admitted Todd Jones.

"What's up, Jake?"

"Balcony railing gave way. Lacey would have fallen three stories if I hadn't caught her."

His gaze darted to Lacey. "Are you okay?"

"Scared me, but I'm fine."

Todd turned back to Jake. "Show me."

The two men joined the manager on the balcony and more discussion ensued.

Wrapped up in the soft, warm blanket, Lacey found herself growing sleepy. The lack of sleep and adrenaline surge combined with the comfort of the bed and warmth had her eyes closing.

She dozed to the sound of men's voices and woke some time later when the manager came into the room, insisting it would be safer if he assigned Jake to another room.

"No," Jake said, voice flat. "Not unless you have two rooms with connecting doors available plus two other rooms nearby for my friends who just checked into rooms across the hall from mine."

Before Jake finished speaking, Graves was already shaking his head. "I'm sorry, but I won't be able to accommodate that request. The hotel is nearly full. I can come up with a room for you, but that's the best I can do."

"Not good enough. I won't be separated from Ms. Coleman. The only alternative is to send someone to fix the balcony railing."

"But the balcony isn't safe as it is."

"We won't go out there until your people fix the railing."

Although the manager tried to insist, Jake stood firm and Graves finally agreed to send up the maintenance team within the hour to begin repairs.

After Graves left, Todd sat on the opposite bed and looked at Lacey. "Are you sure you're all right, Lacey?"

"Positive." Nothing a little over-the-counter pain reliever wouldn't fix. Lacey could handle strained muscles easier than the broken bones she would have suffered had she fallen to the ground. She sat with her back pressed against the headboard and rearranged the blanket to keep it wrapped around her body. The heat felt good.

"Cade was right. This was no accident. Someone cut the railing, hoping Jake or his friend would fall. That same someone wants you. I'm asking you again. Do you know anyone who wants to hurt you?"

Frank's face flashed into her mind, but she pushed the thought aside. Her ex wasn't here and hadn't made an appearance anywhere near her since Adam and Brent confronted him.

"Lacey, tell him about your former boyfriend," Jake said, his voice soft.

"This isn't his work. He's ham-fisted and doesn't plan ahead. He's not smart enough to do this."

"Let me be the judge of that." Todd leaned forward. "Tell me about him."

Knowing it was a waste of time, she told the detective the basics. No need to embarrass herself with her own stupidity.

"He hurt you, didn't he?" The detective's gaze was sharp, knowing.

She nodded. "I let it go on too long, but I realized the truth and walked away. Two friends convinced Frank to leave me alone."

Todd turned toward Jake, eyebrow raised.

Her boyfriend shook his head. "Not me. I heard rumors, but I didn't know Lacey well enough at the time to ask her about the relationship with Frank. If I had known or seen him hurting her, I would have stopped him."

"One of the men is Fortress Security's CEO. The other is Jake's teammate."

A wry smile curved Todd's lips. "Is Frank still alive?"

"He was breathing when they left him."

"Lucky man," he muttered. "I'm surprised you didn't kill him, Jake."

"Jury's still out on that."

In order to make an impression on her former boyfriend, Lacey suspected Adam and Brent had done more than talk, but she'd never pressed for details. As long as Frank steered clear of her, she was thrilled.

Hearing Jake's comment, though, made her realize Frank was in even more danger from the medic than he ever faced with the other two operatives. She would have to be very careful what she told Jake about her months with Frank. She loved the fact he was so protective. On the other hand, she didn't want him in trouble with the law.

"If Frank was in Winston, you would know. He would have asked around town until he located me. Frank has moved on to another woman. He won't think I'm worth the trouble."

Jake's eyes narrowed. "How do you know he's moved on?"

"A friend of mine still moves in his circle. She told me. They appear deliriously happy, but every few weeks, the woman he's dating goes on an unexpected vacation for a week or so." She shrugged. "Same pattern that happened with me."

"He has to want to change."

Yeah, that was never going to happen. Frank was arrogant enough to believe he was in the right, and the woman he was with deserved the discipline he administered. Jerk.

The detective stood. "I'll get my crime scene kit and check for prints before the maintenance people start repairs. All of you need to watch your backs. Especially you, Lacey. If the killer gets rid of your bodyguards, you won't stand a chance against him. He'll do to you what he did to his fifteen victims in the morgue."

CHAPTER THIRTY

Once Lacey was asleep, Jake called Brent and reported the latest developments.

"Did you see the security feeds from the cameras around the hotel?"

"Jones wouldn't let me see them because they were evidence." Jake wondered if Chief Beckett forbid him to share information with outsiders. "The recordings are on the hotel's computer hard drive."

"Perfect. Zane can hack into the system and copy what we need. How is Lacey?"

His gaze darted to the woman curled under the blanket on his bed. "Better than I'd hoped. She's sound asleep."

"Adrenaline dump."

"She was also awake most of the night with Yvonne." When Lacey had napped at the hospital, she woke every few minutes.

"Nothing from Adam and Veronica?"

"A text every hour confirming that Yvonne is safe. Harley went to the garage at noon. He'll return after the place closes for the night."

"What's next?"

"A visit to the Chesterfields after I sleep. Cade takes over the watch in a few minutes."

"I talked to Rafe."

Something in Brent's voice had Jake straightening. "What did he say?"

"The FBI's team arrived and is helping with the autopsies. All the women they've examined were strangled to death."

"Like he tried to do to Yvonne. Do you know if he raped the women before killing them?"

"Inconclusive."

That was not a question he wanted to ask Yvonne. Maybe Lacey could talk to the doctor. Surely the medical personnel asked those questions when she was brought in considering the circumstances.

"Rafe said the killer didn't leave much evidence behind on the bodies."

"In other words, no DNA."

"Not so far."

Might mean he used a condom if he assaulted the women before strangling them. Jake frowned, finding it hard to believe the killer hadn't left a trace of himself behind. If he kept the others as long as he held Yvonne, not leaving evidence was almost a miracle. "Signature?"

"Ligature marks on the wrists, ankles, and bruises around the neck. Each of the women had the letters LC carved into her stomach."

Jake closed his eyes briefly. Another confirmation the man wanted Lacey and the other women were substitutes. "This creep wants my girlfriend, Brent."

A pause. "You and Lacey, huh?"

"Yes. Don't tell me you have a problem with it. I'm not giving her up, and I won't hand over her security to one of my teammates."

"I don't have a problem as long as you treat her right."

He stiffened. "Have you ever known me to mistreat a woman?"

"Doesn't mean I won't be watching."

"I hear you."

"If you hurt Lacey, you'll answer to me."

Jake flinched. "Yes, sir." His boss would beat him to a pulp if Jake was stupid enough to hurt the woman who delved deeper under his armor by the hour. Not going to happen. He had realized he was head-over-heels in love with Lacey Coleman while holding her wrist in a death grip. Nothing like holding onto the woman you loved over open air to clarify your emotional connection to her. Yeah, he was a goner, and he wouldn't fight to save himself. The only thing that mattered in his life was Lacey.

After Brent ended the call, Jake scrubbed his hands over his face, beard stubble scratching his fingertips. He checked his watch.

Cade appeared in the doorway. He glanced at Lacey, his gaze going soft. "How long has she been out?" he murmured.

"An hour. The maintenance people should be here in a few minutes." He turned, considered whether he should move his girlfriend. She wouldn't be able to sleep with the noise sure to accompany work on the balcony. He also didn't want to leave her vulnerable. Yeah, Cade would protect her. Didn't matter. She was his to keep safe, and he didn't want to hand over that responsibility unless it was necessary. "I'll take her into the other room."

A nod from Cade. "Stay with her and get some rest. I'll keep an eye on things here."

Jake lifted Lacey and carried her to the other room. Although Cade had drawn the curtains to block the sunlight, he'd left the bathroom light on and the door cracked.

Perfect. He didn't want Lacey to realize someone was in the room with her and not be able to see who it was. Jake placed her on the beds and cupped her cheek with a light touch. In her sleep, she nuzzled his hand and pressed a kiss to his palm.

His heart turned over in his chest, love for her growing by the hour. He'd soon have to tell her how he felt. Would she one day grow to love him, too? His life didn't bear thinking about otherwise. He longed for a life with her.

Jake lingered a moment before he laid on the other bed. Less than a minute later, he was out. At the four-hour mark, he woke, fully alert. His gaze zeroed in on the bed across from his. Empty.

He swung his legs over the side and a low murmur of voices led him to the other room.

Lacey's face lit when she saw him. "Hi."

"Hi, yourself."

"Hungry?"

He spotted the evidence of room service on the table. "Starved. What did you order?"

"Club sandwich. I wasn't sure what you would like."

He smiled. "That's perfect. Thanks." Jake eyed Cade. "Repairs complete?"

"With a lot of grumbling about me keeping close tabs on them. The work is solid. I checked after they took off."

At least that much was taken care of. Now if he could capture the man targeting his girlfriend and help Yvonne recover, life would be sweet. He'd romance the woman of his dreams and convince Lacey that spending her life with him was worth the risk.

He made short work of the sandwich and chips while Cade and Lacey talked. When Lacey asked Cade if he had someone special in his life, Jake noticed the hesitation before his fellow operative responded.

"Not really." Cade finished the last of his water.

Lacey smiled. "Who is she?"

He rubbed the back of his neck. "A friend."

"Name?"

"Sasha. She owns the coffee shop in Otter Creek."

"Hmm. This sounds promising. Have you taken her on a date?"

Cade's cheeks flamed. "It's not like that. We're friends."

"But you want her to be more?"

One shoulder lifted.

"You should ask her out, Cade."

"I'm working on it," he mumbled.

Jake ducked his head to hide his amusement, replacing the cover over the plate. Not too long ago, he'd been in the same situation as Cade. At least now he didn't have to worry Lacey wasn't interested in him. He no longer had doubts about that, not with her response to his kisses. Man, she burned him up with her reaction to his touch. "I can put in a good word for you," he offered, amused at the horrified expression on Cade's face.

"Pass. I'll find my own dates. I get enough ribbing from my teammates. I don't need you adding fuel to the fire."

"But it's so much fun."

"No." He piled the empty plates on the tray and placed them outside the door. "Yvonne's in pain this afternoon. Other than that, the medical staff says she's doing great."

"The police been by to see her again?"

"Yeah. They weren't happy that Adam and Veronica stayed in the room while they questioned Yvonne. Adam said they didn't learn much. Yvonne remembered a tattoo on the guy's left wrist. An infinity symbol."

"Know anybody with that tattoo?" he asked Lacey.

"Doesn't sound familiar. I've been away from Winston for six years, though, and when I'm here, I spend time with Mom instead of in town. Besides, unless someone has those ink sleeves, I don't really pay attention to tattoos. A lot of Coffee House patrons have them."

When they caught the guy, the tattoo would help identify him. Had the killer talked to Yvonne? Maybe asked about Lacey or taunted Yvonne with her helplessness? Even though Lacey's mother hadn't seen her kidnapper's face, hearing his voice would be another way to solidify the ID.

"Do you still want to talk to the Chesterfields?" Lacey asked.

"I do. Why?"

"They should be home eating dinner now. They are creatures of habit. Paul wants his dinner every night at 6:00 on the dot."

Cade gave a huff of laughter at that.

Jake shook his head. He'd lost count of meals he'd missed while on missions. You learned to eat when you had the chance. "You coming, too, Cade?"

He shook his head. "I need to do some computer work unless your gut says otherwise."

"I can handle it."

"Brent called about the sample we sent to the lab. The substance is blood, but it's not Yvonne's. Wrong type. The lab is running the DNA profile."

"That will take a while." For all he knew, the blood might be from Harley. Might be worth asking if the mechanic had hurt himself in the garage or at least bled on the concrete floor. "We'll be gone a while. I'm driving Lacey to the hospital after we talk to the Chesterfields."

A nod. "I'll let you know if I learn anything else."

"Remy and Lily will check in before they head to the hospital." He escorted Lacey to his SUV.

They drove to her mother's house where he parked in the driveway. "Is there something your mother would enjoy having at the hospital? Maybe a book to get her mind off pain."

"That's a great idea." Inside the house, Lacey went to the master bedroom and grabbed two of her mother's favorite books, and her nightgown and bathrobe.

Once they deposited the items in a small bag and placed them in his SUV, Jake said, "Where do the Chesterfields live?"

"This way." She led the way to the yellow, two-story house across the street with lights gleaming in the windows.

Cheerful place on the outside. He rang the doorbell, gaze scanning the neighborhood. Seemed like a nice place to raise kids. The houses were thirty years old or more, the lawns well kept, the facade of the houses in good repair.

He frowned, feeling eyes on them. Another careful sweep. Nothing. Could be a nosy neighbor. He didn't see curtains moving, but that didn't mean much. Night had fallen.

A chain rattled, the door opened, and a man in his sixties, topped by a thick head of silver hair, stood in the doorway. Icy blue eyes dismissed Jake with a glance, then settled on Lacey. The ice melted, replaced by a heat that set off Jake's instincts. This guy was a predator. What kind remained to be seen.

"Lacey." Chesterfield's voice was almost a purr. "You look beautiful, as always. I was shocked to hear about your mother. Come in and tell me how she's doing."

"Thank you, Mr. Chesterfield."

"Please, my dear. It's Paul. We're more than neighbors."

When the older man reached for Lacey, Jake stepped between them, hand outstretched. "Jake Davenport, Lacey's boyfriend."

Ice crept back in his eyes along with a hard glint of anger. "I see." He turned away without bothering to shake Jake's hand.

Quick footsteps hurried their direction. "Paul, who was at the door?" A soft, round woman rushed into the room and came to an abrupt stop. "Oh." Her hand went to her throat when she saw Jake, then her gaze shifted to Lacey. "Took you long enough to show up. Your mother was missing for days."

Stunned at the viciousness of the attack, Jake laid his hand on his girlfriend's back in silent support. She backed up a step until she was in the circle of his arm.

"I had been calling her for days, Mrs. Chesterfield. Jake and I came as soon as Chief Beckett told me she was missing."

The woman's gaze skated back to Jake.

"I'm Jake Davenport, Lacey's boyfriend."

At his words, the tension in the woman's body melted away. "Yvonne didn't mention you."

Doubt Lacey's mother would have told this busybody even if she'd known. "I've been interested in Lacey for months, but found the courage to tell her recently. Lacey says you're observant. Do you mind if we ask you a few questions about Yvonne and what's been happening around Winston the past few years, Mrs. Chesterfield?"

The woman cast a triumphant look in her husband's direction before bestowing a smile on Jake. "I don't mind at all. Sit down so we can talk in comfort." She gestured toward the living room to the right, furniture still covered in plastic.

Jake resisted the urge to roll his eyes. Barely. Seriously? His mother was a fanatic about everything being in place, but she believed in comfort. Plastic-covered furniture wasn't comfortable. Jake's grandmother had done the same thing, a practice his mother hated. She was told children would mess up expensive furniture in Gigi's house. As a result, Jake's mother felt unwelcome in her childhood home, and vowed she would never treat her own children that way.

He urged Lacey to the end of the couch and sat next to her to prevent either of the Chesterfields from getting close to her. Instead of sitting, though, Paul leaned one shoulder against the wall, his gaze fixed on Lacey. Nora hadn't noticed yet, but it was only a matter of time.

For now, Jake focused on Nora although he kept Paul in his peripheral vision. "May I call you Nora?"

"Oh, please do." The woman's cheeks flushed a pretty pink. "What questions do you have for me?"

"Have you noticed anything out of the ordinary in the neighborhood?"

A frown. "Like what?"

"People or vehicles that don't belong in the area. Someone watching Yvonne's place. Things that don't fit the pattern of what you normally see on your street."

Disappointment filled her eyes. "No."

"What about someone watching Yvonne or her house on a regular basis?"

A quick glance at her husband. She scowled before turning back to Jake. "Yvonne always has people watching her, including the police."

"Are you sure?" Lacey asked.

"A thing like that is hard to miss. I'm sorry, dear, but your mother's past isn't a secret. If your boyfriend doesn't know, you should tell him."

"Mom hasn't been turning tricks or drinking."

"That you know. You don't live here. You don't know what your mother does now that you're gone."

"You think I wouldn't recognize the signs? I lived with her addiction and the downward spiral. That's not what I'm seeing. Besides, I don't think she could hide alcohol abuse or prostitution from Harley."

Another flush in Nora's cheeks, this time from embarrassment. "Perhaps not."

"You said the police are watching Yvonne," Jake said. "Do you recognize the officers staking out her place?"

"I couldn't see who it was. The car was parked in the shadow of a big tree."

"A marked patrol car?"

She shook her head.

"How do you know it's a cop?"

"I saw his badge glint in the moonlight."

"But you didn't see his face?"

"I'm afraid not."

"You're sure it was a man?" Lacey asked.

"Oh, yes. I know a pair of male shoulders when I see them. My Paul lifts weights. I appreciate a muscular man." Her eyes traveled over Jake's body in a leisurely perusal.

Right. "How long have the police watched Yvonne?"

"Years, dear."

His skin prickled. "Guess."

"I don't have to guess. The policeman has been out there a few times a week since Lacey moved to Nashville."

CHAPTER THIRTY-ONE

Jake eyed the woman sitting in the recliner a few feet from him and Lacey. She practically quivered with excitement. He couldn't imagine what her life was like if his questions were a high point of her day. "What do you know about the women who disappeared over the past six years?"

"They're all young and blond." She scooted to the edge of her chair. "Someone killed them."

"Why do you think that?"

"It's obvious to me. I know people say they moved on to another city or state. A few were rumored to have run off with a lover. Some went to help nurse elderly relatives back to health and decided to stay. Most of them were visitors, passing through town on the way to someplace else. But I don't believe a word of it."

"Why not?"

"That many young, beautiful women leaving the area without warning and never returning is too much coincidence. No one heard from them after they left. They made friends here. Some have relatives in the area. No, I'm afraid something bad happened to them."

Smart lady. Jake turned his attention to the man leaning against the wall near the front door. "Do you know anything about the missing women, Mr. Chesterfield?"

A sneer bloomed on the older man's face. "I'm not a gossip and I don't pay any mind to the grapevine in this town. Only weak-minded people listen to that drivel. Those young women were out for trouble, if you know what I mean." The old man's gaze locked onto Lacey.

Jake's muscles bunched. A soft hand on his drew his attention to the woman at his side. Lacey squeezed gently, a smile curving her lips. She didn't want him to react to the deliberate insult. He gave her a slight nod and let it pass. For now.

Although Jake tossed more questions at the Chesterfields, he didn't learn anything more. He stood and held out his hand to Lacey. "Thank you for talking to us. You've been very helpful."

"I don't see how since we couldn't tell you much." Nora turned to Lacey. "How is Yvonne feeling, Lacey?"

"The doctor says she'll make a full recovery."

"I'm glad to hear that." She edged closer. "Is it true what they say, that she doesn't know who kidnapped her? I can't imagine. I guess she was traumatized." Nora shuddered. "She must have been terrified with a madman hunting for her in the woods. Are her injuries severe?"

Jake squeezed her hand. He had a feeling the older woman was an incorrigible gossip, one who would spread information shared around town.

"A few broken bones. Those will mend."

"Did she tell you what happened? Did the man assault her?" She leaned forward a little further. "You know what I mean. It's every woman's worst nightmare."

Lacey's hand clenched tighter over Jake's, the one outward sign of her agitation. "Todd Jones is investigating. He doesn't keep me informed of his findings. My main focus has been on Mom and her recovery."

"Oh, of course. I just thought poor Yvonne would talk to you about what happened."

"I'll tell Mom you asked about her."

"My dinner is probably cold by now. Go reheat it, Nora," Paul said curtly. "I'll see them out."

"Yes, dear." She left the room without a backward glance.

Incredible. If Jake had told Lacey to reheat his dinner using that same tone of voice, she would have dumped the plate of food on his head. He would have deserved it.

As they walked to the front door, Jake kept his body between Lacey and Paul. On the porch, he slowed to let his girl walk a few feet ahead of him and turned to face the other man. "I know what you did to Lacey," he said, voice soft.

A frown. "I don't know what you're talking about. I've never done anything to that girl."

"Oh, yeah, you did. She was fourteen years old and vulnerable. She's not fourteen, and she's definitely not vulnerable. If you ever touch her again, I will rip your heart out of your chest and feed it to you. I care about Lacey, and she is mine to protect. Am I making myself clear?"

Paul gave an audible swallow. "Yes."

With another hard look at the older man, he caught up with Lacey and escorted her across the street to his SUV.

"What was that about?" Lacey asked.

"Don't ask."

"I already did."

Figuring she wouldn't back off, he unlocked the SUV and helped her inside before he caught her chin in the palm of his hand and kissed her. Yeah, he knew Chesterfield was watching, and Jake was staking his claim on Lacey.

Breaking the kiss, he eased back, smiling at her unfocused gaze.

After a couple deep breaths, Lacey's eyes narrowed. "You warned Mr. Chesterfield off, didn't you?"

Another short, soft kiss. “Did you think I wouldn’t? You’re mine to protect, honey, and there may be a time when you visit your mother while I’m deployed. I don’t want you having to defend yourself against a lecherous old man. I think he got my message loud and clear. If he makes another move on you, I’ll be back down here.”

“I can handle myself.”

“I couldn’t be here for you when you were fourteen. You’re not alone anymore, Lacey. We’re a team now. We take care of each other.”

She cupped his jaw with her soft hand. “But I feel like you’re doing all the giving and I’m just taking.”

“You give me more than you can possibly imagine.” A quick kiss, and he shut the door. Driving down the street a moment later, he said, “Where can we find Noah Holt at this time of day?”

Lacey gave a wry laugh. “Probably Sully’s.”

“A restaurant?” He preferred to talk to the man in a quieter location instead of a crowded restaurant. Noah would be more belligerent in a crowd than he would alone. A public venue would also hamper Jake’s ability to secure answers. Hard to apply certain kinds of pressure if a man was surrounded by friends and family who shored up his courage.

“A bar. Unless his tastes have changed, Sully’s is his favorite watering hole.”

Not what he wanted to hear. He’d wait to question Holt. “I’m not taking you into a bar. What is your mother’s favorite comfort drink?” He didn’t think Yvonne would be ready for outside food yet.

She looked sheepish. “Hot chocolate.”

“Sounds familiar.” Jake turned toward the center of town and stopped to purchase coffee, two hot chocolates, and one hot chamomile mint tea in case Lacey’s mother couldn’t stomach the rich drink yet.

Returning to the SUV with two takeout carriers, he set one on the floorboard at Lacey's feet and handed her the other. Ten minutes later, they walked into the hospital and headed for Yvonne's room.

Remy sat outside the door, drawing a lot of female interest as the medical staff and visitors walked the corridor. The Cajun's expression brightened as they approached. "Lacey." He gave her a short hug. "How is your arm?"

"Healing. Jake did a great job."

"Not surprising. He's the best." He eyed the cardboard carriers. "Please tell me one of those is for me."

Jake freed one of the coffees and handed his friend the cup. "How's Yvonne?"

"Seems fine. Since she's skittish with me in the room, I left Lily to keep her company."

"Anyone interested in you or Yvonne?"

A soft snort. "Aside from women and men ogling me? No."

Jake rolled his eyes. Much to Lily's irritation, Remy was a magnet for attention. She said it was the dark hair, eyes, and tanned skin combined with that killer accent. Whatever.

"Cops?"

An eyebrow rose. "Torres and Jones dropped by a few minutes ago, got nowhere with her. Right after Lily and I arrived, two other cops showed up, one in uniform, one not. Uniform was beefy. The other cop was older, looked like he might be a relative of Uniform."

The Becketts. Didn't they have anything better to do? In light of the information from Nora Chesterfield, he wondered which one of the men was Yvonne's watcher. Probably Will.

"Someone in uniform has been watching Yvonne and her home at night several times a week for a while."

Remy's eyes narrowed. "I'll make sure I'm in the room next time they drop in."

"Lily can handle herself."

The operative dropped his voice. "Yeah, she can, but she's my wife."

He understood. Lily was capable, but that didn't mean her husband wouldn't protect her. Jake gave a brisk knock to warn Lily he was entering the room, and ushered Lacey inside.

The female operative blocked his view of Yvonne with her body, hand hovering near her weapon. Lily relaxed when she saw Jake followed by Lacey. "Yvonne, look who's here to see you."

"Lace. Hi, sweetheart." Although her careful movements indicated she was still in a lot of pain, Yvonne's eyes were clear.

"Brought you a hot drink, Mom." Lacey set a carrier on the rolling table. "Would you like hot chocolate?"

Her mother grimaced. "I don't think I can stomach that right now. Thanks for thinking of me, though."

"We also brought chamomile mint tea." Jake handed her the cup. "This will settle your stomach." While she lifted the cup and began to sip, he turned to Harley who sat where Jake left him earlier in the morning. "How's our girl, Harley?"

"So beautiful she makes my heart leap every time she smiles." He winked at Yvonne who had teared up. "She's also a might grumpy."

Chuckling, Jake handed Lacey a hot chocolate, gave Lily coffee, and looked at the mechanic. "You a coffee man?"

"Don't drink no girly stuff."

No tea or chocolate for the tough guy in the corner. He handed Harley the third cup of coffee and took the remaining hot drink for himself. He preferred coffee, but caffeine was caffeine in his book.

Lacey grabbed the bag she'd brought from the SUV. "Jake and I stopped by your house and picked up a few things for you." She pulled out two books, and a nightgown and robe.

Yvonne's eyes brightened. "Thanks, Lace."

They stayed an hour. When Jake noticed Yvonne's eyes drooping, he drew Lacey to her feet. "We should let your mother rest."

Lacey kissed Yvonne's forehead. "I'll see you tomorrow morning, Mom."

"Okay. Love you, Lace." The response was faint, her eyes closing already.

Jake eyed Harley. "You staying again tonight?"

The older man's chin lifted. "Would you leave Lacey in this place?"

His lips curved. "No way."

"There's your answer."

"Need anything before we go, Lily?"

The woman Remy called Elf raised her coffee cup. "This is all I need. Rest, Lacey. Harley, Remy and I will watch over your mother."

Jake had to smile at the way she'd included Harley. Hearing himself mentioned as part of the security detail had the older man sitting up straighter.

In the corridor, he talked to Remy a minute before walking with Lacey to the elevator. As they reached the gleaming silver doors, they opened and a dark-haired man well over six feet tall with steel gray eyes stepped out.

His expression shifted from one of boredom to avid interest. "Well, little Lacey. It's been a long time."

CHAPTER THIRTY-TWO

Ice formed in Lacey's veins. Great. Just the person she didn't want to see right now. "Noah."

"You're looking as beautiful as ever, darling."

"Don't call me that," she snapped.

"It's just an expression of affection." His tone was mild, but his eyes hardened at her words.

Jake's left arm circled her shoulders and he drew Lacey against his side. "I'm Jake Davenport, Lacey's boyfriend."

Lacey wanted to laugh at his blatant claiming of her. Noah's obvious annoyance at Jake's statement brought her a lot of pleasure. Noah Holt had been the bane of her existence in high school. He and Will made it their mission in life to antagonize her. No one dared intervene when the terrible twosome started in on anyone. They were too afraid of repercussions if they interfered.

"Noah Holt. Lacey and I are old friends." He sized up Jake. "How long are you in town?"

"Until Lacey goes home."

A frown at that as he turned his attention to Lacey. "You here to see your mother?"

She nodded.

"How is she?"

"Recovering."

"I want to check in on her."

"She's sleeping. Mom needs her rest."

"I'll look in on her, then. Won't be a minute. Wait for me. We have much to discuss."

No way.

"You won't be allowed in the room," Jake said.

That elicited a scowl. "I go anywhere I please in this town."

"Not this time."

A snort. "Who's going to stop me?"

Jake signaled Remy, who watched the interaction by the elevator, and received a slight nod in response. "The guard at her door."

Noah's head whipped in the direction of Yvonne's room. His jaw clenched. "A guard? Why would anyone want to hurt her?"

"One man already did," Lacey pointed out.

"Some john who didn't like the terms of their agreement."

Rage filled her. She wanted to get in Noah's face, but found herself held against Jake's side. Fine. She didn't have to touch Noah to make her point. "When will your pea-sized brain accept that my mother is not a prostitute?"

Noah surged forward only to find himself blocked by Jake.

"No." Her boyfriend didn't elaborate.

The other man backed off a step, then two. "We need to talk in private, Lacey. Now. I'll take you to the coffee shop if you insist on being someplace public, but I've had enough of your attitude and it's time we hashed this out."

"I'd rather stick a fork in my eye than go anywhere with you. I guess you didn't pay attention to Jake's introduction. He's my boyfriend. I respect him enough not to meet another man alone for anything, including in public. Even if Jake and I weren't together, I don't want to talk. Stay away from me and my mother, Noah."

His voice dropped to a growl. "You might not live here, Lacey, but your mother does. I can make life uncomfortable for her. You might want to think about that the next time you throw insults in my face." With that, he left.

Remy approached. "Who was that?"

"Noah Holt, a jerk I knew in high school. He and Will Beckett are best friends."

"What did he want?" Remy asked, his gaze following Noah's progress down the corridor.

"To check on Mom. I don't know why. They don't have anything to do with each other."

"He acted as though he had authority or power. Does he?"

Lacey scowled. "Only in his mind. His father is Senator Randy Holt."

Jake and Remy grimaced. Yeah, her feeling exactly. Randy Holt was well known in national politics and billed as the next contender for President of the United States. Wealthy and charming, he was thought to be a front runner if he ran for office.

Lacey shuddered. She wouldn't vote for him, the senator too slick for her taste. Didn't matter if he was the hometown boy. He wouldn't change her vote.

"Explains his entitlement mentality." Jake studied her face. "You have a story to tell me about Noah." A statement, not a question.

"Not much of one. I was three years behind Noah and Will. They lived to torment me."

"How?"

"Noah did the same stuff Will used to do, asking how much Mom charged and if she gave discounts to minors. Stupid stuff."

"Words designed to hurt you." Remy laid a hand on her shoulder. "Did Yvonne know?"

Lacey wanted to spout off, but Remy didn't know. "Mom drowned her sorrows in booze when she wasn't working the streets. She couldn't help or offer advice."

"I'm sorry, Lacey."

"It's in the past." Unfortunately, no one in Winston would let the past die. That was why she moved to Nashville. A fresh start and new life far from her painful past.

Remy turned to Jake. "I'll let you know if Holt makes an appearance again."

"I don't want him to bother Mom," Lacey said.

"If your mother doesn't want to talk to him, he won't be allowed in the room."

"Thanks, Remy."

"Later," Jake murmured to his teammate, and turned to the elevator. This time, they weren't intercepted.

Lacey gave the medic a sidelong glance. "Where are we going now?"

"Hotel. I'm hoping Zane sent the security videos. I'd love to know who to point out to the cops." He unlocked the SUV and opened the door for her although his attention focused on a shadowed corner of the lot.

"See something?"

"Someone is watching us." He cupped her cheek when she would have turned to look. "Right here. We don't want him to know we're aware of his presence. Easier to catch him off guard." He dropped a quick kiss on her lips, then closed the door and circled the hood to slide behind the wheel.

Minutes later, they were back at the hotel. At their entrance to the room, Cade glanced up from the bed, computer balanced on his thighs. "How's Yvonne?"

"Same." Jake locked the door. "We stopped by her place to pick up a few things for her. We also visited the Chesterfields."

A smile tugged at Cade's lips. "How did that go?"

"Not like you're hoping." Lacey sat on the edge of Jake's bed. "No punches thrown."

The operative's eyes narrowed at Jake.

"I warned him off. Did Z send the security footage?"

"Yep." A few key strokes later, he set the laptop on the bed for them to see the footage and tapped another key. On screen, people moved quickly in and out of camera range with gaps where no one crossed into view.

Lacey scooted closer to the screen. "That's our hallway."

They watched in silence a few minutes. A figure wearing a dark-colored uniform with a baseball cap pulled low on his forehead moved into view carrying a tool box. With a glance around, the figure slipped a card into the reader, opened the door, and walked inside. According to the time-stamp, ten minutes later, the person left again.

"We can't see the face. That's no help." Lacey had hoped the camera footage would give them a face. At least then she'd know who wanted to hurt her and Jake.

"It tells us more than you think." The medic threaded their fingers together and squeezed. "Our visitor is male and over six feet tall. He's aware of the camera and had access to a master key."

"We still can't identify him."

"Not with this footage," Cade agreed. "Zane sent footage from four other cameras. Hopefully, we'll catch this guy's face in one of them."

"Que up the footage," Jake said. "Let's see if we got lucky."

Lacey wouldn't hold her breath. Not many things had gone their way since this whole mess started with her mother's disappearance. At least Mom was safe, and she had a real chance at a relationship with Jake.

Cade loaded more footage, and they repeated the same process with the view from the hotel lobby. Nothing. Baseball Hat hadn't come through the lobby.

By the time they loaded the final footage, Lacey had decided Baseball Hat was too smart to give them a view of his face. While she was discouraged, the two operatives watching with her didn't seem fazed by the lack of progress.

"Let's see if this one gives us more to work with," Cade murmured. He tapped a few keys and set the video in motion.

Lacey frowned. "Where is this camera?" She didn't recognize the angle.

"Employee entrance at the back of the hotel," Jake said.

She blinked. "How do you know that?"

"When we're on a mission, we memorize our surroundings. We learned the layout of the hotel in case we needed a quick exit."

"When? You've been with me almost every minute since we've been here."

He smiled. "Zane sent me the hotel's schematics and every picture he could find of the hotel. I memorized them while you were napping at the hospital."

"Impressive." Especially considering she hadn't napped long. He'd memorized the layout in less than an hour.

"I'm motivated, Lacey. Learning the hotel's layout means I can protect you better."

Fewer people moved in and out of camera range at the back entrance. According to the time stamp, Baseball Hat entered the hotel ten minutes before he arrived on the third floor.

She groaned. "Still nothing."

"We might have better luck when he leaves the hotel. Depends on which way he turns."

Twenty minutes after the man entered, he left by the back door, his face turned away from the camera almost out of range. He stopped, his head whipping back toward the hotel. Unfortunately, he still had the presence of mind to keep his head lowered. The only part of his face the camera picked up was the jaw line on the right side of his face.

"Precious little to go on," Cade muttered.

"It's not great, but we'll let the techs at Fortress take a crack at it." Jake frowned. "Cade, back up this recording and play it again slow."

"What did you see?" Lacey asked. She hadn't noticed anything to identify the man who broke into Jake's room and tampered with the balcony railing.

"I'm not sure."

Cade restarted the video, this time in slow motion. They watched in silence until Jake said, "There. Back up the feed three seconds and freeze it."

They edged closer to the computer screen. "What is that?" Lacey asked, pointing to Baseball Hat's wrist.

"Can you blow that up?" Jake asked.

Cade worked on the laptop for a couple minutes, then said, "This is the best I can do without degrading the picture quality." He turned the computer around.

The screen shot of Baseball Hat's wrist showed a tattoo of an infinity symbol.

CHAPTER THIRTY-THREE

Jake turned to Lacey in time to see her clamp a hand over her mouth, distress filling her gaze. “It’s not your fault.”

“How can you say that? He’s after you because of me. I’m the reason he tried to hurt you.”

Seeing her this distraught gutted him. He stared at Cade.

“I’ll be back in a few minutes,” the operative murmured and left.

“I shouldn’t have let you come with me,” she said as soon as the door closed behind Cade. “I’m sorry, Jake. I didn’t know you would be a target.”

Jake stood and drew Lacey to her feet. He held her tight against his body. “There is no place I would rather be than with you.”

“You could have been seriously injured. I’d rather have you safe at home than in a hospital bed here. Please, go home. I couldn’t bear it if something happened to you because of me.”

He cupped her face, tilting her head back to look into her eyes. What if she rejected him? “I’m not leaving you.”

"Why not?"

"I love you."

Lacey's eyes widened. "What did you say?"

"I love you, Lacey. So much that it would rip my heart out to lose you. I've been slowly falling in love with you for months. Your heart, your kindness, your enjoyment of the little things in your life, the attention you lavish on Alexa, all those things drew me to you. I wanted to move faster, but I worried you wouldn't let me into your life. The last thing I wanted to do was scare you away." His lips curved. "And I've probably done that by telling you how I feel this soon. Whatever you do, don't run from me. I'll move our relationship as slow as you need, but give me a chance to win your heart."

She shook her head.

His heart stuttered until he noticed she was smiling. What did that mean? "Lacey?"

"You don't need a chance to win my heart. You already have it." She wrapped her arms around his neck. "I love you, Jake. I think I have for a while, but I didn't think you noticed me."

"Oh, I noticed you. How could I not?" His hands shook as he cupped her face between his palms. "Are you sure?"

"How could I not love you? You're the beat of my heart, Jake."

He drew a deep breath and went for broke. "Can you handle my job?"

"What happens if I can't?"

Jake swallowed hard. Man, it would hurt to leave Fortress and his teammates. Bad. Losing Lacey over a job was unthinkable. Although he could find another job, he couldn't replace the woman in his arms. "I need you in my life. I can find another job." He tried to smile though pain ripped through his insides. "I hear EMTs are in high demand."

"Would you really give up the job you love for me?"

"In a heartbeat. I don't want to lose you."

Lacey inched closer. "I love your job and the people you work with. I would never steal your dream. I can handle the absences that come with your work as long as you come home to me."

He shared a series of long, drugging kisses with the woman he longed to make his wife. Soon, Jake hoped. He meant what he told Lacey, however. He'd go as slow as she needed. If that meant a long dating period and engagement, Jake would deal. "Does this mean you'll think about marrying me?"

A broad smile appeared. "Are you asking?"

Oh, man. Did she mean what he thought she did? "Yes, I am. You aren't going to break my heart, are you?"

"Never."

"Will you marry me, Lacey Coleman?"

"I would be honored to be your wife, Jake Davenport."

Thank God. He drew in a deep breath. "Is there a jewelry store in town?"

"Yes, but don't buy anything in Winston. Wait until we're home."

"As long as you don't let some other man steal you away from me."

"Not a chance. I love having my own personal medic."

He stole a quick kiss. "Speaking of that, how does your arm feel?"

"It's sore, but I'll live."

"Still taking the pills I gave you?"

"Yes, sir."

He tapped her nose. "Smart aleck. I'll check your arm before you go to sleep and change the bandage." It would give him a chance to make sure an infection wasn't setting up.

A quick knock and the door opened. Cade walked in, stopped short when he saw them locked in an embrace. “Should I walk around the block again?”

“Not necessary.”

Cade looked at Lacey, then Jake. “Something happen while I was gone for ten minutes?”

“Do you want to share the news, Lacey, or wait?” Maybe she wanted to tell her mother before she announced their engagement.

Lacey smiled at Cade. “Jake and I are engaged.”

His jaw dropped. “Nice work, man. Congratulations to you both.”

Jake pressed a tender kiss to Lacey’s temple. “Thanks. I’ll take watch if you want to sleep.”

“Actually, I need a run.” Cade rummaged in his duffel bag. “St. Claire is a stickler about physical training. I’m not giving him a chance to double my miles as penalty for skipping too many days in a row.”

“I hear you. Adam is the same.”

“Why does it matter if you skip a few days?” Lacey loosened her hold and twisted in Jake’s arms to face Cade. “Wouldn’t your conditioning hold?”

“One or two days off lets your body recuperate. After that, discipline starts to slip. It’s too easy to promise yourself you’ll run later.” He shrugged. “I hate running. I do it because it’s how I keep myself and my teammates safe. We have to be in better shape than the enemy. Sometimes our lives depend on it.”

“Go on, then. I don’t want to be responsible for Sasha not having a date with you.”

Cade’s face flamed as he turned away with his running clothes in hand and headed toward the bathroom to change.

“You need to run, too. Go with him.”

“Not a chance. One of us needs to be with you.”

“I’ll be locked in a hotel room. What could possibly happen?”

"The man who tampered with the balcony had an access card."

"The card won't do him any good if I bolt the doors." She placed her hand over his heart. "Besides, you won't have to worry if I'm running with you."

He frowned. "You feel good enough to run five miles?"

Five miles? Holy cow. She couldn't do that on a good day and this was anything but. "My limit is three. I guess you'll have to go without me."

"What about a compromise? We'll run close to the hotel. When you've had enough, we'll come back with you, make sure you get into the room safely. You can lock yourself in." He'd make sure she had Adam and Veronica's phone numbers programmed into her phone. If a problem developed while he and Cade ran the last two miles, help was across the hall.

She beamed. "Deal. Give me two minutes to change." Lacey hurried into her room.

Cade strode from the bathroom. "I have my phone if you need anything while I'm out."

"You'll have to wait. Lacey wants to run with us."

"She up to it?"

"We'll find out. You scouted a route close to the hotel?"

A nod.

"We'll make sure she gets back to the room when she's tired, then finish the rest of the miles."

Cade was silent a moment. "You're a lucky man, Jake."

"Why?"

"Lacey is protecting you. She wants you to continue training so you're in top physical shape."

"I know," he murmured and turned to his duffel. "I'll be ready in two minutes."

Five minutes later, they started off at a slow jog. The night air felt crisp and clear, the breeze ruffling Jake's hair and blowing the cobwebs from his mind.

Unlike Cade, he loved to run. To him, running equated freedom. Growing up, his mother had been overprotective. She'd had a good reason to guard him and his siblings with the fierceness of a mother bear. His family was wealthy and the threat of their children being kidnapped for ransom was a constant worry.

A nine-year-old boy he'd been friends with was kidnapped and murdered. Marnie Davenport had been afraid to let Jake and his siblings out of her sight for a long while. Finally, Dad had convinced Mom the danger was past once the killer was caught and convicted, and Jake and the other Davenport children were once again allowed outside without supervision. However, during those long months of fear in their community, the only freedom Jake had was when he ran to keep in shape for sports.

Because Lacey's speed was slower than theirs, Jake and Cade matched their pace to hers. Into the second mile, Jake noticed a pair of headlights trailing several lengths behind them. He glanced at Cade who nodded. Jake wasn't surprised Cade noticed. He was sharp and observant.

With a hand signal, Cade broke off and disappeared a moment later.

Lacey slowed, her expression puzzled. "Where is he going?"

"To circle around and get the license plate of the vehicle following us."

"What do we do in the meantime?"

"Keep running unless you need to stop."

"I'll be fine for a few more minutes." She sent him a sidelong glance. "You don't look winded at all. Have you been holding back?"

"Your pace is a little slower than I'm used to. Doesn't matter, though. Adam won't care how fast I run."

"I can speed up."

"Save your strength. Do you like to run?"

"Love it. I don't get a chance to run long distances. I usually have to fit it in between shifts at Coffee House."

"You have good form. You'd be a natural long-distance runner. Unfortunately, once you start college, you won't have time to run a lot of miles."

She didn't say anything for a moment. When the silence lasted longer than expected, Jake asked, "Something wrong?"

"We talked about your career. What about mine?"

Did she really think he would balk at her desire to attend med school? "What about it?"

"I still want to go to medical school. Will you be okay with that?"

He reached for her hand and slowed them to a stop. "Do what you're called to do, honey. If that means being a trauma surgeon, I'll support you every step of the way."

"Even if the studies and interning keep me away from you?"

Jake cupped her cheek with his hand. "I'll help you study. It will be fun and a good review for me."

"Fun." She shook her head. "Your idea of fun is different than mine."

"I want to be part of your life. Studying together will give me time with you. I'll take any time I can get, even if it is studying chemistry and biology."

She placed a soft kiss on his mouth. "I love you."

He grinned even as he slid his gaze to the vehicle crawling their direction. "Remember that when I make you mad one day."

The vehicle stopped.

Jake edged closer to Lacey, his instincts screaming at him.

Behind him, he heard Cade yell, "Gun."

A split second later, a gunshot shattered the peaceful night.

CHAPTER THIRTY-FOUR

Jake dove for Lacey, wrapping his arms around her and taking them both to the ground. He managed to twist them in the air and take the brunt of the impact with the ground.

He rolled them until Lacey's back was pressed to the brick wall of a store and his body covered hers. He wrapped his arms around her head, so no part of the woman he loved was exposed to the shooter.

More shots rang out. Glass broke and the vehicle sped down the street.

Cade raced toward them. "You okay?"

Jake eased back from Lacey, his gaze scanning her body. "Are you hurt, baby?"

"Banged up." She gave him a shaky smile. "Again. What happened?"

"Someone in the vehicle following us fired several shots our direction. Are you sure you're okay?"

"I'm fine, Jake. What about you?" Her small hands gripped his arms. "Did he hit you?"

Knowing the adrenaline surge might have kept him unaware of a wound, he visually checked his limbs and torso. "No. Guess he's a bad shot."

"How can you joke at a time like this? Someone tried to kill us."

More likely, he'd tried to kill Jake. The shooter could have hit Lacey. Jake shoved his anger behind a mental wall. Anger would cloud his thoughts, something he couldn't afford. "He failed. When we're back in the room, I want to check your stitches."

Cade crouched beside them. "Hate to say it, but we need to call Jones."

"He can't do anything."

"Maybe not, but we need the incident on record. I also have the plate for Z to run."

"Traffic cams."

Cade grinned. "Oh, yeah. Zane would enjoy hacking into the system."

Jake reached into his pack and grabbed his phone. He reported the incident to the detective.

Jones sighed. "Someone really has it in for you three. Everybody okay?"

"We're fine. Scared Lacey. Someone is going to pay for that."

"I don't know what you're allowed to do outside the US border, but there will be no vigilante justice while you're in Winston."

Jake grunted without agreeing to Jones' demand for compliance with his edict. No one would touch his girlfriend while he drew breath. Jake had no problem pulling the trigger or wielding a knife defending Lacey.

"Are you safe?"

He hadn't stopped scanning the area since the SUV raced away. "Yeah, he's long gone by now."

"He? You saw the shooter?"

"Just get here. I don't want Lacey out in the open longer than necessary." He ended the call before the detective asked more questions.

"Can I get up now?" Lacey asked.

"Unless you're uncomfortable, you can sit up but stay on the ground." The ground was the safest place for her. She'd present less of a target. "Jones should be here in a few minutes." When she swayed, Jake steadied her with a hand to the shoulder. He called Adam.

"Yeah?" a gruff voice answered on the first ring.

"It's Jake. I'm two blocks from the hotel near the corner of Sharon and Magnolia. I need a blanket and three bottles of water."

"Problem?"

"Yeah. I'll explain when you get here."

"You have backup?"

"Cade's with me and Lacey."

"Three minutes."

A siren sounded in the distance.

Lacey stirred. "The police are coming?" She was looking across the street though Jake didn't think she was focused on anything in particular. How could she be? The vista in front of her was a closed department store.

"Lacey." He tilted her head back. "Look at me."

It took her two beats longer than he liked for her to respond to his command. Lacey was going into shock. One more trauma in a string of them. He couldn't wait to get his hands on the creep terrorizing her.

"There's Adam," Cade murmured.

His team leader ran toward them, his wife, Veronica, on his heels. Vonnie handed Jake the blanket which he wrapped around Lacey. Adam tossed a bottle of water toward Cade who neatly snagged it in mid-air, then handed the other two bottles to Jake. "Sit rep."

Cade summarized the attack, finishing just as Jones arrived at the curb.

Now that Adam and Veronica were on site to help Cade with protection, Jake concentrated on Lacey. He uncapped a bottle of water and encouraged her to sip the liquid.

She blinked when he pressed the bottle into her hand. "Drink. The water will help."

With coaxing, she sipped the liquid. When she started shivering, he sat and gathered her close to his side, wrapping his arms around her to share his body heat.

By the time Jones finished grilling Cade for details of the shooting, Lacey was boneless, the shivers gone. Her eyes were closed, breathing even. Jake's lips curved. Had she fallen asleep? No, he thought. Drowsing maybe, but not asleep.

Jones crouched on the other side of Lacey. "She okay?"

"She said she wasn't injured." Jake didn't completely trust her assessment, though. Shock or adrenaline could mask symptoms of an injury. "We hit the ground hard."

"Better than a bullet. Tell me what happened."

While Jake ran through the events of the past few minutes and what he'd observed, the detective wrote notes in his small notebook.

"Did you see the shooter?"

"Not enough. I focused on protecting Lacey."

"What did you get?"

"Male, big, baseball cap pulled low on his forehead, dark shirt. Cade already told you about the vehicle."

A short nod. "I can already tell you it's Yvonne's SUV. The plates and vehicle match."

"Figured. The killer is desperate to isolate Lacey."

The detective's attention shifted to the woman in Jake's arms. His eyebrows rose. "She's asleep?"

Not willing to confirm or deny the assertion, he said, "Adrenaline dump."

"Sorry, but I need to talk to her."

"I'll do it." Jake ran the backs of his fingers over her cheek. "Lacey."

Her eyelids lifted. She turned her head enough to see the detective. "I'm awake. Ask your questions."

"When did you become aware of the SUV following you?"

A smile curved her mouth. "When Jake told me we had a tail."

"What did you do?"

"Jake and I kept running. Cade circled behind to look at the license plate."

"Do you think he got the plates?"

"I know he got the plates. He's Fortress, like Jake. Child's play for all of them."

He asked her the same questions he'd asked Jake and Cade, received similar answers with one new piece of information.

"I noticed a flash of light on his right hand," Lacey said.

Jake tightened his grip on her. "What kind of flash?"

"He passed under a streetlight about the time he pulled the trigger." She frowned. "Maybe a ring."

"Would you be able to identify it?" Jones asked.

"Not a chance. Everything happened too fast."

Jake exchanged glances with Cade. Zane could help if a traffic cam or security camera resolution was good enough. Of course, the Fortress techs could do amazing things with their gadgets and programs.

After Jones questioned Lacey a few more minutes and learned nothing more, he asked Cade to remain on the scene. "You and Lacey and the Walkers can go back to the hotel. Do me a favor. Stay in your rooms and get some rest. I need a chance to process the clues I already have before you provide new ones."

Jake chuckled as he helped Lacey to her feet. “We’ll do our best to stay out of trouble.” But if trouble came knocking on his door, all bets were off.

CHAPTER THIRTY-FIVE

Jake opened the suite door and ushered Lacey inside. Veronica closed and locked the door. She took a seat at the table facing the door, weapon close at hand.

He motioned for Lacey to sit on the bed. "Let me check your stitches."

"My arm is fine, Jake."

"I need to make sure." He still wasn't convinced he hadn't hurt her when he took Lacey to the ground to avoid the shooter's bullets.

She tilted her head. "Only if I check your burns afterward."

He grinned. Feisty future doctor. "Deal." He helped her take off the lightweight jacket she wore over her shirt. Jake removed the bandage from her arm. Relief swept through him. The stitches held despite the jostling and her wound didn't appear infected. "Looks good."

Taking the opportunity to change the dressing, he used a waterproof bandage this time. "You can take a shower with that one."

Her face brightened. "Really? Thank goodness. Keeping your arm dry while you wash your hair is hard. Your turn. I want to check your back."

"Yes, ma'am." He reached back, tugged off his shirt, and turned. Lacey's soft hands smoothed over his skin, her touch branding him with her sweet heat. "Well, Doc?" That earned him a gentle poke in his side.

"Not yet. Your back looks good." She pressed a kiss to his shoulder blade. "Real good."

Good to know his body appealed to Lacey.

"What happened to your back?" Veronica asked.

"Minor burns from the cabin explosion."

"You need more ointment." Lacey leaned around his shoulder to see his face. "The burns will disappear in two or three days."

He handed her the tube of burn ointment from his mike bag.

"Hard to believe you managed to tick someone off this fast, Jake." Veronica settled back in the chair.

Jake narrowed his eyes. "You're not funny, Vonnie."

She gave him an unrepentant grin. "Adam wouldn't agree with you."

"Your husband adores you. His opinion doesn't count."

Lacey recapped the tube of ointment and handed it to Jake. "His opinion counts more than anyone else's."

He captured her hand and pressed a kiss to her palm.

Veronica's eyes widened. "Something I should know?"

"I'm in love with Lacey and plan to marry her as soon as she sets a date."

Shock kept her immobile for a few seconds. When she moved, Veronica leapt to her feet and grabbed Jake and then Lacey in a hug. "Congratulations. I'm thrilled for you though surprised at the speed."

He shrugged. "I've been getting to know Lacey for months and falling more in love with her every day. It was inevitable. How could I resist her?"

"Do you feel the same?" Veronica asked.

"He's wonderful. Falling in love with him was a slow fall for me, too. After Frank, I didn't trust myself, but I couldn't resist Jake."

"Adam will be happy. He's been concerned Frank would worm his way back into your life."

"Not a chance. He's moved on to another woman. Frank hasn't bothered me since Adam and Brent talked to him."

A knock on the door alerted them to Cade's return. Jake let in the two Fortress operatives. "Anything new from Jones?"

Adam kissed his wife before he replied. "He found a couple bullets, one in a store with a broken window, the other embedded in the wall of that store. Forty caliber rounds."

"Shell casings?"

"None." He took in Jake's bare torso. "You hurt?"

He shook his head. "Lacey wanted to check the burns on my back."

Veronica laced her fingers with her husband's. "Adam, Lacey has something good to tell you."

"I'm ready for good news."

"Jake and I are engaged."

Stunned silence greeted her announcement. Adam hugged Lacey, his embrace loose. "I'm happy for you. You deserve better than Frank. Jake is a good man."

"I paid attention to what you said, Adam." She patted his muscled arm. "That day in Coffee House changed my life. You made me face the truth. Thank you."

"Jake will treat you like a princess." A hard glance came Jake's direction. "If he doesn't, he'll receive a visit from me and Brent."

Jake would never mistreat a woman, especially one he adored. "The boss doesn't know. Let Lacey tell him and Rowan."

"No problem. Have you talked to Zane?"

Jake shook his head. "I was more interested in checking Lacey's arm."

"Call him. We need information. The cops have little to go on."

He called Zane and put the phone on speaker.

"Murphy."

"It's Jake."

"Hold." A muffled murmur came through the speaker, then a series of thumps and a door opening and closing. "Go."

"Sorry to wake you."

"I'm considering it practice for when the baby arrives."

Jake grinned at the reminder that Zane's wife, Claire, was expecting their first child in a few months. Adam grinned at the mention of his future nephew or niece. That baby would have many people vying to babysit. "You're on speaker with Adam, Vonnie, Cade, and Lacey."

"What do you need?"

"Your hacking skills."

A soft chuckle. "Nothing I like better, especially if it involves a fed database. What am I hacking?"

"Traffic and security cams near the corner Magnolia and Sharon in Winston. Drive-by shooting."

"Injuries?"

"No."

Keys clicked for a few minutes.

"Z, are you in your home office or just on the laptop?" Jake asked.

"Office."

"Run the name Noah Holt."

"DOB?"

"Don't know, but his father is Senator Randy Holt."

A soft whistle. "That narrows things down fast. I'll see what I can find on him and his father. Got into the traffic cams. What am I looking for?"

"Black SUV."

"How many of those are in town besides our three?" the tech asked, wry wit in his voice.

"This one is distinctive," Cade said. "The vehicle followed Jake, Lacey, and me as we ran the streets around the hotel." His smile had a hard edge to it. "It also has the back window shot out."

"The SUV is my mother's," Lacey said.

"Get a look at the shooter?"

"Happened too fast." Jake wrapped his hand around Lacey's. "He was aiming for me."

"Wouldn't make sense for the killer to shoot Lacey when his whole focus is capturing her."

Jake tightened his grip on Lacey's hand. "He's a lousy shot. He missed me and could have easily hit her instead. See if you can get me a shot of his face. One other thing. Lacey noticed a flash of light on the shooter's right hand."

"A ring?"

"Possibly."

More keys clicked, then, "Got it. Definitely Yvonne's SUV. Good thing you have fast reflexes, Jake. I'll hunt for security cams along the route, clean up the images. Maybe we'll get lucky."

"How long?"

"Two hours. I'll text you when I finish."

"Send the info to our team plus Cade," Adam said.

"Roger that." He ended the call.

"What do we do in the mean time?" Lacey asked.

"Rest."

She scowled. "How can you say that? The way I feel right now I might not sleep tonight at all."

"You will." Jake squeezed her hand. "When the adrenaline crash hits, you won't be able to keep your eyes open."

Cade handed Jake his phone. "On missions, we sleep and eat every chance we get. At times during a mission, we may not have the chance to do either. We take advantage of the downtime."

"Speaking of sleep, I need more." Veronica rose and kissed her husband's jaw. "Come on, Adam. Jake, if you need us again, we'll be across the hall. Remy and Lily will be here around 7:00."

"Any information comes through, I want to know," Adam said as he and Veronica left.

Jake tugged Lacey to her feet. "If you want to shower, do it now. Leave the connecting door open." After she went to her room, Jake turned to Cade. "I'll take the first watch."

"I'll keep an eye on things while you shower." His friend's lips curved. "I bet you'll finish before Lacey."

Cade was right. Jake had time to shower, dress, and brew Lacey a cup of chamomile mint tea by the time her bathroom door opened. "Let me know when you're ready for company, Lacey."

She appeared in the doorway, dressed in a hooded long-sleeved navy cotton shirt and pants. "Anything from Zane?"

"Not yet." He turned to Cade. "I'll be with Lacey for a while." At least until she went to sleep. Maybe longer. He'd come too close to losing her tonight. He wasn't ready to leave her yet.

Jake carried his laptop and the tea into Lacey's room. He nudged the connecting door almost closed so they wouldn't disturb Cade. "If I check the railing first, would you like to sit on the balcony while you sip your tea? We're protected from the wind on this side of the hotel so you shouldn't be cold."

She smiled. "Sounds good."

"Grab a blanket." Jake carried her tea to the balcony table and checked the railing. Solid. Confirmed what he and Cade suspected. The killer tried to trim down Lacey's protection.

"It's safe," he told her when she came to his side, blanket clutched in her hands.

"Come sit with me. How long will you be on duty?"

"Three hours. I'll sleep until 4:00. We'll figure out our priorities from there." Jake tucked the blanket around Lacey and handed her the hot drink he'd doctored with a packet of sugar.

She snuggled into his side as she sipped. "You sweetened the tea?"

"Yes. Drink it anyway." She didn't add sweetener to her drinks, but under the circumstances she could use the calories.

"Bossy. Good thing I love you."

"The only time I won't budge on an issue is if your health or safety is at risk. Other than that, everything is negotiable."

They sat in silence while Lacey finished her tea. After Jake placed the empty cup on the table, Lacey loosened one end of the blanket and draped it over him.

"I don't want you to chill, either."

Amusement and tenderness ribboned through him. The brisk breeze was nothing compared to some of the downright frigid temperatures he'd endured during missions. Freezing wasn't the norm. Usually, they were sent to hotter climates. No hardship on his part. Jake hated to be cold.

They sat in the quiet darkness, watching the leaves dance in the breeze, and the bushes sway. Off in the distance, a dog barked.

"When will I meet your family?" Lacey asked.

"After your mother is mobile enough to care for herself. We'll make time to visit around my deployments and your schedule at the coffee shop." He turned to her. "We need to go before the end of the year."

"Why?"

"Once you start school, a trip out of town will be difficult."

Her head whipped his direction. "I haven't applied yet."

"That's why you need to start the application process."

"Will Mom be well enough for me to return to Nashville by the first of the year?"

Jake cupped her cheek with his palm, thumb brushing over the soft skin. "Unless she has a major setback, Yvonne should be fine by then. If not, we'll make sure your mother has help to function independently."

"I still don't have the money, Jake."

"Talk to Brent first. If Fortress won't pick up the tab, we'll consider other options." Including Jake paying her tuition. She was going to be his wife. He'd count it a privilege to fund her education. "It's time to go after your dream."

Lacey circled his neck with her arms and kissed him, slow and deep. "Thank you."

"For what?"

"Believing in me."

"I know you can do this. You just have to want it bad enough to not let anything or anyone stand in your way." And that included her mother.

For a few minutes, they discussed colleges in the Nashville area. By the time Lacey was ready to go inside, she had narrowed her choices down to one university for her pre-med studies.

"Is it all right if I sit at your table and work? I'll leave the connecting door open."

She studied his face in silence a moment. "You're afraid to leave me."

"Reluctant is a more accurate term."

Lacey's expression softened. "Stay, as long as you promise to lay down when Cade relieves you."

He nodded. He would have promised her almost anything, as long as he heard her breath and knew she was safe. Once Lacey was under the covers and asleep, Jake grabbed his laptop.

Two hours later, his phone buzzed with an incoming text. He checked the screen, his heart rate ratcheting up a notch. Zane had sent results to Jake's work email.

A few keystrokes brought up the first file. He watched the whole incident from beginning to end several times, each run through reiterating how close he came to losing Lacey.

Finally, he clicked on the second file. Jake's breath caught, fury burning through him.

CHAPTER THIRTY-SIX

Lacey shook her head. “This can’t be.” She handed Jake his phone. “Zane’s wrong.” Wasn’t he?

“I’m sorry, babe. Z double checked everything. He’s the shooter.”

“But why? I’ve never done anything to him. Will doesn’t have a reason to hurt us.”

“The picture doesn’t lie, Lacey.” Cade squeezed her shoulder.

“I’m telling you, something’s wrong. Look at his face. He looks terrified, not like a serial killer out to shoot his elusive target.”

“I noticed,” Jake said. “Let’s find him and get some answers.” His voice was mild, the look in his eyes anything but nonthreatening.

From Jake’s expression, talking was only one thing he had in mind when they confronted Will Beckett. Somehow, she had to prevent Jake from beating the crooked cop to a pulp. He would feel justified, but Lacey was sure Will’s fellow officers, not to mention his father, wouldn’t agree with Jake’s assessment. “Shouldn’t we call Todd? He might find Will faster than we can.”

"We'll call him," Cade said. "After."

Uh oh. That didn't sound good. "After what?"

He just smiled.

She turned. "Jake."

"Trust us. We know what we're doing."

"Don't give the police an excuse to toss you two in jail. You still have the lawyer's name on speed dial?"

Cade chuckled. "I don't think your future wife has much faith in your self-control, buddy."

Jake's lips twitched. "She's probably right. He could have killed her last night."

"He didn't, though. In fact, there's not a scratch on either of you. You think it's possible he deliberately missed?"

"That's one of the many questions I plan to ask." Jake called Zane.

"Murphy. What do you need, Jake?"

"You're on speaker with Cade and Lacey. I need Will Beckett. Find his cell phone number and ping it. Got a few questions for the soon-to-be former cop."

"Hold." Zane was back within two minutes. "Sent you the coordinates and address. He's been in the same place since minutes after the shooting."

"Thanks. If he changes location, tell me."

"Will do. Lacey, how do you feel this morning?"

"Not bad. A little sore in places. Jake tackles like a linebacker. Since he saved me from a bullet, I'll happily take an over-the-counter pain reliever for a few sore muscles."

"Things in Winston will heat up now. Stick with Jake and Cade. They'll make sure you return home in one piece."

"That's the plan."

And he was gone.

Jake checked the information Zane sent. "You recognize this address, Lacey?"

She came up blank. "Sorry." Where was that?

"Looks like it's on the east side of town." He turned to Cade. "Suit up. Let's have a talk with this clown."

Lacey laid her hand on Jake's forearm. "I want to go with you." She saw the refusal in his eyes. "Hear me out. You don't know him like I do. I'll know if he's lying. Besides, nothing will happen to me. Will won't touch me with you and Cade at my side."

Jake listened to her impassioned speech while he strapped on weapons, including a wicked looking black knife with a huge blade. Good grief. "Do you carry that many weapons on missions?" Lacey asked.

"More plus the ammo." He smiled as he tugged his black t-shirt over some kind of vest. "Gun stores aren't handy when we're in the desert or jungle."

When he finished tying his black combat boots, Lacey scanned him from head to toe. Wow.

Jake's eyebrow rose. "What?"

"You look hot."

With a laugh, he hugged her. "You're biased."

Only a little. Whew. He and Cade were built. "Take me with you, Jake. I want to hear what Will has to say for myself."

"All right. Remember to do everything we tell you without question. I don't know what's going on, but there's more to what's happening than we think."

She hurried to her room to grab a jacket and her cell phone. The two operatives were waiting by the door when she returned.

Instead of going to the elevator, Jake steered her toward the stairs. "Don't want to alarm anyone with our gear."

Smart. They looked capable and deadly. They climbed into Jake's SUV. He cranked the engine, entered the information Zane sent him into the navigation system, and drove from the hotel parking lot.

Lacey's brow furrowed as they drove from town and headed toward the mountains. They rode in silence until Jake turned into a subdivision with large homes sitting atop acres of well-landscaped lawns.

"Small-town police work must pay well," Cade said.

Jake drove through the neighborhood until he reached a large three-story house with gray stone on the outside and black shutters at each window. "Beckett is in there." He continued driving to the end of the block and turned the corner.

Lacey frowned. Weren't they going to stop? "What are we doing?"

"Scouting the area."

Jake circled the block and parked three houses down. "We'll walk from here."

"Why not park in the driveway."

"We don't want Beckett to know we're here. He might run."

They exited the SUV. "Wait," Jake murmured. He went to the back of his SUV, rummaged in his Go bag, and returned to Lacey's side. "Take off your watch."

Intrigued, she handed it to him. He flipped the watch over and pressed something to the band. When he was satisfied the object would stay, he buckled the time piece around her wrist again. Jake threaded his fingers through hers as they approached the house. He signaled Cade, and the other operative slipped around the corner of the house, hidden from view.

The shadows were deep and long in the pre-dawn darkness. If Jake hadn't been holding her hand, she wouldn't have been able to see him. His entire body was clothed in black. Nothing on him gleamed or glittered.

They crept along the side of the house until they reached a corner. Jake released her hand and signaled for her to stay in place.

Lacey strained to listen for sounds indicating someone saw them creeping along the house although the effort was futile. The only thing she heard was her pulse pounding in her ears. She wasn't normally skittish at night. Being out here like this, however, was spooky.

Was Will the serial killer? It didn't make sense to her. Will didn't care enough about anyone but himself. He was in law enforcement and knew the chances of being caught were good. Lacey didn't believe Will was smart enough to elude detection this long. From the discussion she and Jake had with Todd earlier, the killer hadn't left any clues behind. Will couldn't have pulled that off. According to rumor around town, he'd failed the detective's exam twice in the last three years.

Jake returned to Lacey. "It's clear," he murmured. "Cade's waiting at the back door."

She followed him around the corner. The other operative stood near the door, his gaze scouring the area.

"Yvonne's SUV is in the detached garage," he whispered when they reached his side.

"Door?" Jake asked.

"Locked. Alarm's been disabled."

A nod. "Turn around, Lacey."

She started to question him, then thought better of it. Protecting her again. Lacey spun until her back was to him. A moment later, he said, "Inside."

Cade slipped into the darkened house first, followed by Jake and Lacey. They walked into a dimly lit kitchen. Stainless steel appliances and granite or marble countertops glistened in the low light.

Jake glanced at her. "Stay behind me." When she nodded, the two men began a cursory search of the rooms on the first floor. No sign of Will down here.

They climbed the stairs to the second floor in silence. Cade took the right side of the hallway while Jake angled toward the left. Jake and Cade cleared each room. Nothing.

Where was Will?

With a hand signal, Jake led the way to the third floor. On this level were four large suites. Again, the two men split up. Jake and Lacey went into the first suite. Beautiful furniture. And the art on the walls? Exquisite.

Jake turned toward the door on the right and twisted the knob. He opened the door just enough to see inside, then backed away. Nudging Lacey against the wall by the door, he pressed his lips to her ear. “Don’t move.”

He left and returned a minute later with Cade on his heels. Jake bent to speak into Lacey’s ear. “Will is in bed in the room on the right. I know you want to hear what he has to say. I respect that, but I don’t want you in his sight. If you wait by the door to the room, you’ll hear everything that’s said. Will you do that for me?”

Lacey nodded. She had a feeling this wouldn’t be the last compromise she made to accommodate Jake’s protective streak.

He pressed a kiss to her forehead in thanks, then signaled Cade. The other operative slipped into the darkened room with Jake a step behind.

Lacey moved to the left side of the door. While she didn’t have a line of sight into the room, she could tell from the shadows on the wall that Jake and Cade had split up and were on both sides of the bed.

She prayed the nightmare ended and her mother would be safe now.

A muffled shout reached her ears.

“We need to talk, Beckett,” Jake said.

More muffled words.

“I’m going to lift my hand. Answer my questions, and I’m out of here.”

“How did you get in here?”

“Doesn’t matter.”

“I’m a cop, you idiot. You’re going to jail.”

Despite his harsh words, Lacey heard the bald fear in Will's voice. Was he afraid of Jake and Cade, or afraid they knew what he'd been up to?

"I know your secret, Beckett."

"You're crazy. I haven't done anything."

"I have evidence that says different."

"You don't understand."

Lacey frowned, wishing she could see Will's face. He sounded desperate. What was going on?

A hard hand clamped around her mouth and something sharp stung her neck. Before she could make a noise to draw Jake's attention, the world grayed, then faded into black.

CHAPTER THIRTY-SEVEN

Jake glowered at the cowering cop pressing himself deeper into the mattress to put distance between them. "Make me understand." He saw the exact instant when Beckett decided to brazen it out.

"You don't have evidence."

"Wrong. Traffic and security cameras caught a great picture of you with a weapon in your hand. You fired at us from Yvonne's SUV on Magnolia seven hours ago. You've been playing a very dangerous game for six years, haven't you, Beckett? The FBI want to talk to you."

"Why did you pull the trigger?" Cade asked, his voice a low rumble. "You could have killed Lacey."

"I don't want to hurt anyone."

Jake analyzed the words, the pitch of his voice, and compared them to his other encounters with Beckett. Lacey was right. Something was terribly wrong. No question Beckett was the shooter, but he acted terrified rather than defiant because he'd been caught. Was he afraid of prison time as a former cop or someone on the outside? "Talk to me or I'll make your life so miserable, you'll wish you were dead."

"I can't," Beckett whispered.

"Someone is targeting Lacey, and I don't think it's you despite that stunt you pulled last night on the street."

"She's okay, right?"

"Your aim is lousy."

A scowl from the sweating cop. "I hit what I aim at."

Now they were getting somewhere. "You aimed at the store window and the wall?"

"That's right. I don't want to hurt anyone," he repeated.

"But you've hurt plenty of people in the last six years, haven't you? You know we won't stop until we find the man who hurt Yvonne. Why did you aim away from us? A smart man would have taken out the threat. But you didn't. Why not?"

He shook his head, refusing to answer.

"Come on, man. The game's up. The only person who matters to me is Lacey. You need to tell us who wants her so we can stop him."

"He'll kill me."

Confirmation of what he suspected. Beckett wasn't in this alone. He wasn't smart enough to pull off so many murders without detection for six years. No question that he was involved, but he wasn't the brains behind this operation. Who was the dominant partner? His father? "Where is your father?"

Beckett shook his head. "I don't know. I haven't seen him since before dinner last night."

Jake had seen the empty police chief's suite across the hall. "Is he the man after Lacey?"

"What? No! Dad would never do something like that. He might have been hot for Yvonne, but Lacey's too young for him."

"Are you sure?"

The cop swallowed hard, nodded.

The skin at the back of Jake's neck prickled. He signaled Cade to keep questioning Beckett. He pulled his Sig and, staying in the shadows, approached the doorway into the sitting room.

He stepped into the room, scanning. Empty. Ice water poured through Jake's veins. Where was Lacey? As much as she'd wanted to hear the conversation with Beckett, she wouldn't walk away. Could they have missed someone inside the house?

Jake hurried to the other side of the suite and checked the other room. No sign of another person. A quick check of the hallway and he had to accept the inevitable conclusion. Lacey was gone. Fear like he'd never known flooded his body. He couldn't lose her. Lacey Coleman was everything to him. Without her, his life would be an eternity of loneliness and heartache.

He rushed back into the Beckett's room and jerked the cop up by his pajama top. "Who else is in this house?"

Will tugged at Jake's wrist with one hand, a ring glinting in the dim light. "No one, I swear."

He leaned closer. "Try again. Lacey was right outside this room and now she's gone. Who else is here, Beckett?"

The other man groaned. "No. Oh, no. You brought her here? You should have taken Lacey back to Nashville. He's always watching the house. He has a key, and now he's taken her. You handed her to him on a silver platter."

Jake twisted the material in his hands until seams popped. "Quite whining and give me a name."

Beckett shut his eyes. "I don't want to die."

"I've got news for you, Beckett. If you don't give me this clown's name, he won't have a chance to kill you. I'll take you out myself in the most painful method possible. Who has my girlfriend?"

"Noah," he choked out. "Noah Holt."

"He's the one who killed all those women?" Jake pressed.

Beckett looked as though he wanted to cry when he nodded.

"He'll go to ground," Cade said. "Where is he going, Beckett?"

"I don't know, I swear."

Jake shoved the pathetic cop away from him before he killed him. Trusting Cade to keep Beckett in place, Jake grabbed his cell phone.

Two rings later, a gruff voice answered. "Murphy."

"It's Jake. I need help."

"Hold on a sec."

He paced to contain the clawing in his gut to do something, anything, to find Lacey. Z was his best chance.

"Go."

"Activate my tracking tag."

Keys clicked. "Lacey?"

"Noah Holt has her."

"He's the serial killer?"

"Looks like it." More keys clicked. "Please, tell me you've got her, Zane."

"Signal is strong and steady. I sent the link to your phone and Cade's. I'll keep monitoring her position from here in case you hit a dead zone."

"Thanks. Tap into the traffic cams. I want to know what he's driving." He ended the call. "Got her." He inclined his head toward Beckett. "Secure him and let's go."

Beckett scrambled back. "Wait. You can't just leave me here. What if he gets away from you? I'll be a sitting duck."

"You better hope he doesn't."

Cade made short work of securing Beckett with zip ties.

Instead of going to the back entrance, Jake ran out the front door, leaving it unlocked to provide easier access for law enforcement. They sprinted to the SUV. Jake cranked the engine as Cade tapped on the link to the Fortress tracking program.

"Got it. Turn right at the entrance to the subdivision. Holt just drove onto State Route 1."

Though it took teeth-gritting discipline, he kept to the speed limit while in the subdivision. The last thing he wanted to do was injure an innocent civilian in his haste to find Lacey. If Holt was driving, he couldn't hurt her.

Once out of the subdivision, he floored the accelerator. Jake activated his Bluetooth and called Todd Jones. "It's Jake."

"Oh, man. I haven't cleaned up the paperwork from the last encounter we had. What now?"

"Lacey is missing."

"How did that happen? I thought you were keeping close tabs on her."

"Never mind that now. We think Noah Holt took her."

"Holt's the serial killer?"

"You can get answers from Will Beckett. He's the one who shot at us last night. Also, he hasn't seen his father since dinner last night."

"You think the chief is involved in the murders?" His voice was incredulous.

"Don't know. At this point, I don't care. That's your problem. I have a tracker on Lacey. Cade and I are going after her."

"This is police business, Davenport. You need to stand down."

"If our positions were reversed, would you?"

Jones uttered a muffled curse, then said, "At least call in Torres. The case is his, and he needs to be on scene to make the arrest."

If there was an arrest. The way Jake felt at the moment, he couldn't guarantee Holt would be alive to face a trial. "I'll call him as soon as I get off the phone with you. You'll find Beckett secured to his bed."

"You're sure he's the shooter?"

"Security and traffic cams don't lie."

"Fortress hacked the cameras?"

Jake remained mute.

"Fine. Have your tech person send the footage to my email from an anonymous source."

"Copy that."

"You better be right about this, Jake, or my career in Winston is toast."

"Later." He ended the call.

"Turn right at the next intersection," Cade said.

Jake followed the instruction, skidding around the corner and racing up the entrance ramp to State Route 1. He activated the Bluetooth again and called the FBI agent.

"Torres."

"It's Jake Davenport. I think Noah Holt has Lacey."

"Tell me everything."

He summarized what they knew and the events of the past twelve hours. "I put a tracker on Lacey's watch. Cade and I are in pursuit."

"Send me the link. I'll be leaving the hotel in two minutes."

"Copy that."

"Jake, I need this clown alive. His victims deserve justice, and their families need to see him behind bars. Don't go vigilante on me. I don't want to toss one of the good guys in jail. You hear me?"

"I got it." But he couldn't make any guarantees. Jake would do whatever was necessary to protect the woman who owned his heart.

CHAPTER THIRTY-EIGHT

Lacey woke in darkness. For some reason, the bed was uncomfortable. Frowning, she tried to find a more comfortable position and failed.

At that moment, she woke enough to realize she wasn't in the hotel in bed. The rocking motion clued Lacey in that she was in a vehicle. Memories of following Jake and Cade into Will's house sparked. She'd been listening to Jake's interrogation of Will. How had she ended up in a vehicle? Maybe she passed out and Jake carried her to his SUV. That would be embarrassing, if true.

Then she remembered a hard hand clamped over her mouth and the sting of pain in her neck. After that, nothing. Her heart rate zoomed into the stratosphere. She didn't pass out. Someone injected a drug in her neck and knocked her out. How long had she been unconscious? Shouldn't the sun have risen by now?

She strained to see in the darkness and realized her eyes were covered by a black cloth. When she tried to raise her hands and remove the blindfold, she couldn't. Her wrists were tied behind her back.

Lacey wrestled down the panic threatening to overwhelm her and explored her surroundings by feel. Carpet covered the floor and a hump dug into her side and hip. Whoever grabbed her tossed her in the floorboard of the backseat. More exploration convinced her nothing was on the floor to use in freeing herself from the bonds.

She considered whether to let her abductor know she was awake and decided against it. If Jake managed to find her in time to save her life, she would insist the medic give her lessons on escaping bonds. No, *when* Jake found her, not if.

She thought back through the seconds before she blacked out and couldn't come up with an identity. She had been inside Will Beckett's house at the time. Is it possible her abductor was the police chief?

Probably not, she decided. Taking Lacey from his own house would be stupid. Jake would confront the police chief in his quest to find her. Had Jake and Cade missed someone in the house in their search? She rejected that idea, too. No way. They'd been almost soundless in their search. Lacey doubted anyone would have heard them soon enough to hide from the two operatives.

The only logical conclusion was the kidnapper had been watching the house. The possibilities were endless, but in that neighborhood, her bet was on Noah Holt. He was tight with Will, had been since they were kids. Noah had enough money that she wouldn't be the least surprised if he lived in this exclusive area.

As she thought about the long-standing connections between Will and Noah, Lacey wiggled her wrists, hoping to loosen the bonds enough to slip her hands free. At this point, she was helpless to defend herself except with her feet. If Noah had taken her from Will's house, she would need more than luck to defeat such a big, muscle-bound man.

Lacey scowled, anger building at the man who was attempting to steal her future. She had plans and dreams, big ones, and she wouldn't give up without a fight. All she had to do was survive long enough for Jake and Cade to find her.

The vehicle turned onto a rough road. At the speed they were traveling, the rutted track strained the suspension system and repeatedly slammed Lacey's already bruised ribs into the hump on the floor.

She rolled onto her stomach. The beating she took wasn't any better, but at least the position gave her ribs a break. Lacey didn't know how many miles they traveled or how much time had passed when the driver slowed to a stop. The driver turned off the engine. A door opened, then slammed shut again. A moment later, the door at her back opened.

Hard hands yanked her backward out of the vehicle, then she was tossed over a muscular shoulder. After the pounding she'd already taken thanks to the lousy road, this latest insult to her body hurt.

The man carried her a couple minutes, then stopped. Keys jangled, then a door was unlocked and she was carried inside. The scent of wood filled her nostrils. The man carried her further inside the dwelling before dragging Lacey off his shoulder and tossing her onto a bed.

She tried to scramble away with no success. Having her hands secured behind her back hampered her efforts. A moment later, the blindfold was removed. Blinking against the sudden glare of light, Lacey's eyes took several seconds to adjust.

She scanned her surroundings. A cabin. Log walls. Wood floor. A colorful quilt on the bed. One window. If Lacey freed her hands, she could escape through the window.

"Don't even think about it," a male voice growled. "You wouldn't get ten feet before I captured you again, and I wouldn't be happy with you."

Lacey's attention shifted to the man who stood feet away from her, arms crossed over his chest. Dread coiled in her gut. "Let me go, Noah."

"Not a chance, sweetheart. I've waited six long years for you to come to me. Now that I finally have you, I'm not letting you walk away."

She needed to keep Noah talking to delay the inevitable. "I don't understand."

"You left me." He edged closer, a glower on his face, anger glittering in his eyes. "After all we meant to each other, you ran away from me."

Cold chills surged up Lacey's spine. He thought they had some kind of relationship before she left Winston? Nothing could be further from the truth. In the best interest of her health, however, she shouldn't enlighten him. Noah had created a relationship out of nothing, and pointing out he was wrong would end in disaster for her.

"I'm sorry, Noah. I didn't think you noticed me."

His eyebrows rose. "How could you not know? You talked to me all the time in school and when we ran into each other in town. I asked you out, but you always turned me down. You shouldn't have done that." His voice rose on those last words.

"I was underage until the day before I graduated from high school. I was protecting you, Noah. Please, don't be angry with me."

"Why did you leave me? We could have been together then."

Oh, man. This guy was seriously looney. What was the safest thing to say to that? "I wasn't strong enough for you six years ago. I needed to stand on my own before I would be worthy of someone like you." Spouting such nonsense made her want to throw up. But if it kept her alive, she'd tell Noah Holt anything his demented mind wanted to hear.

His expression softened as a satisfied smile curved his lips. "I knew there was an explanation for your behavior. However, I'm not pleased about Davenport. I'll have to punish you for spending time with him."

Was he serious? One look at Noah's face, and Lacey had to conclude he was. Time to nudge his thoughts in a different direction. "Where are we?"

"My cabin. I work hard and need a place to unwind." His eyes narrowed. "Of course, you would know that if you'd stayed where you belong."

"Why did you bring me here?"

"We need to be alone. Too many people would interfere."

"Interfere in what, Noah?"

"Training you to be my wife. I'm from an important family, Lacey. You'll be on the world stage from the moment we leave here. My father is going to be the president, you know. Your conduct and etiquette will have to be perfect to make up for your faulty genetics."

"Faulty genetics."

"Don't play dumb, sweetheart. It's not becoming of a lady. Your parents are less than desirable contributors to the gene pool. The only thing they did well was create you. I expect you to avoid any contact with your mother from now on. I won't tolerate her influence in our lives. No prostitute should ever step foot in the White House. If you defy me, I will take care of Yvonne permanently."

"Did you kidnap my mother?"

"I did it for you."

"How do you figure that?"

"The public would love you even more if you were in mourning over your mother's death." He shrugged. "I'll adjust the plan unless you want me to go ahead and take care of her now."

“No, you don’t have to do that. Mom won’t be a problem.” Not once Noah was behind bars where he couldn’t hurt anyone else. “Were you the one who sent Mom the money?”

He grinned. “You liked that gift?”

“Yes.”

“I did it for you. You work too hard taking care of yourself and your mother. I saw how tired you were each time you came home to me. I had to do something to help you.”

She had to get free before Noah decided to punish her for running out on him. “I appreciate that, Noah.” She rolled to her side. “Would you untie me, please? The binding is too tight and my hands are going numb.”

“The front door is locked with a deadbolt and I have the only key. You won’t escape me, Lacey. If you try, I will punish you.”

The same threat. “I understand.” A deadbolt lock meant her only avenue for escape if Jake and Cade didn’t arrive was the window. As long as she was still breathing, she had a chance.

Noah left the room and returned a moment later with a knife in his hand. “Turn onto your stomach.”

The idea of him at her back with a knife made her skin crawl as much as the idea of him touching her in any capacity, even to cut her bonds. Praying she wasn’t making the biggest and last mistake of her life, Lacey maneuvered herself onto her stomach and waited for either her hands to be freed or for Noah to plunge the blade deep into her body.

Hard hands grasped hers. The cold steel of the blade caressed her skin as it slid beneath the binding. A quick jerk, and her hands were free.

Although her first inclination was to run for the window or the door, instinct told Lacey that Noah was ready for any attempt to escape, eager for the chance to exact punishment as he'd threatened several times already.

Instead of running, Lacey turned over to face her demented schoolmate once more. She scooted toward the headboard on the side of the bed nearest the window. A small lamp sat on the nightstand. She could use the lamp as a weapon if nothing else came to mind. "Did you hurt all those missing women, Noah?"

"They weren't you. They acted like they were for a while, coming on to me and confusing me. But I soon learned the truth. They were fakes, hoping to cash in on my family fortune."

"That was clever of you to figure out their scheme so fast." She caught a shadow of movement beyond the door. Was it her imagination or had Jake and Cade found them this fast? "What now? We can't stay here a long time, you know."

A scowl. "Why not? You don't have anything else more important than satisfying my needs and desires. No one else matters in your life anymore, Lacey." He grabbed her ankles and jerked her down flat on her back. In the next instant, he was on top of her, holding her down with his considerable weight.

CHAPTER THIRTY-NINE

"No." Lacey turned her face away from his seeking mouth, body bucking to throw him off balance without much success. Noah outweighed her by a good 80 pounds.

Noah sat up and slapped her. A moment later, his hands were around her throat, squeezing. "No woman defies me, especially not you. You will learn to obey me. Anything and everything I want."

Lacey dug her nails into his hands and scored his skin. He bellowed in pain and rage, ripping his hands from her throat to shake them. She twisted and fought with a determined focus. With one hand, she fumbled on the nightstand for the lamp, grasped the neck, and swung it at Noah's head. She hit him with a glancing blow and managed to dislodge his body enough to bring her feet up between them. When Noah came back at her, hands aiming for her throat again, Lacey used both feet to shove him away from her. He flew back and hit the wall. Stunned, he slid to the floor.

In a flash, she leapt from the bed and lunged toward the window. Noah moaned as Lacey fumbled with the lock.

When it finally gave way, she shoved up the window, hoisted herself over the sill, and slid to the ground.

A howl of fury from Noah sent Lacey into a dead run. No use going for the SUV she saw parked in the driveway. She didn't have a key and, unlike the Fortress people, couldn't hot wire the ignition. Another skill to have Jake teach her.

She veered to the left toward the woods. Hoping the regular forest inhabitants were still asleep, she sprinted into the tree cover.

"Lacey, if you don't come to me, I'll go to the hospital and kill your mother."

Did he think that would stop her headlong flight to safety? Not a chance. Jake's teammates would never allow Noah near her mother. Him threatening her again did give an indication of his position and it was too close for comfort.

Lacey pushed herself to run faster, stumbling over exposed tree roots and skirting a fallen log. She had no idea where she was going. She just knew she had to run from Noah before he hurt her more than he already had.

"You'll never get away from me," Noah bellowed.

This time he sounded closer. Lacey scowled. How could that be? Her old schoolmate was not a jackrabbit. Of course, he was about six inches taller than her. His stride had to be longer which meant he covered more ground with every step.

Not daring to run faster for fear of twisting her ankle or knee and becoming a sitting duck, Lacey angled toward the sound of the water she heard nearby.

"Lacey!"

A gun fired behind her. Bark flew off the tree to her right, sending splinters of wood into her cheek and neck. Lacey darted into a thicker stand of trees and continued her dash toward the water.

She got a stitch in her side, clamped a hand over it, and kept running. She had plans for a future that didn't include Noah Holt.

Lacey shoved through a pair of bushes and skidded to a stop at the edge of a river. She scanned for a place to cross and couldn't find one. Fantastic. Guess she was getting wet this morning. Didn't matter as long as the dunking got her away from Noah.

She took two steps toward the water and a hard body slammed into her from the side. Before she got her breath back, strong hands wrapped around her throat. An infinity tattoo was on one wrist.

Noah's face was above her, his face twisted with rage. "You're like the others. You will learn to obey me if you want to live. Otherwise, I'll end you like I did all of them."

Lacey's vision began to darken around the edges as she continued to fight to free herself. In the recesses of her mind, Lacey recognized that she was losing the battle to stay alive until Jake arrived. Despair filled her. She wanted a life with her medic, one filled with laughter and love, maybe children. She couldn't let Noah steal that from her.

She got a sense of movement from her right, and then a shadow hurtled across the open space and dove for Noah, knocking his body off hers. As soon as his hands were away from Lacey's throat, she dragged in much needed air.

The sounds of grunts, curses, and fists pummeling flesh filled the area as Lacey shook her head to clear the fog of shock and oxygen deprivation. She turned her head in time to see Jake land a punch, flinging Noah against a tree.

Noah shoved off the trunk and came at Jake again, determination mixing with a kind of madness in his expression. The momentum threw both men onto the grass near her feet.

Lacey scrambled away from the fighting men.

"Get her out of here," Jake ordered as his punch snapped Noah's head to the right.

Cade scooped her up from the ground and carried her to the shelter of a tree farther from the action. He set her on the ground, pushing her hair back from her face. "You okay?"

She nodded. "Go help Jake." Her voice sounded raspy. "I'm fine."

"He doesn't need help taking down this clown."

"Then make sure he doesn't kill Noah. I don't want to visit my husband in prison. Go!"

"You stay right here. I'll be back in a minute." The operative raced back to the riverside as flashing lights came into view in the distance. Sirens screamed, growing louder as law enforcement vehicles moved closer. She wanted to help Jake, but knew she would only get in the way. Besides, Jake wouldn't want her near Noah. If he grabbed Lacey and used her as a hostage, he might get away and come after her and her mother again as well as other blond women who crossed his path. That outcome was unacceptable. No, far better for everyone involved if she stayed far away from the fray.

The fight continued for another minute with Cade looking on until Jake landed one last punch to Noah's face. Her kidnapper flew backward into a tree and slid to the ground with a groan. He didn't get up.

Breathing hard, Jake swiped at his face with his sleeve, his gaze locking with Lacey's. "Cade, secure Holt. Once I'm sure Lacey is all right, we'll take Holt to the cops and let them do whatever they want with him."

"Copy that." Cade grabbed Noah and flipped him onto his stomach. He pulled zip ties from his pocket and cinched Noah's hands behind his back, then began searching him for weapons.

Jake crossed the space between him and Lacey in four strides, and dropped to his knees, hands cupped around her shoulders. "Are you okay, baby? Did Noah hurt you?"

"I'm fine, Jake."

He nudged her into a strip of sunlight, and growled. "No, you aren't. Holt hit you." His shaking fingers brushed over her cheek where Noah had slapped her. He continued his examination, checking her limbs and torso for more injuries. "I should have killed him for what he did to you."

"You can't help me study for exams if you're behind bars."

A small smile curved his lips. "True. Come on." Jake stood and helped Lacey to her feet, keeping his arm around her waist for support. "The cops must have arrived on scene by now. I want Holt off my hands so I can concentrate on you."

Cade jerked Noah to his feet. "Move. You have a lot of explaining to do before you go to jail."

Noah fought to escape the operative, cursing loudly, demanding to be set free. "You don't know who you're messing with. I'll have your jobs and your freedom."

"Shut up, Holt," Jake snapped.

"Lacey is mine. No other man is going to touch her. I'm going to kill you, Davenport."

"Yeah? You're welcome to try if you ever get out of prison. Close your mouth and get moving before I think better of my decision to let you live."

Even from across the few feet separating her from Noah, Lacey could see the swelling on Noah's jaw and his split lip. She'd bet there were plenty of other bruises in places she couldn't see. Knowing Jake, he'd made sure Noah would remember his mistake in kidnapping Lacey for a long time.

Cade frog-marched Noah back toward the cabin, easily keeping him in line when the raving man tried to escape. A few feet ahead, Rafe Torres walked toward them with another agent at his heels.

He shook his head as he approached. "Should have known you wouldn't wait for the badges to show up."

Jake eased Lacey closer to his side. "It's a good thing we didn't. When we got here, Holt was strangling Lacey."

Torres shifted his gaze to her. "Is Noah Holt the man who kidnapped you?"

"Tell him the truth, sweetheart." Noah turned to stare at her, a warning in his eyes. "Tell him you came with me because we belong together."

Ignoring him, she nodded at the FBI agent. "Noah kidnapped and strangled me. He also told me he's the one who hurt Mom and the other women."

"No." Noah broke away from Cade and ran at Lacey. "Traitor," he screamed. "You're like all the other women. You deserve to die."

Jake stepped in front of her, blocking Noah. He took her former schoolmate down with a punch to the stomach and a knee to the face.

Torres and his companion hauled the bleeding man to his feet. "Looks like Holt might have a busted nose." Eyes twinkling, he turned to Jake. "I don't suppose you want to render aid to this man."

"Not a chance."

"Didn't think so. You're out of luck, Holt. You'll just have to go to the hospital for treatment. But don't worry. Two FBI agents will be keeping you company."

Torres and his companion walked with Noah between them. The group emerged from the woods to a cabin and yard full of local law enforcement and FBI agents milling around setting up a perimeter with crime scene tape.

"You don't know who you're messing with. My father will have all your badges."

Torres scowled. "Do yourself a favor and shut up, Holt." He signaled to one of the waiting FBI agents.

"Accompany Mr. Holt to the hospital. He's under arrest for kidnapping and attempted murder, and that's just for a start. Read him his rights."

"Yes, sir."

Brent's friend turned back to eye Lacey. "You need to get checked out at the hospital as well, Lacey."

"I'm okay."

"I need your injuries documented for the case against Holt."

Although she didn't need medical assistance, Lacey wanted to help the FBI put Noah away for a long time. She feared if he was released from prison, he would come after her and Jake again. "All right."

"I need you to answer questions before I send you to get checked out."

After a two-hour question-and-answer session, Torres said, "All right. I'm finished for now. Go to the hospital. I'll catch up with you later. Jake, don't leave town until you clear it with me."

"As long as I'm not called up for deployment."

"If you are, call me."

With a nod, Jake clasped Lacey's hand. "Come on. Time to make sure Holt didn't leave any lasting damage."

CHAPTER FORTY

"All right, young lady. You're free to go." Dr. Reacher patted Lacey's shoulder. "Considering what you went through, a few bumps and bruises are to be expected."

At the doctor's words, the knot in Jake's stomach loosened. "You're sure, Doc?"

"Positive. You have one tough lady here, Davenport. She's a keeper."

He smiled at the woman holding his hand. "Believe me, I'm well aware of that. I'm planning to marry her as soon as she gives me the go-ahead."

"Congratulations. Let me know the date of your wedding. I might drop in." He clapped Jake's shoulder and left.

"Told you I was all right." Lacey squeezed his hand.

He knew the truth. One minute more, and Holt could have killed Lacey. From her own admission, she had almost passed out by the time Jake tackled the senator's son.

"I needed a doctor's confirmation." Jake cupped the nape of her neck and drew her against his chest. "You scared me, Lacey. I was afraid I'd arrived too late."

"You arrived in the nick of time. Thank you for saving me again."

"I'm glad I was there. I can't believe Holt had built up an entire relationship with you from minor interactions over the years."

"Me, either. It's creepy. I don't know how he concocted that make-believe world because I wasn't nice to him. When he wouldn't take no for an answer, I became increasingly short with him." She frowned. "Did I cause him to hurt people?"

Jake brushed her lips with his. "No. He's mentally ill and has been for a long time. I think we'll find out his father knew and, rather than getting his son the treatment he needed, the senator kept it quiet."

"I want to see Mom now."

He walked with Lacey to the elevator. Adam greeted them outside Yvonne's room.

"Heard you caught your man. Good job, Jake."

"Thanks. Does Yvonne know?"

His teammate shook his head. "Vonnie and I thought you and Lacey would want to break the news. She'll be relieved to know she and her daughter are safe."

Jake knocked and pushed open the door, ushering Lacey inside.

"Hi, Mom."

"Lacey, what happened to your face?"

"Long story."

"I have nothing but time right now. Sit and spill."

As Lacey's story unfolded, Yvonne's uninjured hand fisted. "That lowlife scum," she said when her daughter had finished. "Where is he now?"

"Getting medical treatment." Lacey grinned. "Jake's handiwork."

Yvonne looked at him with approval.

"You don't have to worry about Holt anymore." Jake pressed her hand between his palms. "He won't bother you, Lacey, or any other woman again."

"What about Will? What role does he play in all this?"

"Will was an unwilling accomplice, blackmailed into helping Holt with his obsession. The Becketts were desperate to keep the power and money rolling in from their association with the Holts. When Will was seventeen, he and Noah were with a fifteen-year-old girl. They got caught up in a sex game that went wrong. That's when Noah got his first taste of killing although Will got the blame for the girl's death. Noah fixated on Lacey, creating a relationship in his own mind. He became angry when she moved to Nashville, and he started taking substitutes and killing them in his rage."

"Did Chief Beckett know?"

"According to Agent Torres, he did."

"He knew Noah had me, didn't he? Wayne left me out there with that crazy man."

"I'm sorry, Yvonne. He will pay for that. The FBI arrested him at the house of his long-time lover."

"We do have some good news to tell you, Mom."

Yvonne wiped tears from her face. "I could stand to hear something good."

Lacey smiled at Jake before turning back to her mother. "Jake and I are getting married."

Surprise, then joy filled Yvonne's face. "Oh, honey. That's fantastic. I'm happy for both of you. Do you have any idea when the wedding will be?"

"I have an idea, but I want to talk it over with Jake before I announce a date."

"Well, I hope I'm out of these casts before your wedding although I won't complain if you don't want to wait." She smiled. "The wedding pictures would prompt some questions from my grandchildren one day."

Mental pictures of a couple kids with Lacey's beautiful features and maybe his hair popped into his head. Warmth spread through Jake's body at the thought of holding his own children, caring for them, loving them. Yeah, he longed to have the privilege of guiding his and Lacey's children to adulthood. The journey was sure to be exciting and full of laughter.

"It will be a while, Mom. I have some schooling to get through before that happens." Beside him, Lacey stiffened, as though waiting for her mother to reject her dream again.

Her mother studied her a moment, then nodded. "It's your life. Do what you think is best." She turned to Jake. "You take care of my daughter."

"She will be my first priority in everything, Yvonne. You have my word."

"Good. I want you to take her home to Nashville."

Jake froze. "Why?"

"She needs to get on with her life."

"Mom, you're going to need help for a while."

"Harley and I talked after you left last night. We're getting married right away." Yvonne's cheeks flushed. "We don't have a reason to wait. Life is short and we're not young anymore. He'll pick up the marriage license today and we'll go to the justice of the peace as soon as I leave the hospital. Harley can help me with whatever physical assistance I need."

Huh. Jake hadn't seen this coming although he should have. Yvonne and Harley had been keeping their relationship under wraps for months. Now that Lacey knew and approved, they didn't have a reason to wait. "We'll stay until you marry Harley at least. In the meantime, Lacey and I will talk about what she feels like she needs to do."

Three hours later, Jake walked into the hotel room with Lacey at his side to find Cade hefting his Go bag over one shoulder. His eyebrows rose. "You're leaving?"

"Yeah. My team is being deployed. I already cleared it with Torres. I have to check with him when I return." He turned to Lacey. "Send me an invitation to the wedding."

"I'll do that." She gave him a hug and stepped back.

Jake shook his hand. "Thanks, Cade. I owe you."

"One day, I might cash in on that favor."

As he opened the door, Lacey placed a hand on his forearm. "Ask Sasha for a date. She'd be crazy to turn you down."

His face reddened as he nodded and walked to the stairs.

Once Cade was gone, Jake shut and locked the door. He wrapped his arms around Lacey, grateful she was safe. "I think your mother will be leaving the hospital in another day, two at the most. What do you want to do after she marries Harley?"

She laughed, the sound a little raspy from the trauma to her throat. "I don't want to interfere with the newlyweds. My main concern was that Mom had someone to help her. I think between Harley and Loretta, she'll be fine."

"That leaves us. You said you had a date in mind for our wedding. What were you thinking about?"

"New Year's Eve. I know it's fast, but what do you think?"

He thought about the logistics, nodded. "That will work. I'll make sure Brent doesn't schedule my team for deployment around that time. Are you sure you'll have enough time to prepare, Lacey?"

"It's eight weeks away. That will give me time to get the ball rolling for school, find a dress, and figure out where we're going to live."

"The last one's easy." He smiled. "I have a house not far from Coffee House. I'm not sure your mother will be out of the casts by the end of the year."

She shrugged. "Like she said, the pictures will give our children something to ask her questions about. Will your family be okay with this?"

Jake kissed her long and deep until she was molded to him, a dreamy look on her face. "They will adore you. If you want, when we leave here, we'll go see my family and you will see for yourself."

He hugged her tight, his cheek resting against her temple. After nearly losing her today, he couldn't think of a good enough reason to wait much longer to marry the woman of his dreams. The chance of a lifetime waited. Nothing would make him happier than to walk by this woman's side for the rest of his life. Oh, he knew they would face difficulties. Their chosen professions weren't for the faint of heart. For the chance to love, honor, and cherish Lacey Coleman, he'd face down any challenge.

ABOUT THE AUTHOR

Rebecca Deel is a preacher's kid with a black belt in karate. She teaches business classes at a private four-year college outside Nashville, Tennessee. She plays the piano at church, writes freelance articles, and runs interference for the family dogs. She's been married to her amazing husband for more than 25 years and is the proud mom of two grown sons. She delivers occasional devotions to the women's group at her church and conducts seminars in personal safety, money management, and writing. Her articles have been published in *ONE Magazine*, *Contact*, and *Co-Laborer*, and she was profiled in the June 2010 Williamson edition of *Nashville Christian Family* magazine. Rebecca completed her Doctor of Arts degree in Economics and wears her favorite Dallas Cowboys sweatshirt when life turns ugly.

Sign up for Rebecca's newsletter: http://eepurl.com/_B6w9
Visit Rebecca's website: www.rebeccadeelbooks.com

Made in the USA
Middletown, DE
02 February 2018